This book is a work of fiction.
Names, characters, businesses,
organizations, places, events and
incidents either are a product of the
author's imagination or are used
fictitiously. Any resemblance to actual
persons, living or dead, events,
or locales is entirely coincidental.

I0657955

This book is Copyrighted Material

All rights reserved. The text of this
publication, or any part thereof, may not be
reproduced in any manner whatsoever without
written permission from the publisher/author.

@2013 by Author Quentin Hartwig, Ph.D.

This is a self published novel

ISBN

ISBN-13: 978-0615859330
(Quentin L. Hartwig Ph.D)
ISBN-10: 061585933X

WINGS OF DANGER

A Novel
By
Quentin Hartwig, PH.D.

TABLE OF CONTENTS

CHAPTER 1

A PAIL OF WATER

November, 1939, A Football Field,
When two linemen tackled him from both sides, the impact knocked his helmet off. He couldn't remember much more than sinking to his knees, seeing flashing lights, and stars going off like fireworks. Numbed, he fell forward on his hands into a crouching position.

Footsteps followed by cold water flooded his head. A faint scent of perfume, a sensual aroma, jarred his mind and reality began creeping back into his consciousness. A person spoke. "Wolfgang, are you okay?"

He looked up to see a statuesque cheerleader, holding an empty water pail.

"When you were hit and fell to the ground, everyone at the bench looked frozen. So I grabbed the pail and just poured the water over you. It's all I could think to do!"

"It's the best thing anyone could have done."
Saw her take the bus. Found her in the yearbook.
Wow, Michele, that cold water felt so good. What's happening on the field?"

"I heard the referee say that after this time out, the Third Quarter will end. *He knows my name!*

"You have a few minutes before the game starts again."

Oh, I'm standing so close to him and he's looking at me, talking to me.

Shaking the water off his head, he stood, gazed into her eyes. "When you get back to the sideline

Want to take her into my arms

"ask Coach to send in the Tim and Allen pass team right after the Fourth Quarter begins."

She looked back into his eyes, nodding breathlessly. "I'm going to the dance tonight!" She flashed a smile and ran back to the sidelines.

Wolfgang never forgot that brief encounter and often recalled it when he needed a boost. Her eyes, such fragrance, and that veiled invitation released adrenaline from some deep, yet untapped recess in his body. A charge of adrenaline he had never experienced before. A moment ago, he didn't think he had the energy to run one more play. Now he had a surge of power that would see him through this last quarter.

As Wolfgang trotted back to the huddle to call the next play, he called some private ones as well. He would look for her at the dance to resume those precious moments suspended just seconds ago.

With that plan firmly in the back of his mind, he returned to his team as their quarterback and captain determined to lead them to victory.

The Chase

The gymnasium swarmed with teenagers busy with chatter and clatter. Music from a Victrola on the stage had already separated girls to one side of the floor and boys to the other.

Above the stage a permanent sign read, BISHOP CARROLL HIGH SCHOOL. Hung on a hook below it a reversible sign read, WINS. Below that a new crayon inscribed sign taped to a wire hanger read, FINALLY.

Wolfgang, with teammates Tank and Carlos, passed the nun's inspection at the door. Wolfgang, blond curly hair and bruised cheek, straightened his dark blue sport coat. Tank, amply named, adjusted the four letter rings stretched frail on the right sleeve of his varsity sweater. Carlos, edgy with dark eyes, ran his fingers through his black, glistening hair like a preening peacock.

As they wended their way to the edge of the dance floor, a boy, with pants reaching only his ankles and jumbled hair pointing skyward, hurried to their side.

His eyes fixed on the four rings, he blurted, "Hey, you guys did good today! I'm halfback on the freshman team."

Carlos edged him aside with, "Good work. Do twenty push-ups every morning."

"See what an occasional win will do. Now we're all heroes," Tank mused.

They reviewed the prospects across the floor. This evening Wolfgang's eyes sought out Michele Lavern.

"Let's see if that hero stuff holds when we ask someone over there to dance," Wolfgang mumbled.

Trying to look nonchalant in his search, he found her already dancing. He took considerable notice of this junior and he was impressed with her style of dance. Smooth-right on the beat and not flashy. Wolfgang didn't like a show-off on the floor. "Didn't take long for her to be asked."

Wolfgang's mutterings were overheard by Tank standing next to him. "Might you be referring to the new water-girl?" Tank inquired nudging Wolfgang in the ribs. "Uh huh."

"If you wanna' move in on that territory you've got your work carved out for you. She's one popular girl in the junior class. Fun to be with, quick on the draw, and doesn't. She's the kind boys like to impress their folks with."

"She can introduce me to her folks," Wolfgang suggested with a happy smile.

Tank and Carlos chorused, "You ain't even to first base."

`"No matter, I'm confident with a capital C."

Tank's own search spotted another couple on the floor. "Who's Jennifer dancing with?" he asked.

Wolfgang shook his head. "Don't know his name.

He's in my study hall. Hangs with guys in the band."

"I know her 'ole man. Seen him at the camp dance hall," Carlos confided. "Likes to get chummy with the migrant girls. Braceros don't like gringos messing with their muchachas. Someday he'll wake up in the gutter with a lump on his head."

"You go to the camp?"

"Sure, I know a couple of guys there from Matamoros. They're here just to make money to send home. It's a lousy life so to even things up they think they have to protect their women."

"I've seen some muchachas at Mass. They're good looking," observed Wolfgang.

"Wanna meet some?"

"And get a lump on my head? No thanks. Wolfgang nodded toward Michele. "He's taking her back."

"So ask her to dance!"

"I am, I am. Gotta wait for the right moment."

"Don't think she has a steady," Tank offered.

"How do you know?"

Tank confided. "My sister Sandy happens to be a good friend of Michele. I asked. She said so."

"Well, we both can't dance with her at the same time." Wolfgang arched an eyebrow. "Wouldn't look right."

Tank knitted his brow and shook his head. "Nah, I want to dance with Jennifer. I don't want to go with someone Sandy hangs around with. If she hears something juicy, I'd never, never hear the end of it. Michele's yours."

"You're so generous! Anyway, my strategy this evening will be to dance with a couple girls, and then sweep Michele off her feet!"

"Sweep? May your ego handle disappointment," cautioned Tank.

"Fear not."

The record player started the next dance with Glenn Miller's Moonlight Serenade.

"Uh, oh, there's Mr. Wilson. If we stay here, he'll come over and talk history. Let's get movin'," Carlos suggested as he plotted his pursuit across the floor.

"Oh, heck, might as well get down to business," Wolfgang said, and the three stepped forward. Wolfgang parted from his friends and began walking toward Michele's group.

The combination of the incident on the football field and the chemistry of the evening defined Wolfgang's intention to ask Michele to dance. As he approached, the group parted creating a path to Michele. Their eyes met and locked.

"May I have this dance with someone who can carry a full pail of water twenty yards and hit a target square on?" Wolfgang requested. The group giggled in response.

Michele glided forward, said, "Yes," and stepped into his arms. "It's a way of life where I live."

Wolfgang smiled. "That exercise is becoming to you!"

Michele shyly darted a glance into his eyes. "You tease."

Encouraged by mutual affection, they danced closer.

The trombones guided the couples with slow-slow-quick, slow-slow-quick. In the meantime, Wolfgang's senses were taking inventory. Tall, engaging eyes, athletic build, hands warm, dry, firm.

She startled him by saying, "And who said football players can't dance!"

"Jealous rumor."

"Do you know the back-around step?" she asked.

"Do I know the back-around?-
Don't ever change that perfume
You bet and after that we'll do the Hampton Stride. Do you know it?"

"You just lead,
I mustn't melt in his arms
"Mr. Captain of the football team!"

After the second dance, Michele said, "I should go back to my group. That was super."

This caught Wolfgang off guard. He hoped he didn't show his disappointment, as his strategy had called for one more dance.

"Of course. I'll walk you back. I hope I've erased that rumor about football players."

"At least one." Turning her head close to his ear, she whispered, "Please ask me again a little later." She dropped his hand and joined her group.

Wolfgang returned to Tank and Carlos and exclaimed, "That sugar is sooo sweet!"

"Indian call Wolf Pale Face no more, say Red Face instead," Tank teased.

"Does it show that much? Wow, it's hot in here." Wolfgang wiped his brow with a handkerchief. "Don't they ever open windows?"

"Pal, you just need another pail of water!" Carlos chimed in.

Tank looked at Wolfgang and then at Michele already out on the floor dancing again. "Seems you ain't the only star in her heaven," he observed.

"I never rush. Maybe sweep, but never rush. I wonder though why she never noticed me before?"

A classmate limped by and brushed against Wolfgang. "Great game, Captain. That tackle in the First Quarter could be heard clear up in the band!"

"Hey, George. Thanks. When you guys play a Souza, it gets us moving," Wolfgang turned back to Tank for further counsel. The classmate limped on.

"Maybe she's seen you with Francine our own Senior Class number one snob." While Wolfgang watched Michele dancing out of the corner of his eye, Tank continued his analysis. "She probably thinks you see her as a farmer's daughter and not worthy of your lofty requirements."

"Lives on a farm? That's why she said something about carrying a full pail. How you know so much about her?"

"Sandy's had her to our house a few times. Guess she was really excited to be elected into the Varsity Cheerleading squad. Not easy to muscle in on that clique. She may be from the country but she's got smarts and a body to boot."

Carlos felt compelled to suggest a game play. "If I were in your shoes, I'd ask her to the Winter Sports Dance. If she says yes, there's hope for you yet."

"Hope?" Wolfgang cast his eyes upward in feigned disgust. "First, I'll gain her confidence in some casual situation. Like a planned accidental meeting. Unleash some charm and, well, then it's all down hill."

"From what I know," Tank cautioned, "be prepared for her lofty expectations. That one has plans. But I do have a suggestion. Sandy could ask her to come to the High Top. We'll show up and let nature takes its course."

"Tank, you are a wizard. We three amigos will do just that. Tell Sandy she's sworn to secrecy."

"Believe me, Sandy loves intrigue. She's got a bookcase full of mysteries," Tank reassured.

"Well men, we're just pumpin' mud here. Let's head back across those choppy waters. She whispered an invitation to another dance so I mustn't keep the little lady waiting."

These two young people will face a future impacted by war, ambition, and deceit that will test their affection for one another.

CHAPTER 2

SECRECY SPAWNS RUMORS

A Few Days Later

"You're paranoid. They're good business for this community and employ a lot of people from town," asserted Howard Manning, the editor of Northern Bend's major newspaper, the Daily Inquire.

"I'm not. They're Germans, they talk dutchy and they all live secluded in that cabbage patch," countered Mayor Cliff Renford of Northern Bend, Indiana. "Something wrong is going on out there. Suspicions started when they bought dynamite and wouldn't say for certain what it was for. You can't see into that depression, the place is all surrounded by hills. That Otto made certain of that. Just to get in you have to pass through a gate. All the markings of trouble with Hitler coming to power. If those Nazis ever invade the U.S., you just wait and see. They'll change their colors. I know. People talk."

"How do you know?"

"I just know. You don't reveal all your sources so I don't have to either."

Manning didn't think much of that comparison, but hit on a course of action. When rumors took on a life of their own, he looked for ways to gain quick access to the truth. Anyway, he was getting tired of Renford's harping on the responsibilities of a newspaper.

"I'm on pretty good terms with the Baron. I'll surprise him with a visit and do some investigating on my own." After a moment of reflection, Manning continued, "For a little guy, he sure can fly a plane. Remember when Rockhaven was surrounded by a flooding storm and the hospital ran out of snake antiserum? They called me all in a panic. Several people had been bitten and there was no way by land to get medicine to them. Did I know anyone who could help?

"I rang the Baron and without hesitation he offered to fly the antiserum to them. Knowing such a feat would make a hot story, I asked if I could go with him. He said we might not make it. I said, let's go. He flew that twin engine through a tempest of wind, rain, and hail."

"Ya, I know, I know. You buttered up that story like he was some sort of hero. Just the kind of publicity they want for their cover-up."

"You and your cover-up stories," Manning countered. "You weren't there. To avoid those violent winds overturning the aircraft on the runway, he practically flew the plane into Rockhaven's main aircraft hangar.

"When the mechanics saw him taxiing toward the hangar, they rolled the doors open just in the nick of time. 'Cause in he came, motors roaring. Once passed the doors he slammed on the brakes, reversed the pitch on the props and the plane spun like a top. The canopy popped off, loose paper and debris flew around in the hangar. Like a bird, it nestled in at the far end of the hangar. Otto sat there for a couple of seconds and, without so much as taking a deep breath, handed the antiserum to a guy in a white jacket. Not so much as a ruffled feather. Wouldn't take any money for the trip. My article was picked up by AP and its appearance in the Chicago press got him some commercial business."

The mayor slapped the editor's desk as if this affirmed his suspicions and said, "You proved my point. He didn't loose, he gained. Those krauts always do. They, and their patents—they make a lot of money. I hear they keep a patent attorney in Washington busy nearly halftime doing their paper work. And what do we get?"

"Well, what should we get? It's their money. It's obvious the Ottos invest it or at least some of it, into their plant. The facility has grown over the years and every year more people outside their community work there."

Manning swung to his intercom and buzzed his secretary. "Jean, anything major on my calendar from now until suppertime?"

After some faint paper shuffling, the intercom spoke. "Nothing I can't reschedule for tomorrow."

"Ah, good fortune. Do it. I'll see you in the morning."

Irritated that this rumormonger had pushed him into a corner, Manning closed the meeting with a curt reproach. "You're always harping on their allegiance. I'm going to test your hypothesis and drive out to your so-called cabbage patch unannounced. They'll have no time to prepare, hide, or whatever you think they'd do if forewarned. I'll tell the Baron I've heard rumors and I want to see for myself. I'll pledge to secrecy anything they consider confidential in the business sense. However, I must be allowed to roam freely. Tomorrow I'll tell you if there is anything to worry about."

The mayor undeterred by the glacial summary nodded approval. "Make them talk in English. Get into Building 6. No one from the community works there! Also the bunker near the water treatment plant that's off limits, too. See it all."

Manning figured he might as well start with the core of the mayor's rumors. If there is anything to them, the mere mention of these two locations should create a climate in the Baron's office giving credence to Renford's allegations.

What He Knew
As Manning drove out of town toward the Sternlicht plant, he recalled in the early twenties

the first time he met the Baron, who introduced himself as Fred Otto. They had both joined the same community baseball team. Otto appeared in some sort of old world soccer outfit that brought forth a few snickers from the regulars. Manning had walked over to the crew-cut, middle-aged stranger and introduced himself. Otto, a good head shorter than six foot Manning responded with a thick German accent. German and with World War One Armistice only four years past, his presence was scorned by three war-scarred players.

Still, desperation calls for desperate measures. The team needed a good catcher. The last one had had his fill of slashes from spiking sliders into home base and was contented to play second fiddle to the right fielder. Otto had a peculiar way of throwing but fired a baseball with impressive speed. Without revealing the hazards, Otto was offered the catcher's position. He accepted and the season began.

Otto worked hard at play. He mastered the rules of the game, batting, and English pronunciation. The accent faded and soon attempts to steal second most often failed. One day an incident exposed a hidden capacity in Otto. A capacity for violence.

A home game, top of the seventh. Visiting team at bat, runner at third, game tied. Runner at third had all the characteristics of a bar bouncer, burly, gnarly hair everywhere, and roustabout paws. Worse, he kept pointing his shoe spikes at Otto. Otto, aware of the implied intentions of the runner, only once warned with a negative shake of his head.

The batter popped a fly straight up and Otto signaled that he'd catch it. Burly charged toward home base. As Otto caught the ball, Burly fell on his back, slid into home, and with his spikes raised high, ripped Fred's leg. A bad decision. Otto slammed his foot into Burly's chest, and grabbed an arm with both hands. With one guttural heave, yanked it free of its socket. As the hapless runner writhed in instant pain, Fred sunk one hand into his victim's throat and would have torn it out had not several players pulled him off. Once away from his opponent, Otto reverted in seconds to a calm player anxious to get the game underway.

In those few seconds, Otto won full acceptance as a player on the Northern Bend baseball team. Even one of the war-scarred patted him on the back. Later, Otto revealed to Manning that instant fury was the power essential to surviving combat. It would be a power Otto would employ to push, cajole, force, his way into lucrative patents, military and civilian contracts. Manning recalled being impressed with all the questions Otto would ask of team members about starting a business. He knew Otto worked at North Bend's major employer, Weinbaum Motor Works, but seemed determined to go it on his own.

One day, at a Chamber of Commerce luncheon, the president of the National Bank had leaned over to Manning and said, "Guess what property the little Dutchman, Otto, bought?"

Manning, unaware that Otto was looking, had to say, "I have no idea."

"The depression north of town near the river. Been a repossession on our books for years. I named a price, he made an offer, we cut a deal and I was glad to get rid of it. Felt kind of bad to sell worthless acreage to a foreigner who's trying to get started over here, but on his behalf, I unloaded it at a loss. Anyway, business is business. I've got stockholders to contend with."

Manning's acquaintance with Otto waned when Otto left both the team and the Motor Works to take up residence on his purchase. Then one day someone mentioned Otto had put up a sign at the entrance through the hills which read,

STERNLICHT
PLEASE DRIVE WITH CARE

Manning smiled at the news. Otto must have known all along something about the property no one else knew. Could it be the little Dutchman pulled something over on a National banker?

At the same time, there was buzz about town by people who had seen Otto and another fellow digging about in the dump retrieving old pipe, motors, and the like. "They come over here only to end up in the scrap heap! Ellis Island should do a better job of screening," some said.

As the road rolled under his car, Manning searched his memory for recollections of the evolution of Sternlicht. The first time he drove there to see the joke for himself, his impressions were on the side of the joke. Hills surrounded the property on three sides and only one road led into the flat stretch of land. It looked pretty desolate with a few huts dotting an area close to a makeshift landing strip. A lone aircraft sat near a hangar with several people working on it. Otto was one of the workers. Howard remembered stopping and talking a bit with him. He asked Otto if he could write an article about the facility. Otto nodded approval. Manning took pictures. The place looked forlorn. He managed to write a positive yet realistic article.

Something <u>was</u> happening. A windmill nearby spinning in the breeze was clue enough that Otto had tapped into Mother Earth for her possession which would sustain life and growth: water.

Manning told his chief editor Sternlicht was, or would be, a story of rags to riches. Reporters of the Daily Inquirer were told to chronicle whatever metamorphosis occurred out there. The problem was getting Sternlicht residents to talk. Everyone seemed reluctant to discuss operations or goals of the organization. About the only way to get a story was to be present when something happened like the flight to deliver the antiserum. Even then, the Baron, as Otto now preferred to be addressed, only wanted to talk about what happened and not about what might.

But Manning made a solid connection with fair articles and kept it alive whenever he saw the Baron. This visit would test the strength of that connection. He had come on the premise of suspicion, and a rather severe one, at that.

Before entering his destination, he slowed to read a sign on the right side of the road. Expanded and freshly painted, it announced,

Sternlicht, Indiana
Sternlicht Aviation Corporation

Watch for children
Airacuda Executive Suite

Indeed, he had arrived. His pulse quickened.

CHAPTER 3

AN UNSCHEDULED VISIT TO STERNLICHT

Both Is Better

Manning marveled at the transformation of scenery that occurred as he drove through the narrow pass into the largely German community. Vegetation was sparse on the outer edge of the surrounding hills yet it flourished inside on lawns, gardens and in the park. The contrast mirrored an oasis in the middle of a dry prairie. He sensed the allowed greenery meant a degree of water rationing. The phrase, waste not, want not, came to mind.

In low gear, he drove along two streets lined with homes framed with tidy front yards and the ever-present gardens in the back. A woman on her hands and knees was washing the front steps of a house. Surely a European custom. Manning couldn't imagine anyone doing that here.

Beyond the residential area, Manning noted an administration building flanked on either side by one storied spacious buildings. Last visit, Manning had counted one hangar, now he could see four. He was awed. One day there was little more than a tinny windmill flapping in the wind. The next visit, a few short years later, buildings, houses, and airplanes on the runway dot the landscape.

A parking lot between the administration building and a hangar seemed the best location from which to view the business sector of Sternlicht. He drove into it and parked at the fence closest to the runway. Hangars lined an asphalt runway that stretched toward the open end of the encircling hills. At the far end, he could see the river glistening its way into the horizon. While scanning the river, Manning

took note of a two-storied building close to the
runway some two miles distant. The high fence
around the gray, camouflaged structure resembled
"Building 6" that Renford had squawked about.

His gaze returned to the hangars. Two airplanes
were warming up near one of the hangars. Several
men were standing near the planes signaling to
the pilots. One walked to the hangar, got a tool,
and made an adjustment on the plane.

At another hangar, a plane was being pulled out
with a small tractor. It looked brand new. A pilot
with a parachute strapped to his back climbed into
the cockpit, checked instruments, and started
the two engines. In an unconventional style,
the motors faced backward with the propellers
pushing the plane instead of pulling it. After
some initial sputtering and coughing, the motors
warmed and settled into a high whine. He watched
the pilot check controls by moving the ailerons,
rudders, and tail assembly. The silver fighter
aircraft rocked as the pilot gunned the motors.
A large barrel protruded from the front of the
fuselage and smaller twin barrels faced forward
from the two motor mounts. "That's gotta be the
Airacuda," Manning murmured.

For a fleeting moment, Manning toyed with the
temptation of pulling up a chair and spending the
rest of the afternoon just watching the comings
and goings of the airplanes, vehicles, and
people. He was tired of spending hours in smoky
offices talking, talking, blah, blah. To sit in
the sun watching those people work on exciting
new technologies would have been a luxury for
him. Yet, the morning's tirade pressed him to get
on with his mission.

Manning walked into the main office building.
Above the front door was a large silver star
emanating rays from all sides. He'd heard that
Sternlicht was German for starlight. Displays,

pictures, and maps highlighting Sternlicht's history lined the lobby.

He approached the receptionist. "Good afternoon, I'm Howard Manning of the Daily Inquirer. I don't have an appointment but I would like to speak with Baron Otto."

"Good afternoon, Mr. Manning. The Baron is in the office of his son, Henry. Just one moment. I will let him know you are here."

Recognizing the advantage of talking with both of them at the same time, Manning quickly suggested, "Both together would be best!"

The secretary smiled, buzzed Henry's intercom and said, "Mr. Manning of the Daily Inquirer is here and he wishes to visit with you and the Baron, if that is possible?"

After a brief pause, the secretary's intercom clicked.

"Sure, show Howard in."

Manning stepped into Henry's office. The large room was brightly lit by spacious windows facing the hangars and runway. Henry, the Baron's older son, was more artistic than his father. The room's decor reflected more the entertainment industry than aircraft. From numerous conversations at Chamber of Commerce meetings, Howard knew Henry ran the corporation's business affairs while the Baron directed the engineering component. He had noticed Henry, as Chamber Treasurer, managed the budget with a sharp pencil, a skill he probably exercised at Sternlicht as well. Manning credited the entertainment-related display to Henry's wife, Mercedes, who had been a singer-dancer in a Luxembourg nightclub when Henry first met her during a business trip in Europe.

Henry was sitting at his desk while he and the Baron, standing beside him, looked up from a blueprint as Manning walked in. They greeted one another with handshakes, and Henry said, "Good to see you, Howard! What brings you to these parts?"

"Well, I'm on a mission of inquiry." Manning's voice, honed from years of experience in asking tough questions, exuded sincerity. "Please believe that I come with no imagined suspicions. However, part of my role as an editor is to seek and print the truth. I'll come right to the point. The mayor has felt pressured to convey to me rumors—and so far as I know—they are only rumors, that somewhere in this facility there is secret activity that could be detrimental to the security of our nation."

Manning shifted in his chair. The only movement by the Baron and Henry was a narrowing of their eyes.

"As you know, there is terrible unrest in Europe. Hitler has already marched troops into the Rhineland and annexed Austria. Some extremists believe, through considerable stretch of the imagination, that the U.S. is also a part of his planned conquests. Should the worst happen, there is fear this facility will become an outpost for his armies or a fifth column sabotage center, or something dire like that."

Manning could see anger in Henry's face as he began to rise out of his chair and said, "We pump a lot of money into Northern Bend. What about the Mayor's business manager's sale of scrap metal to Germany's obvious ally, Japan? Is that sale detrimental to our security or does his job in the mayor's office shield him from suspicion? Damn, I---"

The Baron remained expressionless, silent. Manning quickly raised his hand to indicate he need not finish his statement. "I understand your anger with these rumors. I'm here to clear the air and to keep my readers focused on real problems, not imagined ones."

Before Henry could further vent, the Baron reflected on the situation. "I can see where some might imagine those things taking place here. Sometimes I consider the label, Cabbage Patch, with amusement, but I know with some people it reflects a fear or resentment. I came with little— my wife's diamonds—as a matter of fact, and using them as collateral, got this place started. Some may think our personal property was just a cover for more significant funds coming from Germany. Well, it isn't true. What we started with is what we came with."

The Baron walked to the window and waved his hand at the array of facilities and aircraft. "We've done all this with elbow grease and sacrifice. I was lucky to get good people who had hopes like mine and this place just grew. Any business we do with the Nazi regime is no different than what we do with England, France, and Spain. On occasion, we've peeked into some German secrets. Such snooping could get one shot on the spot. Some day the truth will be known that the Ottos helped British scientists gather data on German low frequency aircraft detection systems.

"Howard, we go back a long way and have always shown respect and trust in one another. Only a few in Sternlicht know about the detection information I just shared with you. If we continue with this interview and a tour of the facilities, what you will see and hear is so confidential that lives will be in peril if such information were disclosed. Thus, are you willing to shake my hand and abstain from printing something that would divulge a military secret or pre-patent developments?"

Howard nodded his head in the affirmative but added, "I want to be free to go anywhere in and about your facilities. Ask any questions, even those that could expose a security risk to this nation. Having a degree in engineering, I feel adequately prepared to conduct this examination. I'm not going to print anything harmful to you or the nation. I trust you won't warn anyone of my coming—trust goes in both directions—and I want all conversations to be in English."

The Baron thought for a moment extended his hand, and they shook in agreement.

Henry, looking for some advantage to this arrangement, spoke up. "Sounds like you plan to write an article."

"Yes. I'm sure there are things happening here that would be of interest to the general public. When I return to your office, we'll talk about my tour and you may have some suggestions about items I could highlight. I'll give you an opportunity I seldom grant to others. You can read and comment on my piece before it goes to print."

"Sounds reasonable, workable. But you're going to need an interpreter. Not everyone here speaks good enough English to carry on a conversation. Dad and I both speak German and French. Would you like one of us to accompany you?" Henry suggested.

"Is your son, Wolfgang, here today? Unless I'm misinformed, he's also fluent in German and French. Could he accompany me?"

"Certainly," Henry replied. "He drives out from town with me every day. Works on some engineering research or development in the morning and then on the grounds in the afternoon. All concerned about being in shape for football, he wants to do hard labor in the afternoon. Today, he's on the ditch gang back of Building 6. Come, I'll drive you over there in an electric cart and I'll tell him to join you and interpret."

Building 6 was the same building Howard had spotted in the distance from the parking lot.

A twelve-foot fence surrounded the two-storied, windowless structure and four barracks. Manning relished the invitation. The mayor's pet riddle was about to be cracked.

Henry parked near a gate guarded by an Army corporal. He turned a serious face to Howard. "Most confidential building at Sternlicht."

They approached the guard. "Good Afternoon, Corporal. This is Howard Manning. We need to enter the compound, to speak to Wolfgang. He's one of the ditch diggers. We'll later tour the facility."

The guard stared expressionless at Manning and then back to Howard. "Good afternoon, Mr. Otto. Does Mr. Manning carry a security release?"

"No, not necessary. He's with me."

The guard unsnapped the pistol strap on his holster. Howard flinched. The guard backed into a metal control booth and closed the door.

"He's concerned security is being compromised," Henry whispered.

"Is his gun loaded?"

"You bet. This facility is top secret. Given our agreement in the office, he did *not* know we were coming. He's on the phone to the Baron right now asking, Sir, your son is here with someone without a security clearance. What is your order?

The guard reappeared with a second corporal. The pistol strap had been re-snapped. "Wolfgang is with the pipe fitters on the north side of the building. Follow me and I'll take you there."

Howard, relieved the pistol had been secured, was anxious to enter the secret realm.

Around the side of the building, they soon were peering into a pit occupied by rusted pipe, new pipe and two bare-chested diggers. Not hearing the visitors' approach, the two in the pit kept tugging at a piece of rusted pipe until Henry called out Wolfgang's name. One looked up and said, "Hi, Dad--and Mr. Manning!" Manning was surprised that Wolfgang knew him.

Henry beckoned. "Wolf, could I speak to you?" With that request, Henry backed away from the pit for privacy. Wolf climbed out of the pit and joined Manning and Henry. This was the closest Manning had ever been to Wolfgang Otto, the college boy he had heard about from several, including his granddaughter, Elizabeth. No doubt Elizabeth will come flying through the door this evening, as usual, to spend a few minutes with her Mimi and Papap so he'll bring up Wolfgang as a subject for discussion.

As Henry briefed Wolf about his role in Manning's visit to Sternlicht, Manning categorized Wolf as a trim, muscular Teuton with blond curly hair. Handsome face until he noticed the scar that ran from his cheek to the corner of his mouth. He remembered how he got that scar—fighting with two thugs robbing his sister outside the Williams Drug Store. It had been a small action story during a slow news week in August, but no one in the Otto clan cared to discuss the incident. Wonder why they don't see a surgeon and have the scar removed?

While the group walked back to the front of the building, Henry outlined its purpose.

"We know when the German Luftwaffe participated in the Spanish revolution in the summer of '36, they conducted most of their immediate battle communications in the clear—that is, in German, rather than in code. Code takes too long to decipher, and in the heat of battle, every second counts. There is the distinct possibility we could be at war with Germany and the U.S. Army needs pilots and radio interceptors that understand German, their slang and idioms. Such knowledge would give our boys an edge in a pitched air battle.

"This Sternlicht facility is an ideal isolated site to train Army personnel in foreign combat language. Many U.S. military and government officials who travel in Europe are familiar with German military jargon. They fly in, simulate military conversation and then fly out unnoticed. That's difficult to do in a metropolitan area with people everywhere and nosy, too.

"The course is intensive, and we house all participants in these barracks. You don't see the students in town because a couple of beers could result in a slip of the tongue. We bus a new bunch into this compound every three months and subject them to an intensive course of lectures, one on one conversations, homework, and experience interpreting real German Luftwaffe communications.

"Conversely, no one is allowed in this compound from town. Non-military types increase the risk for security leaks. Leaks passed to the wrong people in Europe would cast suspicion upon our business reps in Germany. Being under suspicion in Germany can escalate into dire consequences.

"Members of Sternlicht provide another source of instructors. For example, my brother, Emil, just returned from the Heinkel plant in Freiburg. They want to know how we minimize the recoil of the 37mm cannon installed in the fuselage of the Airacuda. In return, we want details of the alloy they use in their engine block. The conversations stalemated, but in the meantime, Emil talked with some of their test pilots and picked up some new lingo. Therefore, he spoke to the students in German as if he were a pilot entering a combat zone.

"If you write an article about Sternlicht, you can't mention the existence of B6. If you do, someone will want to know its purpose, and then, sooner or later, the cat is out of the bag."

As Henry spoke, Manning better understood the reluctance of the inhabitants of Sternlicht to talk about activities other than social ones. The experience he once had at the Cabbage Patch now made more sense. On the first Sunday of every month, the Sternlicht community held a picnic in the park that lies in the center of their residential area. The Baron had invited the Manning family to Sternlicht to enjoy the festivities. In the center of the park was a bandstand with a piano. Volunteers would move the piano to the stand in the morning and as the picnic progressed, anyone who wished to play the piano could do so. Manning was amused at the way parents would encourage their children to perform on the stage. There were people sitting around the bandstand, which gave the children experience in performing in front of an audience. Some kids played the piano. Others recited poems. One group put on a play they had written. If one were willing to talk about little Fritz's recent advancement to second oboe, little Gertrude's interest in history, or one's own child, a conversation with any resident of Sternlicht could go on for quite awhile. Inquiries about the business end of Sternlicht, on the other hand, would be met with a shrug, or, "Entschuldigen Sie, ah, excuse me, I'd like to get some more food." Then the visitor would find themselves alone.

Henry's descriptions were tantalizing morsels to a newspaper editor. Having survived a sentry's challenge, Howard's desire to get into the building was met by Henry's invitation, "Let's take a look around," and Henry led the group through the front door. "We will walk down the hallways and I'll tell you what is going on in the different rooms. If you want to learn for yourself, you can go into any room you wish, Howard, and ask questions."

They proceeded down a central hallway passing, on either side, offices and classrooms. In the classrooms, students in army uniforms were sitting at desks listening through earphones. At the front of the room an instructor sat in a mock cockpit talking into a microphone. Howard stepped into the classroom. Henry and Wolfgang followed.

The instructor was speaking German. Students were listening, sometimes taking notes. After a minute, the instructor stopped and began asking questions, some in German, some in English. Student replies would be in the same language. When the instructor, whom Howard didn't recognize, saw the three standing in the back of the room, he said, "Let's take fifteen," as if visitors were not uncommon. Most of the students took this opportunity to stand up and stretch.

Howard walked over to one young officer wearing pilot's wings on his shirt and a single silver bar on his shirt collar. "You think this kind of training is worth the effort, lieutenant?" he asked.

"Yes, sir. I'm up for promotion to squadron leader and one of the qualifications is combat readiness in a foreign language. Since I'm half German and half Irish, I chose German. If we get into a war it will more likely be with the Germans," he said with a serious face.

The accent sounded familiar. But this kid could be from Frankfurt and just well trained in American English. He pressed for details. "Where are you from?"

"A little town in southern Minnesota you've probably never heard of, Fountain," replied the lieutenant with a smile.

Howard could hardly believe the good fortune in this answer. "Actually I visited there one Christmas with my parents when I was about ten.

My dad's uncle lived there. I remember that visit well because it was cold. I went sledding with a friend across the street. Deep snow and bitter cold." Howard noted this lieutenant's accent sounded just like that kid.

"Did you like to go sledding as a child?" Howard inquired.

"Sure did. There are huge depressions in the earth, you may remember, we call sinkholes. They were great for fast sledding especially the one behind the bank. Sinkholes occur in only a few places around the world," he said with some pride.

"You've been very helpful. Thank you." Satisfied he was an American pilot, Howard walked back into the hallway.

"The lieutenant and I had something in common. We both know about a little town in Minnesota. He seems quick on his feet. I'll bet he's a good pilot."

Henry explained, "They train in Airacudas while they are here. They have to qualify in a variety of fighter aircraft in order to advance to squadron leader. They do a lot of night flying. I know it disturbs several farmers in the area, but the training is a must. If it's okay with you, Howard, I'm going back to my office and leave the rest of the visit with Wolfgang as your guide." Howard agreed and the group separated.

CHAPTER 4

WOLFGANG LEADS

Revelations

Howard saw Henry leaving as an opportunity to gauge Wolfgang as the person in charge.

Howard and Wolfgang climbed into another electric cart. Wolfgang said, "Just point and we'll go there."

Manning was stunned. Given access to the awesome importance of this building struck the core of his journalistic soul. As he looked about, he knew there was more to learn.

"What's that complex over there?" Manning asked pointing to a three-storied building sandwiched between a low multi-windowed structure and a water treatment plant. Behind the building was a huge mound covered with grass. Projecting out of the mound were two large chimneys.

Wolfgang explained, "The facility to the left of the three storied building is the pump station that draws water from the well. The water is distributed to all the buildings in Sternlicht and then the wastewater is returned to the sewage treatment plant on the right. There, the water is treated and blended back into the fresh water from the well."

"And the three-stories?"

"Houses offices, chem labs, shower facilities and lockers. The septic odor sticks to clothing so everyone bathes and changes before going home."

"They mix sewage water with fresh water? Isn't that unsanitary?"

"Dad's chemists tell us the water leaving the treatment plant is as pure as snow."

Wolfgang caught Manning's grimace as they discussed the blending and surmised the thought of sewage in the drinking water ended the editor's interest in the buildings. Now the editor's inquiry shifted to the mound whose apex paralleled the top of the three-storied building.

"It's for ammo storage. Pilots train with live ammunition, and we need it for weapon development. Carl Gottlieb's group has designed a 37mm cannon that can be mounted in the Airacuda carrying enough nitro per cartridge to bring down a bomber. I've worked in that shop. Carl is very strict about the handling of the explosive materials. He's a chemist and makes some of it himself. They've only had one explosion. Even with the precautions, I prefer to fire a 37mm shell rather than load it. You want to go there?"

"Ah, no, but the chimneys?"

"Those are really air vents for maintaining temperature and humidity in the ammunition."

"You assemble planes out here?"

"Yup, in the two hangars next to the administration building. The Weinbaum Motor Works makes the motors in town. The number of planes on order is small enough so their construction can be handled here. If a lot of Airacudas had to be made, I think they would move the assembly out of Sternlicht."

"Your dad said you worked in research this morning. What did you do?"

The electric cart hummed as the two talked while riding back to the cluster of hangars along the path running parallel to the main runway. Their conversation was temporarily halted as two aircraft roared past them down the runway and took off. They watched the two enter a steep climb each trailing two wisps of light blue smoke. The power of four engines at full throttle and maximum propeller pitch thundered across the depression. The two soon climbed out of sight.

"That's a training mission," explained Wolf. "The lead plane was a single-seater with an advanced student, and the two-seater following behind carried the instructor in front with a beginning student in back. The fighter version of the Airacuda is tricky to land because the props are on the trailing edge of the wing rather than the leading edge. It's been designed with the least drag but because of the resulting low square footage of wing, it has to be flown into a landing rather than glided. Great in an approach to a runway whipped with a strong cross wind but bad if both engines quit. It doesn't glide. Drops like a stone. The student has to learn to deal with these characteristics. I prefer to fly the fighter version. From what I know about other fighters like the English Spitfire and the German Me-109, the maneuverability and armament of the Airacuda will give it the edge in combat. And, boy, I can tell you it's exciting to put that power and ammo together."

Imagining the difficulty of performing a power-land the first time, Howard asked, "How is the student taught to touch down?"

"First, there's classroom instruction, and then they practice in a simulator. It's a maneuver that has to be practiced on the ground first because reflexes learned from glide-landing will result in a crash. To prevent newcomers from slamming into the runway, the Baron organized a team of Sternlicht engineers and pilots to design a stationary cockpit that makes the student feel as if he were flying the real thing. There's one in the hangar we just came from and one in Building 2 that some members of the original team are making more sophisticated. I certified in the original one but practice in the one in Building 2. As the engineers improve the fighter, each pilot has to keep updating to remain certified. Flying the real thing gets expensive but practice in the simulator doesn't cost much. In the simulator,

the instructor can cause certain things to go
wrong and the student can practice recovery
schemes. If you fail, at least you don't crash.
You just get corrected by the instructor and you
start over again."

"Is power-landing a maneuver some can't
master?"

"If they can't, the Baron recommends to their
commanding officer that they be trained to fly a
different kind of fighter or be transferred to a
bomber group. He is convinced the Airacuda is the
best fighter-bomber in the world. He doesn't want
crashes scaring off military purchases. Do you
want to fly the simulator? It's a fun experience!"

"No thanks, I have two left feet—not that well
coordinated. Returning to my original question,
what were you doing this morning?"

"I was with Hans Holzhacker who is designing
a rear view mirror for the Airacuda. It will be
attached to the top of the front windshield.
In order to reflect a wide angle, he must first
solve the mathematics of parabolic reflection. He
taught math in Austria before he immigrated to
the U.S. The guy's got a wild imagination that
comes up with the formulas and then I do the
math. I use the slide rule to get approximations,
but sometimes he makes me do it longhand if he
wants exact figures. He also throws in his two
cents worth to a group working on canopy etchings
that will make celestial navigation easier. He's
good, but cranky. A lot of people don't get along
with him. I didn't like him either at first. I
soon learned to get his mind back on track with
some math question associated with the mirror.
Do you want to go there? I'll interpret because
he won't speak English. Do you speak French? He's
pretty good at that.   And if you don't, that's
even better because then I can omit his zingers!"

Howard glanced at his watch. "Let's walk through

Building 2 and if I see something interesting, I'll ask about it."

As they approached Building 2, Howard noticed the lengthening shadow of the trees. He decided if nothing peculiar appeared in the walk-through, he would express his thanks to Fred and Henry, and call it a day. As he walked through the building, he recognized several people from town. They waved, he waved. Howard concluded the mayor was badly misinformed. Maybe maliciously.

He felt relieved. With Cliff, it was always much ado about nothing. But Howard sensed Sternlicht was a potential headliner because positive things were happening here. He knew print referring to a local, expanding industry would be good news in these depression times. And good news sells papers.

"Many thanks for the tour and your explanations, Wolfgang. I'll just say good-bye to whoever is in the front office. Looking forward to your sophomore year at Trinity University?"

"Very much so. This ought to be a good year in football. Lots of freshmen moving up. Always competition!"

"That reminds me. I should know the answer to this question, but I don't. I'll ask. I've heard of a Wolf Pack on the Trinity football team. Does that have anything to do with you?"

"Mr. Manning, Come to a game! The answer is there. Have a nice day." They shook hands and Wolf left the building.

Howard again approached the secretary in the lobby.

"Mr. Otto said to invite you into his office as soon as you came back."

Howard knocked on the door and entered. Henry was writing on a chart hanging on the wall. "Turn up anything you want to know more about or maybe visit?"

"No, I'm quite satisfied. I don't know who the mayor is communicating with, but this visit certainly erased any suspicions he raised with me. I want you to know how much I appreciate your cooperation in this matter. Frankly, I was a bit embarrassed to raise the issue, but as an editor, I felt obliged to examine the charge. As I said in the beginning, I'm going to write some articles about the positive aspects of the area economy and one will be about Sternlicht. I'd appreciate a call when something is happening out here that would be interesting to our readership."

"That sounds good. We'll look forward to your draft. Take care." Henry said as he walked Howard to the door.

Driving home, Howard plotted three action items outloud. He needed to verbalize to drain off his pent-up excitement and hoped no one would see him talking to himself. "If Elizabeth comes over this evening, I'll get her reaction to the name, Wolf. Sara speaks to a lot of women in her club. We've talked about Sternlicht but I've never asked what other women hear and say about the place. Boy, I need to get my ear to the ground on this one. Aside from the anti-snake venom story, I don't know much about the Cabbage Patch. Wonder who came up with that clever term for the major crop coming out of all those little gardens back of every home. Bet every cellar in that community smells the same!

"Cliff Renford. I'll give him a ring in the morning and imply I have something juicy to tell him. He'll be in my office before Jean can bring me my second cup of coffee. I'm going to enjoy watching his face exhibit disappointment when I put the kabosh on his allegation. He turns my stomach with his pasty overweight appearance and malicious comments ending with, "just between you and me, Howard." The guy has a way with words that makes it a bit dangerous to scoff at his accusations without doing a little legwork of my own.

Why have I've missed developments out there? The production of the Airacuda and that executive plane is no secret. One will be in demand if we get into a war, the other when this country pulls out of the depression. Either way, they'll stay in business. Then there's Wolfgang. I've got to nurture my contacts with that Otto crowd. With them, the extraordinary is the ordinary. Could even bring a Pulitzer to my doorstep."

He turned down his street and caught sight of their front porch. "Ah, she has the front light on. Sara is such a gem. It's good to be home."

CHAPTER 5

DIFFERENT INTERPRETATIONS TO THE VISIT

Not All Secrets Revealed

While Henry watched Howard Manning's car leave Sternlicht, the telephone rang. As he picked up the phone, he whispered to the Baron, "Let this be Wolf with good news."

"Yes?"

"It's your son on the phone, sir."

"Vater?" (Father?)

"Jah, was geschah?" (Yes, what happened?)

"Er sah und besuchte nur das Gebäude sechs und zwei." (He saw and visited only Building 6 and 2)

"Gut. Auf Wiedersehen. Später." (Good. Goodbye. Later.)

"Auf." ('Bye.)

Henry placed the phone back in its cradle. "He saw nothing."

On a notepad, the Baron sketched three buildings in front of a high mound. On the middle building he wrote the capital letters, IDC. "Sewage treatment and an ammo dump just doesn't arouse any interest in visitors." He leaned back in his chair with his hands clasped over his head. "Nestled in between is one of the most secret facilities in the Northern Hemisphere, the International Decoding Center.   "He fell for the old ruse just like everybody else. Put up a steel fence around the isolated Building 6, let no one from town in it, and the rumors fly. And as they fly," the Baron continued, as he pointed in the direction of the distant water treatment cluster, "attention is completely diverted from the real story at Sternlicht, the IDC. He must be getting rusty as an engineer. The size of the air vents didn't even raise a question in his mind." The Baron pointed to his son and reflected,

"That's what happens when you don't keep up with your field."

The Baron sat up straight in his chair and vented his feelings about Howard's unexpected appearance. "I put it to him straight when I said, we go back a long way and have always shown respect and trust in one another. I hoped when I mentioned trust that he'd come forth with some sort of apology for not making an appointment. No way. The very next words that came out of his mouth were, "I want to be free to go anywhere!"

"We've known one another for nearly 20 years. Took him on a flight that netted him a story worthy of AP. When he shows up here, he doesn't show one iota of trust. Even wants to prattle about with total freedom. He's obviously more concerned about the Mayor's feelings than ours."

"Let's talk about Emil, dad. Things are getting hot on mainland Europe. I wish he'd wrap up those contracts and get at least to England. I know Mother worries about him, too."

"He'll do all right. He's got a sixth sense about danger. His goal, our goal: learn the alloy in their motor block, then come back. We have a mission, the Airacuda, and that's our guiding light."

"I gotta say, Dad, sometimes that mission takes on the aura of a fixation, no matter what."

The Baron dispatched Henry's concern with a wave of his hand. "You worry too much."

"I know you love him but he's my brother and he's one of a kind. For Mom and my sake, get him out of harms way while the gettin's good."

"All right, all right. I'm going home now. Annie has planned an early supper. Stations of the Cross are at 7. By the way, tell Mercedes she was breathtaking in that blue suit at the dance. She seems prettier now than when you brought her over."

"Every night I count my blessings!"

A Second Impression
That evening as Howard and his wife, Sara, ate supper, he mentioned his afternoon excursion.

"I drove out to Sternlicht after lunch and met with Fred and Henry Otto."

"Oh, at whose invitation?"

"Well actually, no one's. I just wanted to chat with them."

"You don't go anywhere uninvited just to chat- at least not this afternoon. You had a meeting with that railroad exec about the train derailment. What's up? You on to a story?"

"Before I tell you why I went, I'd like your impression about the place."

"What do you want to talk about?" She tapped her fingers on the table for emphasis. "And you must promise that after we talk, you'll tell me why you went there. I'm not going to wait until I read it in the paper."

"Okay, I reserve some reservations you'll understand after we talk."

"Double okay. Let's talk." Sara's eyes narrowed. "Now I am curious."

"Fred's wife, Annie, is a member of the Women's Club. Does she talk much about what goes on at Sternlicht?"

"Not really. When we attended their Sternlicht picnic last summer, she asked if I would nominate her for membership into the Women's Club. She felt more women in her community should participate in town activities. Too much isolation, she said. The children get to know town children in school but the same opportunity doesn't exist for the adults. Not everybody gets involved in PTA and that doesn't meet very often. I did, and now several ladies from there are active."

"What did you learn about Sternlicht from

them?"

Sara folded her napkin. "The usual. They talk about what women often talk about, their children and what they are doing. Wish their husbands didn't work so much. Cooking. They get along with the town crowd about as good as the town crowd gets along with itself.

"You know, several of the town club members work at Sternlicht. Men from town work there, too. Seems to be a good place to work. Very clean." Sara brushed some table crumbs onto a plate. "They tell me it's not unusual to find a cleaning lady from Sternlicht scrubbing the toilet floors on her knees. I'll bet they don't scrub the toilet floor on their knees at the newspaper!"

"No, they don't. Do they ever mention what their husband's jobs are?"

"They work! Engineers, I think one's a chemist, one lady's husband is a tool and die maker. They make airplanes, and they fly them."

"*Tool and die maker. A die is a tool to shape material. Do the town club women that work there ever talk about buildings they can't get into?*"

Sara smiled. "I think we just reached the core of this apple. You mean, do some think something nefarious is going on out there? Okay, how about this. Not long ago, Henrietta said to me, in her low hoarse whisper, They're making bombs out there!"

"That's true. They are. They're experimenting— attempting to make more effective bombs."

"But Henrietta added, in a worried whisper, to bomb Northern Bend when the Germans come!"

"You've never told me this."

"Didn't believe it. However, if you want me to become like Cliff, then I'll tell you every tidbit I hear and expect you to investigate each and everyone of them."

"Lord, no! One like him is one too many already. As I think about it, I admire that in you. I imagine women come to you with all sorts of things about their neighbors and such, and hope you'll pass it on to me. Then scan the paper for the dirt they've spread."

"Oh, I get hints from time to time, but they never comes from Sternlicht. I imagine they have their problems like everyone else. A couple of weeks ago, I overhead a conversation between two women from Sternlicht in the Club's coatroom. They spoke about someone having a drinking problem. I'm sure they thought it was private but I happened to be standing just outside and couldn't help but hear it. Sternlicht is a whole other world and conversations with them can be more interesting than with many of the hens in town."

"I'll take that as fact rather than rumor. That's why it's a chore accompanying you to your couple's card parties."

"Jane Winters mentioned to me once that some areas are restricted to only certain people. Most assume this is expected in a company doing research. Patents and all that. I think if something bad was going on, someone would notice. And anyway, unemployment is still high, and people are happy to work even if they have to bicycle or walk to Sternlicht. That's all I know. So what do you know?"

"I can tell you some things. It all started when Cliff Renford called me this morning and said he wanted to stop by my office. I replied it had to be now. In he pops, closes the door and unloads rumors he's heard about Sternlicht. Rumors to the effect that the Cabbage Patch, as he calls it, is a bee hive of Nazi sympathizers and in a war, they'll take over and shoot us all!"

"How does Renford keep getting elected? His style is to direct attention away from himself. He doesn't do diddle for the community but loves to socialize and gossip. Most of what happens in this town should be credited to the Chamber of Commerce and, if I may say, the Women's Club. You canceled the meeting and drove out there. Then what?"

"I can tell you one thing, for sure, the Nazi thing is kaputt. In fact, they're doing a lot of good stuff. Some confidential. Exciting. I'll be writing a series of articles on companies generating jobs for the area. Sternlicht will be first, and this is what will grab the readers attention." Howard then outlined the contents of the article he planned to write.

He got into as much detail as Sara wanted to hear, and then remarked, "Henry's son, Wolfgang, was my interpreter. He's quite the young man. Just finished his first year at Trinity University. Although he was quite accomplished at Bishop Carroll, I must admit we didn't report much about Bishop and I'm beginning to think that has been a mistake. The visit accomplished a lot. If Elizabeth comes over this evening, I'm going to mention his name and get her reaction."

"She'll be coming over soon and you'll get a reaction. This afternoon, I helped her pick out a dress for the dance she is going to next week. Again with Jerry. She likes him."

As they ate, Howard mused further. "This afternoon was fun and interesting for once. I understood most everything they talked about, weapons development and faster aircraft. It's their business.—I kinda envy Wolfgang. Right in the middle of so much activity. I guess his dad rotates him through the plant in the morning and work details in the afternoon. Probably grooming Wolf to take over when Henry retires.

"Such a difference from talking with Cliff,"
Howard sighed, leaning back in his chair. "I have
to talk with him to know what's going on in his
administration. Cliff has some deep-seated fears
about war and fighting. I think that's why he sees
goblins at Sternlicht. What a contrast between
Cliff and the Baron. Where one would jump under
the bed at the sight of an enemy, the other would
march forward guns blazing."

Sara agreed. "From what Annie's said, that
sounds pretty accurate. She worries about his
flying those fast planes. Thinks he's getting too
old for that. Well, anyway, I baked some cookies
before we went to the Francis Shop. Would you
like some for dessert?"

"Smelled them when I came in. Thought you'd
never ask."

A Granddaughter's Version

She walked to the cookie jar, placed several
on a plate and set the delectables on the table.
Each took a cookie and ate it with their coffee.
They smiled at one another as they heard footsteps
on the back porch. The unmistakable approach of
their granddaughter, Elizabeth. After a quick
knock and a "come in", Elizabeth entered the
dining room. A vibration example of youthful
enthusiasm.

"Hi, Mimi and Papap!" She quickly gave Sara a
kiss and asked, "Have you shown him the dress?"

"Not yet. He'll want you to model it."

As her grandmother spoke, Elizabeth walked
around the table to her grandfather, and pressed
her cheek to his. "What, pray tell, did my big
Papap do at his big paper today? I count on you to
give me some scoop so I can impress my friends!"

"I went out to Sternlicht this afternoon."

"You did? You haven't been out there for a
long time. Why did you go? Who did you see? You
got a scoop to tell me?"

"Saw Wolfgang Otto. Talked with him quite a bit."

"You did? Oh, oh, did you mention my name? You know one of your duties as my Papap is to mention my name with pride to such available bachelors!"

"Ah, I didn't but I can assure you that if I see him again, I'll mention your full name and list all your charms."

"This time I will forgive you. I think he's taken, anyway."

"What do you know about him. You've mentioned his name before but I didn't have the impression you were in the same crowd."

"Not until recently. When I went to Northern Central, and he to Catholic, our groups never got together. All that rivalry and stuff just kept us apart. But since we've graduated and attend different colleges, we've started to get together, like at the Big Top Cafe."

"Have a cookie, or two or three," Howard offered.

"They look yummy. I shouldn't. I already had a piece of Mom's cherry pie. But just one." Elizabeth took a small bite out of a cookie, chewed, closed her eyes. "Oh, so good. I have such a sweet tooth!"

"Would you like a glass of lemonade?" Sara asked as she began to rise out of her chair.

"Yes, Mimi, but you sit. I'll get it."

Elizabeth rushed into the kitchen with her short hair bouncing in the light as she continued her reactions to Wolfgang. "Jerry played against him in football and the other night when we went for a soda, Wolf was there with some friends. He asked us to join them. We did. Had such a good time.

"He's soo' good looking. That scar! I asked him if it hurt? He said no and said since it ties his mouth to his ear, he'll never lose either.

"Then his girl friend, Michele, quickly popped in with, 'I suppose when you have a mouthful, you get an earful.'

"He replied laughing, 'That's right. As long as I eat, I'll never be deaf.'"

Elizabeth returned from the kitchen with a glass of lemonade and took another nibble from her cookie. She tucked a lock of auburn hair back of her ear. "Jerry and I sat across from him and Michele at that large round table in the back of the restaurant. She lives on a farm and is a senior at Catholic. She's blonde and very pretty. Do you know how they met? Can you imagine?"

"No, I can't recall any of my reporters telling me," Howard replied.

"See, that's why you should have someone writing a gossip column for your paper. Now, that's interesting stuff."

"When you finish college, you come to my office and we'll discuss that possibility. If there's anybody who knows the teen world, it's you."

"Can you believe she threw a bucket of water on him at a football game!"

Sara's eyes widened. "I hope you don't do that sort of thing at the games."

"Nooo," Elizabeth assured. "Jerry and Wolf talked about their battle last fall when at the end of the game everyone was pooped. I guess Wolf went back to pass and he was tackled so rough, Wolf's helmet was knocked off and he sank to his knees in a daze. Other players were on the ground, too. The scene was so messy that the trainers and coaches just stood looking at the downed players. So exciting! Then Michele—she's a cheerleader- ran out on the field," Elizabeth described as she rapidly walked her fingers from her cookie to her lemonade, "with a bucket of water to Wolf and pour it all over his head."

At the word pour, Elizabeth raised an imaginary

pail and mimicked how Michele doused his head. "Wolf said the coach is always telling him not to drink too much water and after the game said, 'I hope you got enough water this time!'"

Elizabeth, with a hint of envy, spoke of Michele and Wolfgang's relationship. "I couldn't help watching those two. Sort of teasing one another. Can you believe it: she's taking flying lessons at the airport. Wolf told her to call him when she plans to fly so he can stay on the ground out of danger. She says, Danger, you say! Then stay on the runway! I guess he landed one day, the brakes locked or something and he skidded off the runway at Sternlicht.

"Once, at the Big Top, he said something to her in French. I don't think anybody saw this."

Howard interrupted, "I can't imagine anything getting past you!"

Elizabeth smiled at her grandfather, gently tapped his hand and continued. "She looked at him, paused and replied in French. It was like a golden moment. He said something again in French. They just looked at one another in that special way, you know. She replied, 'That's a certain!' and they joined the table chatter. I think they're meant for each other.

"I'm happy with Jerry—at least for the moment. Now, I'm going to model the dress that Mimi picked out for me!"

A Rumor Set Aside

True to Manning's prediction, the following morning Cliff Renford appeared at the editor's office before his second cup of coffee was delivered. Without even prefacing with a good morning, Cliff pulled up a chair close to Howard's desk, leaned forward with eyebrows lifted in hopeful expectation and asked, "What happened, what did you see? Should I be in touch with the

Governor to bring in the National Guard? We need to nip this in the bud before it gets out of hand!"

To counter Cliff leaning forward, Howard pushed his chair back and exclaimed, "We? Back off, Cliff. You're all in a lather about nothing! You've let your imagination run wild without an iota of evidence to support it. I'm not part of your 'we.' I'm a reporter who tries to be objective and see things as they are, not as others think they are. Sit back in your chair and listen to what I have to say about my visit to Sternlicht.

"I went to Sternlicht unannounced, just like you said. I met with Fred and Henry and they agreed with my terms of the visit. Their only condition was that I not reveal anything of a proprietary or security nature. I agreed. I'm not going to publish any industrial secrets that could let someone else jump the gun and get a product out before Sternlicht. Lord knows we need the jobs.

"I've been at this game a lot of years and have heard about as many variations of the lie as there can be. I didn't detect any. I walked into laboratories, asked questions and everyone spoke in English. Some were hard to understand but that place is on the up and up. They have sensitive U.S. military contracts keeping us in pace with developments abroad. If we ever go to war, Sternlicht will be a major player in our victory."

"That little patch of hangars is going to make the difference if we go to war?"

"In a heartbeat, Cabbage Patch, as you call it, could expand production of their very successful fighter-bomber in some facility outside Sternlicht. I don't want war, but if it comes, jobs will come with it, and I'd want to see that plant located in or around Northern Bend. We can't take these people for granted. With their contacts and communications equipment, they could build plants anywhere."

"Sounds like blackmail to me if they hinted such a possibility. I'll not alter my duties as Mayor. You may be star-struck with their glitter. I'm not. They're a disaster waiting to happen, and when it does, I'll be prepared to blow the horn."

"Where they may build a plant is only my extrapolation of what I learned during the visit. They're too forthright to engage in blackmail. When something needs to be done, they do it. As far as I can see, they've always made the right decisions, and they've been right for Northern Bend.

"Finally, Cliff, you need to be more skeptical of your rumor sources or your crystal ball needs polishing. Spreading unsubstantiated rumors about Sternlicht or anyone else isn't becoming of you. Time has sort of jaded your perception of things. You need a more positive outlook."

"Thank you for that psychiatric evaluation. It's not what I'm hearing from others, but I'll keep it in mind."

"It's precisely those others you should be evaluating as your sources."

"Thanks, anyway, for the coffee and the description of your afternoon jaunt. Just the same, I'll remain vigilant. Such is the responsibility of a mayor. See you at the chamber luncheon?" Cliff asked as he was leaving.

"It's on my calendar."

CHAPTER 6

DISASTER STALKS NORTHERN BEND

A Nice summer day, 1939

In the Baron's opinion, Cletus Bauerman was the best pilot in the Cabbage Patch. Bauerman's special skill was that of a marksman. His side vision was immense and looking straight ahead, Cletus could gauge the movement of a plane approaching from the side with such precision that he need only fire a two-second burst ahead of the plane. Without exception, the burst and plane would cross paths at exactly the same time. Scratch one plane.

During peacetime, development of the Airacuda as a fighter-bomber required frequent testing of its firepower. Instead of bullets, the Baron outfitted the Airacuda with a camera. When the electric fire button on the control stick was pressed, the camera aimed over the 37-mm cannon captured the image of the plane attacked. By triangulation, one could calculate a hit or miss. Bauerman held the best record of anyone in the Patch.

The Army planned to select a new generation fighter-bomber and had asked several aircraft companies to demonstrate their latest models at Wright Field Army Air Base near Dayton, Ohio. The Baron selected Bauerman to demonstrate the firepower of the Airacuda IV.

The Sternlicht team knew they had a winner. To stay in the race until that big contract came along, they modified the Airacuda design to also serve a commercial role as a two engine six passenger aircraft. The United States was slowly emerging from a dark depression and aggressive manufacturing managers needed a rapid means of travel from one plant to another. Billed as the

Executive Suite in the Sky, commercial sales of this passenger configuration kept Sternlicht in the black.

The day he was to leave for Wright Field, Bauerman had a severe pain in his right lower abdomen and felt chilled. Passing under a motto hanging over the door at Hangar 1 he read once more, *Be at your best when the best is needed!* Bauerman translated that into a motto his father taught him, Work is the first duty. Arbeit ist die erste Pflicht! With that command in the back of his mind, he filed a flight plan and took off. The next day, in pain, feverish, and at less than his best, he still topped the competition.

Too sick to remain alone at Wright Field, he climbed into the Airacuda and tuned his short-wave radio to the Sternlicht frequency.

"Bauerman to Sternlicht. Come in."

"Sternlicht here."

"I must speak with the Baron."

"I'll connect you by phone." A pause. A faint sound of dialing. Conversation. Bauerman's torso quivered from a bone-rattling chill.

"Baron here."

"Baron, I took first in the competition. General Ward has to grant you the contract." Bauerman stiffened as a sharp pang traversed his abdomen. "I've got severe pain in my belly and don't think I can stay for the briefing tomorrow. Could you come?"

"Of course. You get yourself to a hospital."

"In the time it would take me to get to a hospital here, I could be home.

"Cletus, just leave the plane."

Cletus flinched again from another stab of pain. In his altered state of mind, he thought the Baron said, "Cletus just <u>fly</u> the plane." so Cletus broke in with, "All right, Baron, that's what I'll do!" and tuned the radio to the Wright

Field air controller.

"Wright Field air. This is Airacuda IV requesting take-off instructions."

"You are cleared for runway four."

Cletus taxied to runway four and headed back to Sternlicht.

As he approached Northern Bend, he retched from nausea. He had to land soon. Delay could be followed by unconsciousness, collapse and the loss of Sternlicht's only Airacuda IV. Northern Bend's airport was closer than Sternlicht's so he brought the Airacuda down to a bumpy landing, parked in a row of other aircraft, and deactivated the armament system. Duty done. Exhausted, he radioed the control tower for help, then slumped forward.

Within two hours, Bauerman's black, ugly, ruptured appendix was in a surgical pan, and he, sound asleep in a hospital bed.

A Crisis Relayed At 0920 Hours, Saturday

"This is Captain Smithson. I'm placing a call to Baron Otto for General Wolford. Tornado."

Phyllis, the Baron's secretary, knew Tornado was code for urgency. "He and his son, Henry, are at a briefing at Wright Field this morning, Captain. The number for that conference room is Cincinnati 282."

"Thank you." The captain then rang the new number. "Good morning, this is Captain Smithson. I'm placing a call to Baron Otto for General Wolford. Is he there?"

The captain heard a muffled voice, "Baron Otto, I have a call here from General Wolford." The captain handed the phone to the general.

The Baron ranked Wolford as part of a new breed of Army aeronautical engineers that fully comprehended the growing menace of the German Luftwaffe with its impressive array of fighters and medium bombers. Gone were the days of coddling aircraft designers that hadn't had a new idea in years. Only innovative aircraft designers could match the menace on the horizon. He knew Wolford was impressed with the Airacuda but lacked the authority to award a significant order. It would take some kind of calamity to produce a shake-up in Army command. So with a ray of hope, he took the call.

The Baron answered the phone at the receptionist's desk, tipped the receiver so Henry could listen and declared, "This is Baron Otto."

"I've got one hell of a problem," the General began, voice quivering. "I had arranged with the Navy to anchor an old destroyer in the northern waters of Lake Michigan. We loaded a Martin B-10 with 500 pound bombs and had planned to guide this unmanned package of explosives by radio control from a two-man fighter. Radio control of this bomber into that tin can would render the Army's new Norden bombsight obsolete. Give us real accuracy. The B-10 took off fine and guiding was on target when for some reason its transmission failed. The fighter went in to shoot it down only to have its electrical firing mechanism jam. Now this two-engine flying bomb at an altitude of 20,000 feet is headed south over Lake Michigan in the direction of Northern Bend. My ops exec calculates it will reach land by 1130 hours. This promising project would be sunk if the plane reaches land and out of gas. I'm thinking Sternlicht is the closest field with something that could intercept it. You got an armed Airacuda that could bring it down before it reaches land? This whole thing is Godawful! Right now, you're my only hope."

The Baron smiled as he saw this as an opportunity to demonstrate an Airacuda's firepower. In a confident voice, he asserted, "General, we've got the right weapon, an Airacuda IV parked at the Northern Bend airport, but I've got to figure out how to get it airborne. I'll call the tower there and see if anyone is servicing it. Chances are it will be someone who can carry out the mission. You're at your office? Good, I'll call you back when I have some information."

0930 Hours

The Baron grimaced as he checked his watch. "Two hours to landfall. That's like no hours. With luck someone will be at the plane now intending to fly it back to Sternlicht." Henry pointed to the airport number in an address book for the Baron, who then dialed zero.

"Operator, this is an emergency. I need to make some long distance calls. Can you stay on the line until I have finished all of them?"

"Yes, but there will be an extra charge."

"Of course. Please ring Northern Bend, Indiana, 920."

A ring, two rings, connection.

"Control tower, Northern Bend."

"This is Baron Otto. Is anyone at the Airacuda?"

"Good Morning, Baron. Let me look."

A pause.

"No, I don't see anyone."

The Baron put his hand over the phone and looked at Henry. "No lucky break. No one there. It'll take nearly an hour to get someone there from Sternlicht. That's 1030. 1130. One hour. We still could make it." He spoke again into the receiver. "I'm dealing with an aircraft emergency. Please don't let anyone tie up your phone for the next half hour. I'll be back to you with instructions."

"Yes, sir."

0940 Hours

The Baron hung up and looked at his watch. "Ten minutes wasted." His hands felt sweaty and his heart thumped.

Turning to Henry, "Where's Wolf?"

"He and Tank went hunting. Where I don't know. Probably shooting gophers at Sternlicht. He'll be tough to find," Henry replied. "Today is the Saturday meeting of the Woman's Club. Mercedes and Mom will be there."

The Baron imagined the consequences. "If that loaded bomber crashes into town, the blast will shatter windows for fifteen blocks in any direction. The flying glass alone will be like bullets. I'll call the club as soon as I can get someone to the plane. Damn, who can fly it? Since Phyllis called last night and said Cletus was in Northern Bend General, he's out. Flying back was stupid! Well, who is left? Granger, Lieutenant Granger. I know he's fired at targets flying an Airacuda. Operator, are you still there?"

"Yes, what number do you want?"

"Give me Northern Bend 229." The Baron could hear the phone ring, ring twice, ring three times. "Pick it up," he pleaded.

After the fourth ring a voice answered, "Security."

"Security, this is Baron Otto. Is Lieutenant Granger there?"

"Yes sir, he's just down the hall in a meeting."

"Good, bring him to the phone ASAP." The Baron winced as Security hastily dropped the phone on the table to fetch the lieutenant. "When you try to get someone on the phone, getting the connection is like the tortoise and time is the hare."

His watch now read 0950. The Baron shook his head, pursed his lips and whispered to Henry, "We aren't going to make it."

0950 Hours

A horse and buggy clopped down a street and stopped in front of a two-storied home separated in back from the river by a spacious, manicured lawn. Michele stepped out, waved to her father and said, "Thanks, Dad. I'll look for you at 4 o'clock." Michele walked past tall, white porch columns and rang the doorbell.

Cori Jameson, a classmate, opened the front door and greeted her visitor. "Hi, Michele. I like that jacket! Come in, come in."

They walked through a short hallway lined with coat hooks into an expansive living room furnished with sofas, easy chairs, abstract paintings, an area rug, and a spiral staircase. Whenever she visited Cori, Michele learned what it was like to live in the lap of luxury.

Michele removed her jacket and handed it to Cori. "Bought this at the Francis Shop. They just got a new line in. You should go there. Really swell stuff. Oh, hurry, turn on the radio to WNBX. They should be playing dance music now."

Cori gleefully cried, "Yes!" and ran to a console radio standing along the far wall. "You teach me the turnaround and I'll teach you to drive."

"Didn't your father take the car to work?"

"No, I convinced him to walk. Good for your heart, I said. You should have seen me pushing him out the door. I could hear him mumbling all the way down the sidewalk."

"If he finds out I drove his car, he'll really have something to mumble about!"

"Worry not, he's mere putty in my hands," Cori reassured as she molded imaginary contents in her hands. Turning the radio on, she began to rotate the dial to the WNBX frequency. As she tuned to each station, a glow tube above the dials changed from a very broad band of blue light to a very thin band once the receiver was exactly on the station's frequency.

"That blue light is just the cat's meow," Michele exclaimed. "Our old radio doesn't have one. We still get a lot of static. We pretend the noise is part of the music."

Cori widened and narrowed her eyes mimicking the light. "It's called the Magic Eye. At night when the lights are low, it's kinda spooky." She fine-tuned to the WNBX frequency and turned up the volume.

Diminishing static gave way to a clear voice. "Welcome once again to WNBX-the station tuned to you to entertain and to inform! Here, at the top of the hour, and for an hour, we play the nation's top dance music for your enjoyment. Roll up the rug, dance a tune or two, or just sit back and listen. Our first melody is by the master of the trumpet, Harry James, as he plays 'One O'Clock Jump'!"

At the announcer's suggestion, Cori rolled up the area rug in front of the radio.

Michele started the instruction. "I'll lead. First the basic step and then the turnaround. Quick, quick, slow!"

The two glided across the shiny oak floor. The first turnaround ended with Cori tripping Michele, who fell into a couch, Cori into another, both laughing at the failed first attempt.

Michele, through her giggles, "No, turn to the left, to the left."

"I will, I will."

Again, they glided across the shiny oak floor. This time, the turnaround was executed without mishap.

Cori asked, puzzled, "That is such a swell step. Where did you learn it?"

"From Wolfgang."

"Where did he learn it or did he make it up?"

"His mother was a Rockette in New York, and when they flew there not long ago, he learned it from one of the dancers."

"Are you his girlfriend now?"

"Well, we've gone to a couple of dances and I've had dinner with his parents. But I'm not going to be *just* one of his girls. I keep my nose a little high, if you get my drift."

"Oh, that's exciting. Just a tad aloof. I like that. Carlos needs some adjustment. I'm going to teach him this step, and then I'll smile at some other boys. I'm not going to be *just* one of his girls, either." Sharing a conviction, the girls shook hands and chuckled at their plotting ways.

Michele jumped out of the couch with, "Let's perfect the step before the song stops."

They began to glide across the shiny oak floor when the music was suddenly replaced with an anxious voice, "We interrupt this broadcast-"

"Not again!" Cori complained. "Why do they always break in."

0955 Hours

Cletus gently rolled onto his left side and turned on the radio next to his hospital bed. Yesterday's nightmare of flying with a ruptured appendix and late night emergency appendectomy was behind him. Today he would relax. Soon, his wife, Gertrude, would be at his side.

The first station was broadcasting pork belly futures. "Bierbauch's besser," (Beer belly's better) he grinned. "Nope." He really wanted something soothing.

The next clear station was Let's Pretend. "Children's hour. "Nein." (No.)

Further rotation of the dial brought him to a WNBX announcer forecasting the weather. "Today will be bright and cheerful with a noon temperature of 72 degrees. Don't forget, at 10AM, we will feature dance music. Stay tuned!"

"Gut," (Good.) Cletus exclaimed as he rolled back and waited in sweet expectation.

0955 Hours

"Lieutenant Granger here."

"Lieutenant, this is an emergency," the Baron commanded. "Take a car and without delay go to the Northern Bend Airport, start up the Airacuda parked there and then call the tower for instructions."

An excited voice replied, "Yes sir!" and hung up. Henry showed his father the number of the Women's Club. "Operator, give me Northern Bend 345."

The Baron could hear the operator dial the number, a pause, then a busy signal.

"I'm sorry, sir, that line is busy."

"Ring 920." The Baron could hear it ring, ring twice, then a pick up.

"Control Tower, Northern Bend."

"Control, this is Baron Otto again. A Lieutenant Granger will arrive in a few minutes and start up the Airacuda. When he radios for clearance, give him these instructions."

As fate would have it, a reporter from the radio station in Northern Bend, WNBX, was interviewing the tower air controller and overheard the Baron's first call to the air controller. Sensing an opportunity to bring some life into WNBX programming, he called the radio station and convinced the station manager to turn up the volume on the telephone line and broadcast the conversations from the control tower. Startled but eager to claim an exclusive story, the station manager threw some switches and the discussions outlining the problem were now being heard by all tuned into WNBX.

"We interrupt this broadcast to bring you an

important discussion taking place at the Northern Bend Airport control tower. An unmanned loaded bomber is flying across Lake Michigan in the direction of Northern Bend. Efforts are underway to shoot the bomber down before it reaches our city. Now listen to the telephone conversations."

Listeners heard the Baron say, "Tell the pilot a Martin B-10 with a loaded bomb bay is flying over Lake Michigan in the direction of Northern Bend. The plane is estimated to make landfall at 1130. Tell him to fly the Airacuda up the Northern Bend River to gain speed before going vertical to break cloud cover at 10,000. Then take a heading fourteen degrees to an altitude of 20,000 and make visual contact."

At the Jameson residence, the girls were, at first, disappointed when the music was interrupted by talk. But when they understood the issue, they both ran to the riverbank. After all, who had ever seen a plane flying low over the river? Exciting!

1000 Hours

The hospital radio beside Cletus Bauerman's bed was still tuned to WNBX. He would rather have been listening to some soft Brahms but since he and his wife enjoyed dancing, Harry James would do. He was startled out of his reverie when the music was interrupted with a report of a looming disaster. He considered who would be available to gun down the bomber. Few had his flying skill. Damn, he remembered only six 37mm shells were left in the cannon magazine after the target demonstrations at Wright Field. The cannon would have to be fired manually, one at a time. On automatic, a single burst could empty the magazine. If all six bullets miss in the first attempt, the pilot would have to fly closer to the bomber in order to bring it down with bullets from the six 50-caliber machine guns mounted in the wings. Should the bomber explode, the Airacuda could be destroyed by the expanding, pulverizing fireball.

Arbeit ist die erste Pflicht! (Work is the first Duty!) Feeling duty bound, Cletus pulled the iv out of his arm and sat up on the edge of the bed. The room began to swirl. He gripped the side rails. A minute passed. He felt better. He went to the bathroom, dressed and looked into the hallway. A doctor and some nurses were busy talking at the nurse's station. No one noticed him. He went back into the room and leaned against the bed to steady himself.

"How to get to the airport?," he muttered anxiously. "A cab, no. No bus. I'll have to call someone. Sigmund!" Cletus ran his finger down a list of names in the phone book until he came to Gauss, Sigmund. He picked up the phone and gave the number to the operator. He could hear the phone ring. Be home, be home.

His knees began to shake. He sat on the bed.

After three rings, a high-pitched feminine voice answered, "Hello?"

"Hello, Flo?"

"Yes, Cletus? It's so good to hear your voice."

"Quick, is Sig there?"

"Yes, why?"

"Please, I must speak to him now!"

In an unhurried, melodious tone, "Ziggy is shaving."

"Flo, please, *now*!"

With a hint of disappointment, "Well, just a minute."

Seconds passed like hours.

"Cletus, what's the"—muffle, grunt—"what's the rush?"

Cletus imagined Sigmund wiping the shaving cream off his face. Cletus' voice began to tremble. "Sig, I must get to the airport, now. Now! Pick me up in the alley behind the hospital as quick as you can."

"Behind the hospital?"

"Sig, PLEASE! NOW!"

Cletus knew Sigmund recognized the urgency when he uttered in a lowered determined voice, "Ich werde in zehn Minuten dort sein!" (I will be there in 10 minutes!)

Cletus urged, "Schnell, bitte!" (Quick, please!) He hung up and walked to the door. Each step pulled on the stitches in his lower right abdomen. Movement was painful.

Cletus slipped into the hallway, took the elevator to the ground floor, walked to the end of the hallway and exited through a back door into the alley. He leaned against the building then looked at his watch.

<u>1015 Hours</u>

That left him but seventy five minutes to get airborne and up to 20,000 feet. A tear ran down his cheek in fear he might not succeed, and disappoint the Baron.

The alley was still.

A gray cat slinked from behind a garbage can holding a wiggling mouse in its mouth.

For a brief moment, Cletus was in the presence of another hunter, this one successful.

Cletus smiled. "Gute Kätzchen!" (Good Little Cat!)

The cat heard the voice, stopped, looked at Cletus, and scurried away.

"Wish me luck, Kätzchen!" Cletus whispered as the cat, mouse still wiggling, ducked behind a shed.

A black, two-door Model-T rattled into the alley and skidded to a stop in front of Cletus. The motor sputtered in idle. Sigmund pushed the passenger door open and Cletus grabbed the door jam and eased himself in.

"Cletus, what are you doing here?"

"Drive me to the airport as fast as you can."

In haste, Sigmund's foot slipped off the clutch, lurching the Model-T forward. Jolted, Cletus groaned.

"Sig, you spend too much on Flo. This bucket of bolts begs for repairs."

Sigmund ignored Cletus' observation. "You're in no condition to fly!"

"Just do it," Cletus urged pointing in the direction of the airport with his index finger. "I've got to shoot down a runaway bomber."

"Du bist verrückt!" (You are crazy!)

"Schwiegen!" (Quiet!)

Sigmund glanced at Cletus and was shocked at his friend's condition, a pale face etched with pain. "Hey, this could kill you. Call Sternlicht and let someone else do this. You're gonna pass out in flight and its curtains for you and the plane. You might even crash in town killing others."

"Kein Zeit (No Time)-it's the only way. I'm okay. Feeling better already. You can drive me right up to the Airacuda. That side gate is always open on Saturday morning."

They arrived at the plane and both walked over to the cockpit.

"Boost me up," Cletus requested. Sigmund helped him get in, then got back into the Model-T and drove it clear of the plane. Sigmund waved at Cletus and motioned he would stay until Cletus returned.

Cletus closed the canopy, and activated the firing system. A green light glowed. The weapon was ready. He started the engines and taxied to the main runway. He radioed the tower of his intentions and they cleared him for take-off with, "Good hunting!"

Advancing both throttles to maximum, the Airacuda jumped forward and raced down the runway. The acceleration pressed Cletus back into his seat. The seat belt gripped his abdomen, reminding him of an incision that had only been closed less than a day.

He guided the aircraft to 30 feet above the water and accelerated as he flew up the river.

1040 Hours
Standing on the bank of the river, Cori and Michele looked downstream to the distant bend in the river where the plane should first appear. All they saw was a barge carrying a tall crane being pushed upstream.

Michele shaded her eyes with her hand. "It's still too soon for the Airacuda to appear."

"When he flies by, he won't be much higher than we are," Cori exclaimed. "I'll be right back. I'm getting the camera. What a shot!"

The word camera sparked a fantasy in Michele's mind. What if she was the reporter at the airport? She imagined herself running to the Airacuda and shouting over the engines, "Can I go with you?"

"This is a dangerous mission, Miss."

"I want to take a picture of the danger!"

"Okay, get in behind."

Better yet, what if she was a pilot and had responded to the Baron's call? What if he were to say, "This is a dangerous mission, you'd-"

Emotional tears came to her eyes for she knew she would counter with, "I can handle it." She could picture herself confidently climbing into the cockpit and…

Glistening in the sunlight, a low flying airplane appeared at the distant bend.

1050 Hours
"Cori, hurry, it's coming!"

The back door of the house flung open and Cori ran toward the riverbank. She aimed the box camera on the ever-enlarging silver streak. The plane got bigger and louder as it charged toward them. It was exciting to watch it fly so low!

The girls, in their horror, could see the plane was headed directly at a tall crane parked in the river.

"Look out," they both yelled. As if the pilot heard them, the plane banked away. In doing so, the plane now faced the girls and drew nearer to them at increasing speed. The thought it could crash into them became frightening. As they were about to run, the plane banked back straight up the river.

Seconds later, the plane roared by Michele and Cori. The pilot was wearing dark glasses. His face was partly covered by a mask with a tube running from it. "That's his oxygen mask," Michele shouted over the pounding beat of twin 1400 h.p. engines at full throttle. He looked at them and waved!

Click!

"I took the picture just as he raised his hand," Cori cried.

The Airacuda maintained a low course over the river until it reached another bend. At that point, the plane pull into a steep climb and penetrated the cloud cover.

The sound of its engines changed into a deep roar. The sound echoed along the river valley accentuating the power. Above the clouds, only the fading sound of the engines gave proof of its existence.

1120 Hours

Breaking through the clouds, Cletus looked around for the bomber. Nothing. Nothing but a bright blue sky. His watch gave him ten minutes to find the errant bomber and nail it before it reached land. He leveled off at 20,000 feet, checked his oxygen pressure, and again glanced at the little green light above the altimeter. He relished all the power at his command.

His compass continued to show a heading of fourteen degrees. As he scanned the sky, it seemed someone to his left wanted his attention by flashing the sunlight at him with a mirror. There! The twin-engine bomber was approaching from the left gleaming silver in the sky. It had not been painted, so its aluminum skin reflected the sun's bright rays.

Setting the 37mm trigger on manual, Cletus wanted to make certain the plane was destroyed with his meager supply of shells. He counted on the small charge carried in the 37mm projectile to detonate inside the bomber's fuselage and ignite the explosive load. One hit amidships, and BOOM, the whole aircraft should fall like a stone into the lake.

Cletus was closing in fast. He fired. To his amazement, the projectile flashed in front of the bomber. Chagrined, he knew they'd tease him about the miss when they did an ammo count back at Sternlicht,

He fired the second shot. Astonished, he watched the projectile pass through the fuselage without exploding. A dud!

Dangerously close to the bomber, he fired the third shot. It struck behind the forward cabin, detonating the bomber's deadly cargo. The aircraft disintegrated in a thundering flash. Still in radio contact with the airport, Cletus was unaware his thoughts had really been spoken words. As a consequence, his efforts to hit the target were heard by radio listeners. "Missed! A dud! Getting too close. A hit! BOOM", Static.

"Airacuda IV-come in. Airacuda IV, can you

read me?" The control tower operator's attempt to make contact with the Airacuda was in vain.

To keep listener interest until contact with the Airacuda was regained, the radio reporter decided to return to regular programming. "Judging from what we heard from the pilot of the Airacuda, he was successful in shooting down the bomber but the explosion must have disrupted radio communication with him. When we make further contact with the pilot, we'll return to live broadcast so stay tuned to WNBX, the radio station first in breaking news and top Ten music."

*   *   *

Unable to avoid the expanding fireball ahead, Cletus ducked down in the cockpit as his aircraft flew through fire and debris. Large pieces of bomber parts slammed into the Airacuda causing it to rock violently. A portion of its canopy was ripped off, flooding the cockpit with an angry rush of searing wind and smoke. Hot debris struck his hands and jacket setting fire to his sleeves.

The pain and fire brought Cletus close to panic. He slapped at the burning sleeves—then remembered the small fire extinguisher behind his seat. He pulled its safety pin and sprayed carbon dioxide fog until the flames were gone.

His plane diving, he saw the river rush up as he burst through the cloud cover. He painfully hauled back on the stick to level the plane just above the water.

His call to the airport for landing instructions was garbled. A gash opened over his cheek had filled his oxygen mask with blood. He quickly disconnected his mask, spit his mouth clear and pressed his flying scarf over the wound.

The Airacuda IV right engine quit. The plane dropped closer to the water. He punched the right

starter button. The right coughed into running
for a few seconds. This repeated frantic effort
kept the plane a few feet above water. He just
needed to reach the end of the runway. Cletus'
energy level was bumping on empty.

The girls had begun to walk back to the house
when they heard a distant boom. Its echo along
the valley walls caused them to turn back and run
to the river. Searching the sky they saw nothing
because of the cloud cover.

Poof! The Airacuda dove into sight trailing
billowing black smoke. They gasped as it fell like
a scorched gull. What looked like ruffled feathers
turned out to be, as the plane approached, a
mangled landing gear. This time, the fighter
looked more like a wounded bird rather than a
sleek predator. As it drew nearer, the girls
heard the starter laboring to re-ignite the dead
engine. "Tang…tung…tung…rrrrrRRRROOOOORRRRrrr…"

That laboring sound of desperation Michele
would hear once again in a location halfway
around the world.

As the plane passed the girls, the pilot glanced
their way. This time they saw a face in pain.

Click!

The plane continued to rumble down the river
in the direction of Northern Bend's airport.
Michele and Cori gasped as the plane faltered,
rising and falling, until it turned out of sight
at the distant bend in the river.

"Did you see his face when he looked at us?"
Cori asked. "It was awful. The picture I got was
blood all over his face and jacket. I wonder if
he made it back to the airport. We didn't hear
a crash or anything but then we're pretty far
away".

"If that boom was the bomber blowing up, maybe
his plane was hit by fire and stuff flying around,"
Michele gestured by throwing her hands before her

face. "Sure was covered with soot. Such a mess. I wonder where that bomber would have crashed if he hadn't shot it down? But the pictures. A perfect before and after."

"Wasn't that lucky!"

"Take them to the newspaper! You'll get your name in print. I can read it now, 'Cori Jameson captures the drama of air battle on film.'"

*   *   *

The continued loss of blood pushed Cletus' endurance to the edge. His hands burned, his cheek gooey with fresh blood and his right side pained every time he moved the rudders with his feet. He hurt all over and his vision was blurring. Deja vu! Once again a race to see which would lose first, man or machine. As Cletus struggled to keep the plane airborne, he wondered how long he could manage the controls. Systems were failing and he couldn't lock his landing gear into place.

Turning to follow the bend in the river, the end of the runway came into sight. At first relieved, then struck with horror. A passenger plane was taxiing on the other end of the runway. Cletus strained to bank the Airacuda away from the landing strip onto the adjacent grass. His brain deprived of adequate blood flow, everything seemed to spin: the field, the runway, the nose of his plane. A few feet above the ground, he cut his engine, and trusted in God.

The aircraft slammed into the grass, bounced, dropped hard onto the ground, and slid forward on the fuselage's belly almost to the end of the field. At the first bounce, Cletus passed out.

Veering away from the runway by the crippled fighter onto the grass ended the possibility of a collision with the passenger plane. The crash landing, however, was news enough for the radio reporter to again connect with the radio station and broadcast the events that had just unfolded before him.

The airport fire control and rescue team sped to the crumpled Airacuda. They extracted the unconscious Cletus from the cockpit and doused a small fire burning in the right engine. As an ambulance carried Cletus away, the Airacuda remained behind looking triumphant but scarred.

After receiving several pints of blood, and a return to the operating room where the surgeon closed a torn appendectomy incision, Cletus returned to a hospital bed, sound asleep.

*   *   *

The radio report of a crash landing brought a flood of people to the airport. A photographer from the Daily Inquirer gladly accepted Cori's negatives and then interviewed the reporter from station WNBX. The full story of the laden bomber and the successful Sternlicht pilot consumed nearly all the front page of the Daily Inquirer that evening.

Renford Lingers in Denial

When Dorothy Renford, wife of the mayor, read about the episode, she considered Cletus Bauerman a hero. Within hours of an appendectomy, he had shot down a bomber that could have killed many had it crashed into the city. Her teeth hurt imagining the pain he must have endured walking to, and flying a plane, which, in the end, crash landed.

But not Cliff Renford. He had long hoped someone from Sternlicht would do something he could become righteously irate about. He hadn't been aware of Cletus landing the Airacuda, following the competition, at Wright Field until he read the newspaper account that evening at supper. Away for the afternoon, attending the dedication of a new lakeside resort, he first heard of the runaway bomber when he came home. His wife Dorothy met him with the headline of the evening newspaper, Sternlicht Fighter Destroys Runaway Bomber. He grabbed the paper and scanned the article and accompanying pictures. He stood exasperated, florid. "More free publicity. They get it the easy way, and I have to work for it."

"Clifford! Is that what you think when you read this article? What if that bomber had crashed into a house and killed people because Sternlicht wouldn't send a fighter after it. Would you have said that was a good decision?"

"So they shot the bomber down. Why not? That's what they build those planes to do. Let's hope they only shoot the bad guys in the future. Who was the pilot? I missed the name when I read the article. The Red Baron of Sternlicht?"

His wife, annoyed with his sarcasm, replied sharply, "No, a pilot named Cletus Bauerman. And just imagine, he had been in the hospital recovering from an appendectomy. What courage!"

"That's what they want you to believe. And anyway, that's what he is trained to do. I learned to do my job in the school of hard knocks. If he hadn't shot that plane down, he wouldn't have been doing his job."

As Renford was explaining his view of the event, a new and far more entertaining thought popped into his head, one that he shared with his wife and son, Allen. "That armed military aircraft at Northern Bend's municipal airport could have presented a menace to the citizens at the airport. What if one of those guns had gone off and struck a loaded passenger plane as it waited to take off? What if the shell exploded in a crowded waiting room?"

Why," he emphasized by slapping both hands on his chest, "I would be remiss as Mayor of this community if I did not bring this breach of safety to the attention of the Chief of Police and the city attorney. In fact, why haven't they brought this to my attention this evening. This lawless conduct should have been clear as crystal to them." He lowered his paper. "Did I get a phone call from them while I was away?"

Allen weighed in with his mother. "Dad, those guns don't just go off. You've got to have a key or something."

Dorothy echoed her son's reaction. "What kind of a viewpoint is that? This Bauerman is a hero. Why make something out of nothing? Guns just don't go off. You've got a loaded one in the dresser and that's never gone off. And I don't like it there!"

"You just reinforced my point. It could go off and maybe hurt someone. That's my viewpoint on the armed, loaded plane at the city airport. It could go off and hurt someone."

"I don't like the gun in the dresser for a different reason. You get shaky when you're scared. If you pick up that gun when you think there's a burglar in the house, and pull the trigger, no telling in what direction that bullet will go."

The contest of opinions continued during supper.

"You just don't appreciate the responsibilities I have as an elected official." He dabbed his oily forehead with an Irish linen napkin. "Being Mayor means I must look out for the well-being of the city. In the morning, I need to discuss this matter with the city attorney and the Chief of Police."

"Good Heavens, Clifford," his wife exclaimed as she put her hand to her forehead in disbelief.

"Don't make a fool of yourself on this one. If they didn't call it's likely because they didn't think it was necessary to do so. And remember, when you pick the wrong issue to go public with, it not only hurts your career but your family as well."

Clifford punched at his potatoes. "Pass the gravy, please."

Dorothy held the gravy bowl short of Clifford's reach until she had explained her admonition. "I have to face those ladies at the Club and, believe me, when your feet are in the mud, I hear plenty."

With his parents preoccupied, Allen speared the last pork chop. With the tasty morsel in his possession, he continued to caution his father's intended action.

"My friends don't say much to me at school, but I get the impression people think you play favorites in what you support, and go after those you don't like. I like Wolfgang Otto. He was always helpful to me in football."

"Aren't you listening? I'm not talking about Wolfgang Otto. I'm talking about that pilot, Cletus-ah--ah--what's his name--he's responsible."

"Bauerman, Cletus Bauerman," his wife hissed.

"If you go after Mr. Bauerman, you're taking on the Ottos and I don't want to lose Wolfgang's friendship," his son pleaded. "In the last game of the season with Northern, he could'a called in Willie and Jake for the pass play. But they were seniors, so he choose me and Tim instead," Allen accentuated by pointing to himself. "At the football banquet, he said he did that because he knew we'd pull off the pass play and that would give us and the rest of the juniors determination next season. That's the kind of guy he is. He's popular and now he goes with Michele Lavern who-"

"Lavern?" his father interrupted. "I thought you said he was going with Francine Wellworth."

"Na, I think he dated her because they sang in a couple of school musicals together."

"She's the kind you ought to date! Chris Wellworth is well-heeled, and I could use some financial support in the next election."

"Dad, I can't date just the girls whose parents can give you money! Anyway, Francine is away at college and a snob." Allen took the paper from his father, turned to the second page, and waved at the before and after pictures of the Airacuda. "Look, these pictures were taken by Cori Jameson. She's really nice and I'd like to ask her out."

Dorothy put her arm around her son, "Allen, you date whoever you want."

"That's right, just leave me to fend for myself," Clifford whined as he threw his napkin on the table.

"Clifford, that's totally unfair. You've got an office of employees. Put them to work on your campaign fund," said Dorothy.

Allen joined in. "There one more important thing about Wolfgang. Some kids thought he was stuck-up because he didn't hang out with them all the time. Once, I asked Tank where Wolf was. Tank said he bicycled to Sternlicht right after practice to do something out there like fly planes. Imagine, when he was in high school, he was flying," Allen's voice lowered to a wishful tone. "I sort of envy him. He leads a pretty exciting life. I think I'd like to work there someday." Allen stared at his plate. "So don't ruin my chances!"

"Oh, don't be paranoid the both of you. I'm not going to do something that will interfere with your lives. I just don't want to be criticized for not being a watchful Mayor. Calm down," Clifford pleaded, "Let's have some pie".

   Gauging they accepted his intended caution,
Cliff changed the subject, but held firm to his
intention to call in some key people the next
morning. With dramatic flair, he would ask, "Can you
believe? That Sternlicht crowd left an unguarded
armed aircraft at the municipal airport!"

CHAPTER 7

THE MAYOR PLAYS HIS TRUMP CARD

Now I'll Get 'Em

Mayor Renford felt smug this morning. He had a trump card to play. And play it he would. An opportunity to hold that Otto clan up to public scorn. The nerve to leave a dangerous aircraft unguarded at Northern's Municipal Airport.

His secretary greeted him with a broad smile. "Good Morning, Mayor. You're looking jubilant this morning. Happy the bomber didn't hit Northern Bend yesterday?"

Disappointed that she, too, hadn't recognized the real danger in the whole episode, his smile convulsed into a frown. "Get Olowski and Patterson in here ASAP. Everybody's all a twitter about a Sternlicht fighter shooting down a bomber. In the meantime, that armed fighter has stood unguarded at the airport loaded with ammunition that could go off and hurt people! I want this disregard for the safety of Northern Bend's populace to be explained by those responsible for its presence at the airport, period."

Nancy's cheerful smile vanished along with her dream of a hero's welcome. She imagined herself riding in a convertible following the one carrying the Mayor and the victorious pilot through throngs of grateful citizens lining Main Street. "Yes, sir," she responded in a dismal tone.

Nancy's calls to Oskar Olowski, Chief of Police, and Chester Patterson, City Attorney, caught both of them just arriving at their offices. They agreed to a quick meeting.

Once he had the two seated in front of his desk, Cliff described the potential danger of the unguarded, loaded gun at the airport. In a grave tone he implied a breach of responsibility. "Frankly, I'm surprised and disappointed that you didn't recognize that danger. When I got home last night Dorothy met me at the door with the disturbing news. My first question was to ask if either of you had called and she said no. Where are we on this?"

Oskar responded first. "We? I don't see where we have a problem here. Nobody called me about the fighter being at the airport. I've seen fighters there before. The Ottos have contracts with the Army Air Corps and Army people fly here in all sorts of aircraft to attend meetings at Sternlicht. Henry gives me a ring when he thinks I should know about their comings and goings, and until they screw up, that's good enough for me. I have a lot less trouble with the Otto crowd than with some of the schweinkopfs (pig heads) in this town, to use a Cabbage Patch term."

"Let's not get complacent, Chief." Clifford turned to his city attorney. "Chester, what are our ordinances about loaded guns, dangerous weapons—you know what I mean," searched the Mayor.

"Well, there's a slight hint of endangerment here but given the circumstances surrounding this whole issue, I think it would be counterproductive to try to dig up a charge. It wouldn't be popular and would cost more money than it's worth."

"You don't sound cooperative in this matter, Chester. You're being paid to support the Mayor in legal issues and you're falling short on this one. Numerous attorneys in town have given me their business card. Therefore, your job is one others would like. Now, can you give me some help, or do you give me no alternative but to restructure my office? You know what I mean?"

Chester had wrestled with this kind of dilemma before. The mayor springs a malicious idea, and then threatens Chester if he don't carry them out. The scheme knotted his stomach. He offered a delaying tactic. "We need some collaborating evidence. Maybe the manager of the airport is concerned. I'll give him a call this afternoon."

"Good idea. You call from Nancy's phone right now, and I'll listen in on mine. Don't tell him I'm on the line," the Mayor smirked.

Thwarted, Chester left the Mayor's office and placed a call from a telephone in the outer office to Frank Hastings, manager of the Northern Bend Municipal Airport.

"Good morning. This is Chester Patterson, City Attorney in the Mayor's Office. May I speak to Mr. Hastings?" A pause, then Hastings answered, "Frank, here. Chester, what's up?"

"I'm in the Mayor's office and there is concern the unattended, but armed Airacuda fighter parked at your facility could pose a danger to anyone in its vicinity. Is this a concern to you? I would press charges if you thought so." Chester hated to add the matter of charges but he knew that the Mayor would expect him to say it.

"Na, they always lock the guns in some way only their trained pilots know the sequence of steps needed to activate the firing systems. Every now and then, the Army flies a fighter, or sometimes a bomber, in here and even though they're armed, their safety procedures exceed my standards. Tell the folks down there is nothing to worry about."

Chester caught the Mayor's emphatic motions signaling him to press the issue. "If you think these armed aircraft are a threat, I'll issue an injunction prohibiting such aircraft from entering your air space," Chester offered.

Listeners in the mayor's office could hear Frank angrily sucking in air in preparation to respond. "Look, back off. Don't mess up a good thing. Sternlicht is a cash cow for this airport. They teach night flying, and pay me to allow their aircraft to touch and go, especially at night. They've set up radio transmitters that the pilots can follow at night to guide them to the runway. Their money has enabled me to maintain landing lights all night and pay for tower operators around the clock. That in turn has provided the necessary capability,"—both listeners could hear spit hit the speaker on the other end as Frank stormed on-

"to attract both Allied and Winthrop Airlines to add us to their night flights. All this has boosted our revenues so much that I'm smiling every time I go to the bank. Don't give me trouble. If those contracts go elsewhere we'll have to rent this place out for pasture. Tell your Mayor to keep his nose out of my business. I don't answer to him, I answer to my own airport authority. They're behind me one hundred per-- who coughed? I know that cough! Are you listening in, Renford? You too chicken to make this call? I!--You--" Frank slammed the phone down so hard both Chester and Cliff jumped from the pain of the noise.

The rejection of his concerns didn't deter Renford from pressing a final alternative to his quest. "Sternlicht isn't going anywhere. This airport is too convenient. I'll settle for an apology from the pilot. Call the Ottos, explain my strong objections to this intolerable use of our airport. Hint that I would forget the whole issue if the pilot apologized for his lack of concern." Stretching his office's authority, Cliff extended the phone to Chester. Chester did not accept it.

"I'm not going to present your ultimatum over the telephone. I'll drive to Sternlicht and explain your position to their front office. I think this is a mistake but since it's a concern of this office, I'll go."

"Don't give them any slack. Do your duty," Renford warned.

Chester left the office, but Olowski remained behind. When Chester had closed the door, Olowski's eyes narrowed as he addressed the Mayor. "You're way out of line on this one. If Chester doesn't come back with someone for you to castigate, don't look to me to do your dirty work. You don't push me around like you do Chester. I'm elected, he's not." Then, in a whisper, he added, as he poked the Mayor's chest with his finger, "Remember, I keep files and you're in one of them."

Without a good-bye, he left the office. As he passed Nancy he waved and exited with a cheerful, "You have a nice day!"

Painful Experience

Chester Patterson woke up the next morning with the unpleasant task in the aching forefront of his mind. This is one day he wished he could stay in bed. He struggled to invent a strategy blunting the confrontation so everyone would save face and he would keep his job.

Chester first called Sternlicht to see if the Baron would be able to see him. The Sternlicht secretary informed him the Baron was visiting Mr. Bauerman at the hospital, and she wasn't certain when he would be back.

"I might as well see them at the same time. I'll make the contact at the hospital," Chester concluded. He drove to the hospital, parked, and walked to the front desk. "What room is Mr. Bauerman in?" he asked.

"210B. Take the elevator to the second floor, turn right, and it's the fourth door on the left."

"Thanks."

Chester's hands began to sweat as he rode the elevator. The door opened and he followed the receptionist's directions as he counted "1, 2, 3, 4," walking down the hall. The fourth door was open so he walked to it, and peered into a brightly lit room. A man, likely Bauerman, lay in a hospital bed with an IV inserted in one arm. His head was bandaged. He appeared alert and looked at Chester in the doorway. Next to the bed was Baron Otto, a woman, probably the pilot's wife, and a nurse attending to the I.V. bottles.

The Baron noticed Bauerman looking, so he turned to the door, but didn't recognize the person standing there. The Baron addressed the stranger. "This is Mr. Bauerman's room."

"Mr. Bauerman is the gentleman I wish to see. I'm Chester Patterson, City Attorney from the Mayor's Office."

The Baron's face flashed a puzzled smile, but he made introductions. "I'm Frederick Otto of Sternlicht and this is Mr. Bauerman," pointing to the occupant in the bed. "And his wife, Gertrude. I'm impressed the Mayor is showing concern for Mr. Bauerman. We're pleased he's off the critical list and resting comfortably."

Chester shook hands with Gertrude and the Baron.

The Baron noticed that Chester was nervous. Little beads of perspiration dotted Chester's forehead and his hand was sweaty when they greeted. The Baron braced for the drop of the other shoe.

Chester turned to Cletus. "I'm grateful for what you did. You saved lives by your heroic action."

Cletus smiled and whispered, "Thank you."

"Unfortunately, I must continue with the purpose of this visit. The Mayor is both grateful for Cletus' service to the public but at the same time is very concerned that the Airacuda he piloted had been left armed and unattended.

Armed, the plane presented a potential danger to those in its vicinity and thus constituted a criminal act. The Mayor believes Mr. Bauerman should not have landed the aircraft at the municipal airport, but at Sternlicht instead. Mr. Bauerman's heroic act yesterday softens the Mayor's position. Therefore, he doesn't want me to press charges. He'd settle for an apology from Mr. Bauerman instead."

Hearing the suggestion of a criminal act, Gertrude's face went white and she slumped against the bed. Cletus choked.

The Baron, speechless for a moment, stepped between the Bauermans and Chester.

"I can't think of a more inappropriate time or place to deliver the Mayor's reckless grasp for attention!"

The Baron teetered on his toes like a panther about to spring on a cowering rabbit. "I'm in charge of Sternlicht's operations. I knew Mr. Bauerman landed the Airacuda at the municipal airport in a state of desperation. Given our armament safety procedures, I was confident the plane represented no danger to anyone, including your Mayor. Bauerman is an employee of Sternlicht, and as a result, I take full responsibility for the presence of that plane at your airport. Mr. Bauerman will not appear before your Mayor or anyone else. He has committed no criminal act. The man was sick and landed the Airacuda at the nearest airfield. Please leave and inform your Mayor of my reply to his thoughtless charge."

"May I speak to you in the hallway, Mr. Otto? I truly want to get this whole sorry accusation behind all of us," Chester pleaded.

The two stepped into the hallway. "Personally, I detest the Mayor's petty charge. But if somebody doesn't speak to him, he'll push me to dig up some ordinance and press charges. If he does, I won't have any choice. There's always an ordinance or two that can apply to just about any situation."

"Bauerman doesn't need to answer to anyone," the Baron snapped. "The mere mention of criminal action will devastate him. This threatening ploy is despicable. Still, I don't want this charge, ridiculous as it is, to go to court. Tell your Mayor I'll speak to him about this matter at 9AM tomorrow in his office. Good day."

Disgusted, the Baron turned his back on the hapless Chester and re-entered the hospital room. The Baron pointed a finger at the pale Cletus lying in the hospital bed and sternly commanded, "I want you to erase that last scene from your mind. The Mayor should be locked up in an insane asylum for making such an accusation. You are a hero and don't you forget it. I'm off to let the Mayor know that, too. You get well in mind and body. I need you, Cletus."

"Thank you, Baron. I'll always do my best for you."

*   *   *

While the Baron drove back to Sternlicht, the muscles across his shoulders ached from the turmoil created by the Mayor's lackey. His stomach churned, his heart pounded, and his mind reeled with angry thoughts chasing one another. This episode struck him as a perfect example where life can be stranger than fiction. He couldn't imagine why someone would want to besmirch such a valiant deed.

He decided to grit his teeth, give the apology and that had better be an end to it. Better be.

*   *   *

Back at Sternlicht, as the Baron, deep in thought, walked passed his secretary, she cheerfully waved a message pad to catch his attention. "General Wolford would like you to call back as soon as you get in, Baron. And," continuing to wave the pad, "they brought the Airacuda back on a flatbed. It looked awful!"

The Baron nodded, entered his office, and closed the door with a soft click. He slumped into his chair and remained motionless. The room was quiet. He liked it that way when he needed to gather his thoughts, plan, plot. Tick, tick, tick. The wall clock caught his attention. He watched the second hand tick its way around the circumference of the dial. At his desk, with telephones, intercoms, and red buttons, he allowed each tick to remind himself of his authority at Sternlicht, and the first rate performance of his work of art, the Airacuda. Nothing so small as a twerp would stop him from being acclaimed a first-rate aircraft designer. Focused, he sat up straight, readied a pencil and pad, and buzzed his secretary.

"Put in a call to the general."

Moments later, a red button on his telephone console lit up.

"General Wolford, Frederick here."

"Frederick, Good morning. I want to talk with you about a contract regarding the damage to the Airacuda. I see Cletus' experience as an illuminating opportunity to study the effects of a piloted aircraft passing through an exploded bomber fireball at high altitude. Never in my experience has this happened, and it would likely occur in combat. It's an event our fighter aircraft should be prepared for.

"I would like you to examine, in depth, the effects on your pilot and aircraft. Then make recommendations."

"I just got in, general, but my secretary tells me the mechanics brought the plane back here a few minutes ago. I guess it looks pretty banged up. When we finish our conversation, I'm going over to the hangar and size things up. I appreciate your contract offer, and we'll get right on the job. I agree there is much to be learned from this experience. You can expect a substantial report on your desk shortly."

I'll wire you an advance so you can get started right away. Does Cletus have a telephone in his room? I want to express my appreciation."

"No, but if you call the hospital, they'll put one in it. My secretary will give you their telephone number. He'll be pleased to hear your voice. His wife's name is Gertrude. She may be there. A devoted couple. We're very proud of them. Good talking with you, general."

As the Baron hung up the phone, Henry walked in. The Baron held up his note pad. "I've got good news and I've got bad news. The Baron reiterated his conversation with the General including the part about the advance.

"I hope it's sizable. If we start everything you've mentioned, a cash flow crunch will rear its ugly head right quick if we don't have a check balance to back it up," Henry cautioned. "What's the bad news?"

As the Baron described Chester Peterson's visit to Cletus' hospital room, Henry shook his head. "What asses they are. For the Mayor to press such a charge? Is he a total airhead? And Chester, I would have thought he'd have more sensitivity than to barge in like that! It smacks of a desperate move on Renford's part. Hey, let me go and talk to Cliff. I know him better than you do."

"No. I told Patterson I would speak to the Mayor in the morning. It's all stupid, it upsets me, but I don't want Cletus to be charged with anything. Cletus was shaking when I left. He's one fearless pilot, but the thought he could be charged with breaking the law just terrifies him. In his mind, a good citizen just doesn't break the law. I'm going to give the Mayor the words he wants to hear and then I'll scream and holler all the way back in the car. Let's get rolling with things that really matter. You free to look at that plane now?"

*   *   *

When the Baron walked into the Mayor's office the next morning and saw Renford sitting behind his desk, the Baron concluded the Mayor not only looked like an ass, but a pompous one at that. Chester Patterson was sitting on the edge of a chair next to the desk. To the Baron, he looked smaller than the day before. The Baron only nodded a greeting to both men.

"Good Morning, Mr. Otto. I'm assuming you are here regarding the armed, unguarded aircraft at our airport." The mayor began to extend his hand but dropped it as he could tell the Baron was in no mood to perform the ritual.

"Yes. I'm here because I take full responsibility for any of our aircraft that land at the municipal airport. The plane was secured before Cletus left it. Only a trained pilot could activate the weapons system. We've never had, nor have I ever heard of, ammunition spontaneously exploding. Thus, the plane, in my mind, did not pose a threat to anyone or anything. However, Mr. Peterson informed Mr. and Mrs. Bauerman, and me, that you had considered pressing charges against Cletus for landing and leaving the Airacuda at the airport. If anyone should have posted a guard to the plane, it would have been me, not Cletus. Therefore, I am prepared to express an apology with the condition that when I do so, and we shake hands, this matter will go no further."

Chester looked hopefully at the Mayor.

The mayor relished the moment and wished Chester had thought of a photographer. "Of course, I've had to spend considerable, precious time deciding this case. With some reluctance, I have arrived at a decision. Given all the circumstances surrounding the issue, I'm willing to accept your apology."

"I apologize for leaving the armed aircraft at the airport unattended. Sternlicht will never repeat such an act again." The mayor stood up and they shook hands. The Baron said, in an even voice, "Good day," and left.

When the Mayor's door closed, Cliff looked at Chester and said, "You've just seen the power of the mayor's office exercised in the best interest of the community!"

Chester chose not to respond. In silence, he hoped this stupid move would someday come back to haunt the mayor.

CHAPTER 8

THE CHURCH

The Power Of A Quiet Moment With Him

The apology, given for the sake of expediency, created a mental turmoil in the Baron that was obvious to his secretary when he returned to his office. "Are you all right, Baron?"

"Not really but it doesn't concern you. I don't want any calls for awhile." He closed his office door behind him.

His indignation was at a point of boiling over. He had to do something physical like chop wood, dig in the garden, or take a long walk to purge his frustrations. Staring at the wall wasn't releasing the tension. He told his secretary he was going home for the day.

Annie saw a troubled husband the moment he stepped into the house. Unusual for him to come home this time of the day, she asked, "Fred, what's wrong?"

"Can't talk about it right now. Too upset. I'm going out back and chop wood for awhile".

The cord of maple looked big enough to shake out the demons so the Baron began to chop non-stop. After an hour of work, he had converted much of the cord to fireplace-size, but the demons were still at work in his head. Such an apology was the first in his life, and he didn't seem to have a clue as to the method of exorcism. Even a long walk in the hills failed.

Back home, Annie directed him to a dining room chair, sat down opposite him and asked, "Fred, what's wrong—and don't get up and walk away!"

Fred's face darkened as he recounted Chester's visit to the hospital and the apology that followed. "He was totally oblivious to the crushing distress he heaped on the Bauermans by pushing Chester into that hospital room to mouth a fabricated ultimatum. I can get upset when someone goofs, but after I've had my say, I forget it. But, here, no one goofed and I had to get down on my knees because a vindictive twerp could still derive pleasure by mounting a legal case. Such a lawsuit wouldn't see the light of day in a court room because of its laughable nature. It rankles me no end that I have no recourse!"

"Forgive and forget," Annie suggested.

"Right now neither is possible. Forgive and forget—that's easy to say," Fred countered.

"Look, you're in a terrible state of mind, and it makes me feel awful when you are. I want to help but judging from this conversation I'm not going to be able to. There is much deeper meaning to this whole thing so you need the counsel that only God can give. Go to the mission and just sit in a pew and look at the cross. Comfort will come."

"I'm in no mood to do that."

"I'm not asking, I'm telling. Mood or no mood. Just go."

Fred looked at her resolute face. In those times when he believed a problem insurmountable, she always had a suggestion that might not solve the problem, but it kept things going until a solution surfaced. At the moment, even though sitting in church didn't seem too promising, the Baron drove to the mission.

St. John's Mission was a small parish two miles from Sternlicht serving farm Catholics and some from Sternlicht. The Ottos attended the small white church from the time they arrived in Indiana. The sun was low in the sky, and the tombstones in the graveyard on the side of the church cast long shadows. The name on one blurred into his own name. Would he die before Anne?

He walked up a short flight of stairs to the front

door. He tried the door; it wasn't locked. Father Prokas was a trusting soul. The congregation knew it was his way of encouraging troubled minds to visit.

He entered the vestibule of the church. It was small and quiet. The far wall was lined with wooden pegs for coats, hats, and whatever parishioners wanted to leave behind before entering the church proper. The first time Annie and he entered the vestibule to attend Mass those many years before, there was one empty peg left at the corner of the room. A man was hanging his coat next to it.

The Baron walked to the peg, pointed to it and said, "Hi, I'm new here. Is this peg free or will someone be using it?"

"First come, first pick," the man said smiling.

The Baron quickly noticed he was someone used to hard labor. About fifty, his face was ruddy, tanned. "Gonna live in these parts or just passing through?" the man asked.

"Hope to make this area my home. Thought we'd go to Mass in the country because I'm looking for some land. Figured the parishioners would be the best to ask about available property."

"You don't look like a farmer, but then, farmers come in all sizes and shapes as you can see when you look around. What kind of farming you planning to do?"

"I'm not planning to farm but rather to start an airplane business. For a long runway, I need flat land that doesn't cost much."

"You might be pretty close to what you want. Take that gravel road a piece thata way and you'll come to a ring of hills. They almost surround a large flat piece of ground that ain't much good for nothin'. Seldom rains there so crops don't grow. Bank owns it. Haggle for the price. They'll be glad to unload it. This is a friendly parish.

Hope to see you and the missus again."

When Mass ended, they drove to the ring of hills. He parked on the outer side of the hill and walked to the top. When he looked over the vast, flat expanse, he knew he was home.

He and Annie liked the mission. It was a mixed crowd of Polish, German, and a few Hungarians. Mostly farmers, and remarkably cooperative. If someone's horses went lame, there would always be a team for loan until recovery. The Polish dances were best. Polkas always made him sweat.

All these cleansing thoughts ran through the Baron's mind as he entered the church proper. Light still radiated through the stained glass windows illuminating all but the front of the large crucifix hanging over the altar. The face was not clearly visible and required close scrutiny if one wished to study it. The Baron wondered if Father Prokas planned that effect to motivate contemplation.

Forgiving something he felt was right was new territory for the Baron. He needed guidance on this one.

The Baron looked up at the Cross. The thought struck him that this man got nailed because he told the truth. Yet, the face looked calm and peaceful as if some major assignment had been accomplished, despite the final pain and suffering.

The eyes were cast downward and the Baron's eyes followed them to a missal lying next to him on the pew. He picked it up to place it in the book rack. A small white prayer card stuck out of the book. He flipped to it. At the top of the card bold letters proclaimed, "The Prayer of St. Francis." Pausing to read, he connected with the verse, "It is better to understand than to be understood."

"To understand." He'd read that prayer before, but this time the phrase meant something immediate.

He pondered the relevance of the phrase as an approach he should take with Cliff. It seemed a stretch to believe the armed plane was like a loaded gun. He believed a big difference existed between a disarmed Airacuda and a gun that only needed to be cocked to fire. Still, he saw a modicum of similarity. Maybe he should have sent someone to guard the plane until they removed it the next day. If for no other reason than to shoo off souvenir hunters.

The tilt of the scale of judgment suggested he bear some responsibility in provoking Cliff's ire. He leaned toward understanding the mayor's position.

He took score. The apology pacified the mayor. Cletus was off the hook. He could forget the matter and get on with his mission. Most of all, he hoped he hadn't hurt Annie with his anger.

He looked up again, at a face continuing to exhibit calm and serenity. The Baron now became aware that he, too, felt again relaxed and positive about the future. He felt thankful for the opportunity to do many things others could never even dream of doing. He took pride in converting an arid patch of ground to a thriving aircraft factory. This accomplishment had opened doors even he hadn't imagined possible. He was appreciative and made the sign of the cross.

The Baron left the church and drove back to Sternlicht. This time Annie saw the personality she loved enter the Otto residence. The Baron took her into his arms, looked into her eyes and said, "I'm at peace now."

CHAPTER 9

THE BARON SUGGESTS A SOLUTION

Frederick Otto's secretary leaned toward her intercom to talk. "Baron, Ernst Weinbaum wishes to speak with you. Line two."

The Baron pressed key two and picked up the phone. "Good morning, old friend."

"Good morning, Fred. Uh, can we get together? I need to speak with you in private."

"Sure, when and where?"

"Could we chat in the park?"

Not an unusual request. From time to time when they wanted to talk business or present an idea where no one else would hear, they would meet in the park.

"You name the time, and we'll meet at that bench at the bend in the river. Annie and I are having dinner at Henry's this evening. I could drop Annie off at their house and meet you at 5:45PM. How's that?"

"Just fine. See you then."

At 5:45PM, the Baron parked and walked to the bench where he met Ernst Weinbaum, President of the Weinbaum Motor Company. The Baron pondered the purpose of this discreet meeting. If it were about a problem casting motors for the Airacuda, he carried a folder of relevant blueprints. As the Baron approached, Ernst stood up and they shook hands warmly.

"Ernst, you've got that worried look again. What could be bothering an old fighter like you?"

"It's my brother, David. These are horrendous times for Jews in Germany. He should have left when I did, and I've been after him to immigrate ever since. But no. As a metallurgist, things were going good at the Pflug plant and at present, he heads up a group developing a spectrometer for measuring the quantity of elements in alloys. Because he's the best in the business, they allow him certain privileges not afforded to other Jews. He writes encoded letters to us reporting these dire times."

Weinbaum twisted a handkerchief in his hands. "But he fears privileges will end once the spectrometer is up and running. Then God only knows what will happen to him. He writes that Jews simply disappear and few seem to care. I love my brother. He's all that's left in the family. I've got to get him out of Germany."

Ernst turned to the Baron. "You're the only one I can discuss this with. Believe me, I hate to impose upon you, but I can't leave any stone unturned. Can you think of any way he and his wife could be smuggled out? He has no passport, and his travel is restricted to Germany. He's afraid to attempt political asylum in any neighboring country. Everybody is afraid of German retaliation, and he would just be sent back. And that's treason and certain execution."

With that, the two friends sat in silence, the Baron thinking and Ernst hoping. They gazed at the peaceful river drifting by. A fisherman offshore in a rowboat looked up, waved, and then stared at his bobber.

The Baron unbuttoned his jacket. "They say somebody caught a four pound bass here a few days ago. Do they have any children or anyone else that is expecting to come with them?"

"No".

"Then a small three passenger plane would be enough. Think he could arrange a business trip to Freiburg, which is in der Schwarzwald, ah, the Black Forest, near the southern border of France? Say, late this summer about five months from now. Maybe set up a conference on some technical problem he knows isn't going to be solved by then? This would assure his presence in the area at a specific time. Arrange it over a weekend. Best on a Saturday when he and his wife could picnic in the Black Forest. Would be seen as harmless enough. They would never suspect he would try to walk across the border in such terrain.

"Cletus Bauerman was born there. Immigrated to the U.S. in his late 20's. It's a mountainous region. He should be able to recall a flat open area, at about a 500 foot altitude, and large enough for a small plane to land on. Our pilot would fly across the border at dusk, land, and fly them back into France. Disguise them as American tourists and bring them back in some group that is returning to the U.S."

Weinbaum shifted on the bench and uttered fervently, "Ingenious!"

"I know there are German-Americans from Chicago who vacation in France and Germany. I could make discrete contact and get your brother and wife in with them. They all speak German and so another couple joining them in France would not be unusual".

At the mention of Chicago, Ernst felt some of the weight lift from his shoulders. "They would blend in great with a Chicago group. They could feign sickness like food poisoning or seasickness enabling them to be apart from the group most of the time."

The Baron cautioned. "It's absolutely paramount they don't disclose their true identity to anyone. There could be passengers on the ship who would like to get attention by turning them into authorities. German bureaucrats can be quite lavish with rewards if they are handed a big fish."

The next thought brought a halt to the Baron's

rescue scheme. He lightly poked a pencil on his forehead as he considered the crucial question. Who would fly the plane?

He expressed this quandary to Ernst. "Who wouldn't draw attention flying a small plane from France to and along the German border? Emil says there are German spies everywhere in Europe. They're methodical and keep records on everything. They know who flies in and out of airports in France. Especially small planes. The plan must be perfect. No one must connect the disappearance of two vacationers with a pleasure flight of a small plane from an airfield 100 or so miles away. German reaction to a connection would be swift, lethal and no telling who would suffer the consequences.

"Since Cletus once lived there, he can't be the pilot. He'd be recognized right away and suspected."

They slipped into thoughtful silence. Ernst leaned his elbows on his knees and looked at the ground as the Baron got up and walked to the water's edge. Nothing moved, not even the bobber. Only the river drifted by.

After a few minutes, the Baron returned to Ernst. "I have a sketch of the idea, and I think I know who could fly the plane and not draw attention. But the pilot of that plane must have a reason to be in the area of France adjacent to Freiburg for a period of about two months. This would give him time to find the area he would land on in Germany. The Black Forest is remote. Hopefully, the pilot can cross the border, and locate the proposed landing strip without being detected. If he crosses the border and is not questioned about it, the rescue should succeed. Here's an arrangement I have to make." The Baron emphasized this point by touching his index fingers together. "Do you know Pierre Lavern, the farmer just west of town?"

"Yes, we've bought eggs from them."

"His brother, Victor, has a farm Colmar, France. There has to be an airfield around there. Pierre will need to be convinced to contact his brother and arrange for our pilot to work on the farm during this coming summer. However, Pierre has always been angry with me because he thinks I shot down and killed his oldest brother in a dogfight during World War I. I shot down four French planes but I don't know who the pilots were and Pierre doesn't either. I'm thinking of a person who could talk to Pierre's wife paving the way for me to talk with Pierre. That's Mercedes, Henry's wife. Yet I know when I share the whole scheme with her, it's going to create an emotional crisis."

"Why?"

"Because, in my opinion, only her son, Wolfgang, can pull it off."

Ernst gently touched the Baron's shoulder. "I hated to involve you, Fred. But as I searched my acquaintances, only you surfaced as the individual who could and would see this through. If you have a fault, it's that you never back away from something you think you can do. If you do back away, I'll fully understand, my friend. It's a mission that could be catastrophic."

"Annie and I are dining at Henry's this evening. I'll broach the subject after supper and see what happens. I can't tell you which way it will go. I'm quite certain Pierre's wife is in the Women's Club and Mercedes could speak with her at one of their meetings. As I outline the plan, the danger of the mission will become crystal clear to her. The crisis point will surface when I mention Wolfgang as the pilot. Talk about a mother bear protecting her cub. That's how she feels about her Wolfy. But her Wolfy is the one who could pull it off."

Just then the fisherman gave a whoop and the two watched him pull a fish out of the water into his boat. The two onshore hoped his catch signaled a good omen for the enterprise they were about to undertake.

"I'll be in touch, Ernst. If it's a go, I'll give you a call telling you the die is cast. You'll proceed to contact your brother setting up a correspondence enabling you to monitor his progress. No luggage, just them, nothing else. Those French four passenger planes are under-powered as it is. Also, you'll have to arrange for bogus U.S. passports."

Dusk began to fall as the two parted. Emotion welled up in Ernst as he glimpsed a ray of hope in this exchange. "God speed!" he whispered.

                    *   *   *

The darkness over Europe was of a different kind as the Nazi machine began flexing its intentions of conquest.

CHAPTER 10

THE DANGER IS CRYSTAL CLEAR TO HER

"Guten abend, bonsoir (both Good Evening), wie geht's (how's everything), and tres bien (very good)," were followed by hugs and kisses as Fred and Annie were greeted into the home of Henry and Mercedes. Walking into the living room, Fred asked about the children.

"Jacqueline ate early and is at ballet practice. Wolf begs his pardon because he is meeting Carl and Tank at the Big Top for hamburgers. Don't let on that I told you, but he wants to be there. He thinks Michele will also come with some of her friends and hopes they could all eat together. We've met her. She is both talented and beautiful. Speaks Parisian French, which of course, delights Henry and me. Such savoir-vivre! (good breeding) We approve," she stated laughingly nodding her head. I know we are all hungry, so let's go to the dining room and partake of a roast baked in the luxurious Luxembourg style".

During the course of the meal, Mercedes mentioned a trip she and Wolf would be taking. "Kathleen Temple called last night, long distance from Manhattan, and invited me to join the Starlets chorus line again for the Thanksgiving weekend. Two of the dancers will be absent, and she wants to make certain their replacements are prepared. I said, of course, I'm flattered, and yes, I'll be there. It is so much fun. And more! She is sending me the words to a French ditty she wants me to solo. She is such a good friend! She suggested I bring Wolfy again. Seems several of the dancers were really impressed with him last year. We all went to the Hudson Ballroom after the show, and they had such a good time dancing with him. He's such a charmer! Wolfy will fly me up the Wednesday before Thanksgiving and Henry is taking the evening train."

As Mercedes expressed enthusiasm about the forthcoming trip, Fred became more concerned about how he was going to convince her that her Wolfy would be the right pick for the rescue. He knew this sell would take all the tact he could muster.

At the end of dessert, the women began clearing the dishes. The Baron motioned them to sit down because he had a matter he wished to discuss. "If it's business," Mercedes gestured negatively, "I'd like to take mother into the den and show her the dress I just bought. I didn't have time before supper."

"It's a matter we should all talk about. Pour a little more coffee, please, and I'll explain."

The women sat down at the table and the Baron described his meeting with Ernst Weinbaum and the rescue plot they had worked out. He left out the name of the proposed pilot.

"That sounds quite exciting but dangerous. Those Nazis guard their borders with a sharp bayonet," exclaimed Mercedes.

"That's why I chose the adjacent cities of Freiburg in Germany and Colmar in France. It's a mountainous region that makes walking across the border difficult. Thus, the Germans concentrate their vigilance on the roads and railways. It will be easier to fly from an airport, cross the border at dusk, land, pick up the two, and make it back without being seen. At the airport, the couple will leave the plane at the end of the runway. The plane then taxis back to the hanger with as many occupants as when it left".

"Freiburg?, isn't that where Cletus Bauerman was born and raised? How fortunate, you not only have a plan but a pilot as well. What's to talk about?" asked Mercedes.

The Baron bit the bullet. "The first part of your assessment is correct, the second is not. If the pick up succeeds, Cletus would be suspect. Since his combat flying in the '36 Spanish conflict, his presence milking cows and pitching hay on the farm wouldn't make sense. No, it has to be someone who would be free to spend a summer on a French farm to, say, polish his French but happens to be a pilot as well. And in this case, a skilled pilot who can remain in control in the presence of danger." The Baron stopped and let everyone draw their own conclusions.

A skilled pilot? Each listener speculated from their list of candidates for this mission.

Henry knew whom the Baron would suggest. He averted his wife's eyes fearing she would immediately guess. He would let her draw such conclusion by herself.

Mercedes tapped her finger on her cheek as she considered the few she knew. Suddenly she thought of the one person who the Baron could trust without qualification and she blanched. "Are you thinking of my Wolfy?"

Knowing the anguish that was engulfing her, he tried to soften his affirmative answer by whispering, "Yes."

Mercedes began to cry. Then Annie. Tears came to both Henry and the Baron. After a few moments, the Baron cleared his throat, wiped his eyes and presented the reasons for his choice.

"The four of us, and those close to us, have a destiny to fulfill. We had no say in whom our parents would be. But from the moment of our birth, God's plan has brought us together, each with unique and compelling talents to be leaders, capable of inspiring others to achieve their best. Annie and I came with nothing more than her jewels, but God put those jewels into her hands for a reason. I am convinced that reason is Sternlicht. We were destined to come to America and put right all the things our misguided brethren in the Fatherland are doing wrong.

"We can't do it all, but because we are of German heritage, we must prepare for the conflict will come. God sent Weinbaum to me. I know this with all my soul. There is a reason his brother and wife must be brought to America. I don't know what that reason is, but time will tell. God works in mysterious ways. I have faith God will see Wolf through this trial.

We all know there is something special about Wolf. One could believe Michele was brought into our lives because only a special woman is deserving of Wolf. As Emil is my son, I do feel, deep in my heart, the love you must feel for Wolf, Mercedes. I am painfully aware Emil is skating on thin ice when he conducts business in Europe, especially in Germany and Austria. If they should uncover any relationship between Emil and our Army intelligence, he is a dead man. Let me conclude, I will not send Wolf on this mission unless I think every piece of the puzzle is safely in place. He's my grandson, too."

As Mercedes listened to the Baron's reasoning, her world became unreal. She felt herself floating. The Baron's voice sounded as if he were in a distant barrel. She could only think, my cherished son?

"My Wolfy?" she asked the Baron. Her body felt numb. Squinting at the blurred forms sitting at her table, she quietly said, "Entschuldigen Sie" (Pardon Me), walked into the kitchen and closed the door. Silence again reigned at the table.

Annie broke the silence with "Fred, is there no one else? What about Kermit Schneider?"

"Kermit doesn't speak French, negating the idea of him working on a French farm. I've thought of others, but I still come up with Wolf as one person who would attract the least attention. He's been flying the 'Little Grasshopper' more than anyone else. He's familiar with short landings and takeoffs which will be the hardest part of the trip."

Elbows on the table, the Baron gestured the absence of likely pilots with a flair of his hands. "Other pilots Wolf's age? I've considered some but their parents would be equally distressed with such a request. They'd think, Why not Wolfgang? It's his grandfather's agreement."

"There's Carl Sepler," the Baron speculated. "He could do it. Got all the qualifications. But he has a wife and two children. What would they think? In war, you can be a hero to many. The secret rescue of two in the shadow of certain execution or imprisonment is not likely to attract any takers."

The Baron paused, then added, "If Henry and Mercedes say no—end of discussion.. I'll understand and come up with another plan."

When the Baron finished, they sat thinking and listening to the faint steps of Mercedes as she paced the kitchen floor. They imagined her mind grappling with the conflicting thoughts of a protective mother and an opportunity to do good in the face of evil.

Henry suggested a further dimension to the effort. "David Weinbaum is a metallurgist and there is the possibility he may have knowledge of the alloy the Germans use in their motor blocks. Their engines run hotter than ours, don't seize, and thus achieve greater efficiency and power from their gasoline. If our engines ran as hot as theirs did, we'd be one rung up on the Luftwaffe. If we go to war with the Axis powers, this edge will guarantee a major production contract for the Airacudas. This may have a mercenary ring to it, but we aren't doing this in some sort of vacuum. A lot more is at stake. However, given all that has been said at the table, I don't think we should say anything to Mercedes when she comes back. She's making a decision, as we speak, and we will honor her decision, Dad. It we were at war, I'd say, go. But this is different."

The pacing in the kitchen quickened. Everybody at the table prayed she would come back and join them. Mercedes entered the dining room, face red from crying, handkerchief in hand, and sat down at her place at the table.

"Wolf has been such a wonderful gift to Henry and me. Jacqueline, too, of course. His talent in music is so dear to me. We play the piano together and sing in French. Such enjoyment. I just can't bear the thought of losing him." With that last dreadful thought, Mercedes began to cry again.

The table fell silent.

After a moment, she straightened up in her chair and spoke to the Baron. "I know you mean well and I appreciate your concern for me. As I follow the events in Europe, I feel us being drawn into another terrible war and many of our young people will again have to pay the ultimate price. I guess my only solution to the darkness over Europe will be to enjoy my children while I can. God willing, he will come back to us."

At this point, Annie indicated, by clearing her throat, she wished to comment. Mercedes paused and all waited for Annie's reaction. "We're here, talking about someone embarking on a dangerous mission and that person isn't even here to comment. Maybe he wouldn't want to go."

The Baron quickly rejected her caution. "He'll do it."

Mercedes slid back into her chair to distance herself from the Baron's presumption. "We would be hasty to assume Wolf's decision. Henry and I will talk with Wolf and let him decide."

The Baron slowly placed his hands on the table. "I need to know--soon."

No one spoke. There was no logical reaction to the Baron's request other than to wait for the conversation with Wolf.

Always the gracious host, Mercedes changed the direction of the conversation by suggesting a game. "We are all together now. Let's do something to give relief from these trying times. How about a few hands of bridge?" As she ended her reaction to the Baron's troubling plan with a smile, the other three responded with a cheerful, "Yes."

Henry set up the card table and handed the cards to the Baron. As the Baron dealt the first hand, each, while watching the cards fall before them, reflected silently on the emotional discourse that just occurred.

The Baron. God, it was awful to put Mercedes on the spot. We need more skilled pilots at the level of Wolf and Cletus. The choice could have been someone other than family.

Annie. I know what she is going through. Emil is always the one who travels in Europe to do the Sternlicht business. Everyone knows danger is at his heels all the time. I wish he'd come home and do his work in America. That's why we came here!

Henry. We'll have to count on the Lord to get Wolf back home safe. I hope Weinbaum understands what we have to go through to fetch his brother who should have come here a long time ago. Spectrophotometer. If we could get a piece of that Messerschmitt 109 engine block, he'd be able to tell us what metals are in it.

Mercedes. My Wolfy. I hope Michele showed up at the Big Top tonight. He needs more time to be with his friends. They always keep him so busy at the plant or flying. I know that Wolfy and Michele are made for one another. I do want grandchildren.

Cards went well for Mercedes and the Baron. Fred sensed their good fortune helped her think more positive about the task soon to be asked of Wolfgang. They won two games straight so Mercedes suggested they conclude the evening with some dessert. She and Annie went into the kitchen to prepare it leaving Henry and the Baron at the card table.

"I still have to ask Mercedes to contact Zelia and obtain Pierre's cooperation. Time is of the essence."

Henry agreed. "I don't suppose tomorrow or the next day would be any easier on her. If she is resigned to this matter, she'll do it. Maybe she'll feel more confident about the whole thing if she can play a part in it's organization. Here they come."

"Carrot cake is the tasty morsel I've prepared for the winner's circle and the pair second best," quipped Mercedes.

"We'll expect the same when we take honors, right, son?" Annie asked.

"Thou speakest the truth, Mutti!" Henry returned.

They chatted as they ate the carrot cake. About to finish, the Baron turned to Mercedes and said,"There is still one piece of unfinished business I must conclude. The plan as I see it, begins with a contact by you."

"Frederick!" Annie whispered, "She's endured enough for one night!"

Mercedes lowered her fork on her dessert plate, placed her hand on Annie's, and looking at the Baron asked, "With whom?"

"Zelia Lavern. Pierre is still upset with me. Thinks I shot down his brother. You can be persuasive and I'll wager, if you spoke to Zelia about the importance of this mission, she might agree to take a positive approach with her husband. Maybe stress national defense for both France and the United States.

"The pilot, if it is Wolf, has to work on a farm near the German border. Pierre Lavern's brother owns a farm near Colmar. She must ask him to contact his brother and arrange for the pilot to live and work there in preparation for his mission. You can assure her that every precaution will be taken to avoid any danger to his brother, Victor, family and farm."

"Baron, I hope you're right in all this. What if something goes wrong?" Mercedes queried.

"Something could go wrong. Can't say nothing will. We'll build escape hatches in the plan to provide safe abort should a condition dictate," assured the Baron as he tapped his fingers together. "Emil will be in Europe at the time. He's adept at gleaning information from his various contacts that might indicate such a mission is suspected."

"Women's club meets tomorrow. I could give her a ring and ask her to drop by the house before she goes to the meeting. It's not something I would want to talk about there."

His mission completed for the night, the Baron suggested they leave as the morrow always brings challenges that are best met after a good night's sleep. After hugs and kisses, the Baron and Annie drove back to Sternlicht.

After their guests departed, Henry helped Mercedes clear the table and wash the dishes. As Mercedes stood at the sink, Henry put his hand on her shoulder. She pulled her shoulder inward, but he continued contact anyway. "I didn't know Dad had met with Weinbaum this afternoon and was going to spring this request on us tonight."

"If he's anxious to find out the composition of the metal, why doesn't he fly them out?" Mercedes demanded as she scrubbed a plate.

"Well-"

"Please, don't give an excuse. It's our son that is being asked to take chances."

Henry raised a finger to emphasize a point but Mercedes turned her head away. He knew no further comments would be exchanged until Wolf returned home.

Choirs finished, Henry read the paper while Mercedes played a piece by Chopin. For both, the hall clock ticked slower than usual.

An hour past. Time for Wolf to return.

Car lights moved up the driveway. A door opened and closed. Mercedes stopped playing. Both heard footsteps on the porch.

Wolf, smiling, came through the front door. "Hi, Mom and Dad." He hung his jacket in the hall closet and pointed to the hall clock. "Right on time. Any carrot cake left?"

"In the frig. Did you have a good time?" Mercedes asked.

Wolf opened the refrigerator and withdrew a cake pan three-fourths empty.

"Ya. Everybody was there. Bet Grandpa ate two pieces. What a bunch! Sandy, Tank's sister, was telling how she is trying to teach their old dog new tricks. Well as the old saw goes, it wasn't working, but the way she told it, we were all in stitches."

"Was Michele there?"

"She wasn't there at first and I thought, Darn it! Finally, she came in with Cori Jameson and we all sat in that big booth in the back. After Sandy talked about her dog, Michele chimed in with her attempts to train horses. I guess she's gotten bumped around but doesn't seem to mind."

"Trained to do what?"

Wolf set the cake pan on the kitchen table, picked up the cake knife and began to cut a piece. Henry reached over and covered a corner

of the cake for himself. Wolf cut teasingly close
to his father's hand.

"No skin Wolf, just cake for yourself," Henry
cautioned.

"Dad, so little faith! Ah, things like accept
the bit and follow her without reins, whatever
that's all about. Anyway, I asked her to come to
the picnic at Sternlicht Sunday. She said yes.
Can I pick her up first, and then, come and get
you?" Wolf asked as he pointed to his parents.

"Sure, that's okay, Wolf. We have something
to talk about. It's a decision you have to make.
Your choice will be fine with us," Henry's voice
trailed off with the last sentence.

With a mouthful of cake, Wolf garbled, "Wha'
bow?"

"Wolf, please!"

Wolf quickly swallowed enough to say, "Sorry,
Mom."

"Never, never."

"I know, mom, never talk with a mow' ho!"

Mercedes' eyes filled with tears and one ran
down her cheek.

"Mom, what are you crying about? I'll do
anything you ask!"

Mercedes knuckles went white as she gripped
the arms of her chair. Her mouth opened, her lips
trembled, but no words came out.

Wolf, with grave concern, turned to his father.
"Dad, what's up?"

Henry summarized the earlier conversation.
"This afternoon Ernst Weinbaum came to your
grandfather with a very difficult, and I might
say, dangerous request." He paused.

"To do what?"

"To fly his brother and wife out of Germany."

"Can't he buy them a train or plane ticket?"

"The German border is closed to any Jew trying
to leave. Furthermore, his brother is a noted

spectroscopist, and Ernst thinks the Germans will use him until he's of no further use, and then, send him and his wife to concentration camp.

"Why Jews?"

"It's Hitler. He thinks Jews are their problem and he's made life miserable for them. Apparently even killing some of them."

"What's this dangerous request?"

"Your grandfather wants-ah." Henry hesitated as he looked at Mercedes. Although her lips were gray and her face tense, he had to continue. "He wants you to work on Pierre Lavern's brother's farm near Colmar, France, and fly the couple from an isolated field in Germany to the airport at Colmar. Your uncle, Emil, will be there with a car to drive them to Cherbourg where they'll board a liner to the U.S."

Wolf gave a confident shrug to his shoulders. "I'll just rent a plane and be back in no time. Work on a farm? I don't know anything about farming. What would I do there?"

"The plan is, if you go, to work on Pierre's farm, here for about a month to learn the ropes and then sail to France mid-summer."

"Work on Lavern's farm and see Michele everyday? Sounds good to me!" Wolf exclaimed with a big grin. "When can I start? And a summer in France? Wundervoll!"

"This rescue scheme is fraught with danger. That's what has both your mother and I concerned. We know of the risks from the messages we intercept in the Decode Center. People are being killed for aiding Jews. You'd fall in that category. If caught, tragedy."

Mercedes reacted to the word "caught" with a sucking gasp.

"Hey, I speak German and French. I'd know what people are saying. I'd watch my back. The rescue time shouldn't amount to more than a couple of hours."

Mercedes shook her head in dismay. "It's so risky. Instead of saving two, three could be shot. Furthermore, I'm not convinced saving the Weinbaums is uppermost in the Baron's mind. He seems driven to spare nothing in making the Airacuda the best to win a big contract for his company."

Henry expressed his dilemma. "That's where I'm in a crummy situation. You're my son and Sternlicht is our bread and butter. You and your mother decide."

Wolf stood up and put his arms around his mother. "Mom, this doesn't sound all that tough. When I'm there and I think I can't do it, I won't. Believe me, I won't." They hugged one another.

Wolf turned to his father. "What's the next step? Do the Laverns know I'm coming? Michele sure didn't give any hint."

"Not yet. Tomorrow your mother will meet with Zelia and broach the matter with her. If Zelia agrees, then Zelia will have to convince Pierre to set up your visit with his brother."

"Mom," Wolf asked, "will you do that?"

Mercedes looked at Henry and then at her son. With obvious reluctance to becoming a participant in such a hazardous plot, she replied, "Yes."

CHAPTER 11

WOLFGANG LEARNS HIS DISGUISE

<u>In The Beginning</u>
"Mama, who was on the phone?" Michele inquired.

"It was Mercedes Otto. She would like me to stop by her home for tea before we go to the Women's Club meeting," her mother answered after hanging up the receiver.

"What did she want? Why did she call? Did she mention me?" Michele asked.

"She didn't say. I sensed some urgency in her voice, but she didn't mention your name. Could be something about the coming election of the new president. I've heard her voice concern about the direction of the club. She asked if I would come about eleven this morning.

"By the way, Michele, you seem a bit tense lately. Every time the phone rings you jump a foot. Something bothering you? Should I know something?"

"No, Mama," Michele replied. "Nothing's bothering me. Well, I feel uneasy about somebody. When the phone rings, I think it's somebody. It's so silly."

Zelia sat down at the kitchen table and began to peel apples. She motioned Michele to sit down, too.

"It's not silly if it makes you jump a foot. Is that somebody Wolfgang?"

"Yes, it is, but not why you might think."

"What might I not think."

"That his parent may have the notion I'm not good enough for him."

"Not good enough? I should think so! You feared her call was to convey such a message?"

"When I had dinner with his family the other night it was like--I don't know--a movie. All night we only spoke French. Like we were in France or something. The conversation began with how Mr. and Mrs. Otto met in a night club in Luxemburg. She was a dancer, and he had forgotten his hat. The talk shifted to Wolfgang flying a glider. Then Mr. Otto asked me what I did on the farm."

Michele rose out of her chair and paced about the kitchen. "Oh, my, after all that talk about Luxemburg and flying gliders, how was I to talk about picking up eggs at the coup? Bedding the horses? Please, Mama, I really like Wolfgang, but sometimes I wonder if they'd rather he'd date a banker's daughter, or maybe a movie star. Someone sophisticated. He's witty, thoughtful. He could go with anyone."

"Have they said anything to you that would make you think this way?"

"No, but it's times like that that I feel-- small. I don't like that feeling. Yet, when I got on the cheerleading squad I knew I could be somebody, be one of them. Lately, I've thought about being somebody. Somebody you'd be proud of, somebody they'd want in their circle. It's weird. I want to date Wolfgang, be his girlfriend. Still, it gives me mixed feelings. I like him a lot, but I want to do things before I get married, have children, settle down."

Zelia handed Michele a bowl and knife and motioned her to cut the peeled apples for a pie. Reaching across the table, Zelia squeezed Michele's hand. "To begin with, your father and I couldn't be more proud of you. The fact they invited you for supper says a lot. A feather in your hat. They may have chosen to speak French to make you feel at home. Doesn't sound like vain parents to me. And just what do you want to be before you get married?"

"You'll die when I tell you!"

"No, I won't. Maybe your father will."

"When I saw Mr. Bauerman fly that airplane up the river—a shiny powerful machine—I wanted to be flying it! He put it on its tail and shot through the clouds. That's got to be exciting. It's something I'd like to do—be a pilot."

"Girls don't fly planes. You can still fly but as a stewardess. You'll have to become a nurse-first."

"I don't want to be a waitress in the back of the plane. I want to be a pilot in the front of the plane!" She finished slicing one apple and picked another. "There are women pilots, like Helen Richey and Jacqueline Cochran. They fly and do such exciting things. Mama, I love you and Papa but I want wings to go places, do things and be somebody."

"Dad will bring up Amelia Earhart missing in the Pacific."

"Runaway teams kill farmers, too!"

"I know. It's just so different."

"Please talk to him. I haven't asked for much. This is something I want."

"We've talked about you being a nurse or a teacher, but a pilot? Mon Dieu. (My God.) What a difference a generation makes. I want you to do the things you dream about. I'll think of a way of convincing your father to allow you.

"Oh, Mama, I know I should have mentioned this sooner 'cause you're easier to talk with than papa. I feel better already and I won't be jumping the next time the phone rings."

After I talk with Mercedes about her matter, I'll hint about your feelings for Wolf. We both have such gems as children."

As Zelia patted her cheek, she gazed lovingly at Michele. "So we're going to talk about something she wishes to be held confidential?" She rubbed her hands together. "Now I'm getting excited to find out what she has to say!"

*   *   *

Pierre drove Zelia by horse and buggy into the Northern Bend suburb where Mercedes Otto lived. Embarrassed by the loud clickity-clack of the metal shoes on the pavement, Zelia asked Pierre to let her off a block from her destination. She walked toward a modest home with a manicured lawn and bright flowers ringing a sidewalk that curved around the house to the backyard. A black Buick sat on the paved driveway outside an attached garage.

To Zelia, the modest home masked the far more complex and adventuresome lives of its occupants. She knew Mercedes was from Luxembourg and enjoyed speaking French with her whenever they conversed at the Club. With an air of excitement, she walked to the front door. The front of the house was dominated by two large picture windows. A grand piano was visible through the right window. She pressed the buzzer and heard footsteps approaching from within.

Mercedes opened the door and cheerfully greeted with "Bonjour, Zelia. Thank you for coming on such short notice. Please come in."

Zelia entered into a hallway and followed Mercedes through the first door on the left into a large brightly-lit living room. The setting was graceful. Zelia imagined the décor' nurtured conversation, participation and family tradition. To the left, the grand piano. To the right, a fireplace provided the setting for a coffee table encircled by a sofa and an array of chairs. A tea set and plate of cookies sat on the coffee table.

"Please sit down, Zelia. May I pour you some tea?"

"Of course," replied Zelia as she made herself

comfortable in an upright chair near the coffee table.

"I appreciate your coming on such short notice. I will be frank. I have something to ask of you." Mercedes paused while pouring two cups of tea. "You may wish not to do it, and I will understand. Please believe me when I say, I will understand. Whichever way you decide, I must request you keep this matter in total confidence, not to be mentioned to anyone outside your immediate family. I apologize for this rather abrupt request, but when you hear what I have to say, I believe you will understand my caution."

"This all sounds very serious. I don't know what my reaction will be, but I can assure you, I will keep this conversation confidential."

Mercedes, moving to the edge of her chair, related the whole plot beginning with the meeting between Ernst Weinbaum and Frederick Otto. "We sat at that table last night." Mercedes said pointing to the dining room table in the next room. "The Baron eventually discussed who would pilot the aircraft. Given the site where the rescue would take place, I immediately assumed Cletus Bauerman would be the pilot because the Baron had mentioned he was from that area. But the Baron proceeded to say Cletus would be suspect if a rescue was successful. At that, the table went silent as we all imagined who the pilot would be.

"At first, I didn't understand the silence. I thought everyone was trying to come up with a name. The moment I looked at Henry, he looked away. When he did that, I knew whom the Baron had picked. Our Wolfy. I went limp, felt cold. Of all the pilots, they had to choose from to carry out this mission, dangerous as the two men at the table knew it to be, the Baron had picked his own grandson.

"I asked the Baron if he was thinking of Wolfy

and he said yes. I was shaken by this decision. I began to cry and had to go into the kitchen. In the kitchen, my mind was a jumble of thoughts. At first I wanted to go back to the table and emphatically reject Wolf flying the mission. There! Choose someone else. However, I began to consider the request. It was made to the Otto family, and if the Baron agreed to attempt the rescue, then it should be an Otto that flies the plane. Once the choice was narrowed to the Otto's, there was only one logical person who would draw the least attention of the German authorities. My Wolfy.

"I thought about Wolfgang. He's twenty now and such a dear to Henry and me. Such a big boy. An accomplished pilot and doing well in college. With the growing potential of war in Europe and the Pacific, there is little a mother can do to protect her child from all the dangers in life. I decided since we have had Wolfgang for twenty wonderful years and hopefully for many more to come, I cannot continue to control his life. This was a decision he would have to make. I returned to the dining room table and said Wolf must decide. Wolfy is very dear to me as I'm sure Michele is to you, I still can't bear the thought he might not come back."

Mentioning he might not come back again brought Mercedes to tears and she held her face in her hands. The trust Mercedes had shown Zelia in revealing the emotion surrounding the previous night's dinner, and the affectionate reference to Michele, caused Zelia to cry, too. For a few moments, the two women, on either side of a coffee table, cried for the safety of their children.

"We mustn't cry too much or our faces will show it at the meeting," Mercedes suggested weakly.

"This is the request. Your husband's brother owns a farm near Colmar, France. Would Pierre contact his brother and ask if Wolf could work

on his farm for the month of August? He will help
with the harvest and pay for his room and board.
He would need to be free on Saturdays to fly a
rented airplane from a nearby airport, locate
the landing site a few miles inside Germany, and
practice travel time.

"Presently, the plan calls for Wolf to fly to
a small, flat area in a mountain range inside the
German border at about dusk. The couple will be
waiting there to climb into the small airplane
as soon as he lands. He will then take-off and
fly back to the airport in France. Upon landing,
he is to taxi to the end of the runway where Emil
Otto, Henry's brother, will be waiting for them
in a car. By then, it will be dark. No one should
notice a couple going from the plane to the car.
Next, Wolf will park the plane and return to the
farm. A week later, he will board ship back to
the States.

"Could you persuade Pierre to contact his
brother and arrange for Wolf to work on the farm?
The Baron is making this request through you and
me because he believes Pierre is still angry
about his brother's death."

"I don't think Pierre harbors that grudge
anymore. Time has had a healing effect. I have
always told him he doesn't know who shot his
brother down. This approach may be better anyway.
He just received a letter from Victor—that's
his brother on the farm. He writes that they're
really upset with the German border guards. One
day, nice as can be, and the next, acting like
thugs. Victor sells produce in two little German
villages, Waldkirch and Breisach, located across
the border. Victor likes to trade there as the
people are friendly and pay his price. The police
and Brown Shirts are something else. They are curt
and rough. The people don't dare say anything,
or they get into trouble. Ever since Chancellor

Hitler came to power, the German officials act as if they can do or say anything. Their behavior really upsets Victor. So pompous-like. He may welcome the opportunity to tweak their noses. I will talk with Pierre this evening and call you. If he agrees, I would only ask, that in return, we be kept appraised of the progress of this mission. Pierre is also knowledgeable of the area and may have some valuable information or ideas to offer."

"A good suggestion. I will relay your offer to the Baron and Henry. By the way, Henry and I are pleased Wolfgang has had the good fortune to meet Michele. We are impressed with her. So refined and so French. Her Parisian accent is delightful!"

"They do make such a nice pair. I will convey your kind words to Michele."

Mercedes rose smiling. "Come, I'll drive us to the meeting."

*   *   *

Although Zelia didn't appear any different to her friends at the meeting, inside she was thrilled to be a part of something much more intriguing than anything she had been involved in before. Her life took on global proportions over a cup of tea. She has been drawn into a secret effort to whisk a couple out of troubled Europe and bring them to the United States. The thought of talking with Baron Otto and Henry Otto about such a plan gave her a refreshing sense of worth. One day, she's not much more than a French peasant's wife, and the next, she's helping plot an international conspiracy! She began to gain insight into her daughter's hopes and aspirations. If she catches Pierre in the right mood, they both will be a part of something big.

*   *   *

Pierre had been in town all day at the packing plant selling a dozen hogs. He picked up Zelia, and they arrived back at the farm just as Michele and Tim were walking to the barn to do the milking. He was pleased with his sale of the hogs, and told Michele she needed only to feed the chickens and then help her mother prepare supper.

Michele flew between the granary and the chicken coop to learn why Mercedes Otto wanted to talk in private with her mother. Once in the kitchen, Michele inquired, "What did you and Mrs. Otto talk about this morning?"

"Two things, one of which may be of concern to you and the other, of special interest to you. Rather than tell the story twice, the one of concern, I'll wait until your father has had his supper and we can talk as a family. The other item is that Mr. and Mrs. Otto are very pleased Wolf has dated you. They think you are so refined and speak with, in her words, a delightful Parisian French accent."

Michele gave a big sigh of relief. "When I'm with them in their home, and even when his grandparents are there, I do have a good time."

Michele wanted to ask her mother for details about the other matter but thought better. They talked of different things while they made supper and set the table.

Zelia knew the profitable sale of the hogs had put her husband in a favorable disposition. After supper she asked all family members to sit down in the living room because she wished to relate a conversation she had this day.

Pierre sat in his favorite chair because it placed him closest to the radio. In the evening, he enjoyed lighting his pipe and listening to comedy or plays.

"Someone told me of a plan for next summer to secretly rescue a couple from Germany. They asked me because they knew we were familiar with the border, where the rescue would take place," Zelia began.

Pierre took the pipe from his mouth. "What part of the border and who is the someone?"

"The border is between Colmar and Freiburg and the 'someone' requested I keep their identity confidential for the meantime."

Pierre looked perturbed. "That's near Victor's farm. Who knew such information?"

"I've heard you tell numerous farmers, and even the auctioneer at the packing plant, you have a brother who is a farmer in France."

"Did I mention Colmar?"

"In some detail. You take some pride in telling people you came from France, especially if you know neither they nor their parents did!" Zelia reminded.

"Oh, well, people don't seem to mind to brag about their farm. I'm not going to just stand there and say nothing."

"They're going to began asking when you plan to use the tractor you won that just sits in the machine shed. If you think their bragging is annoying wait until they tease you about a piece of equipment you don't know how to run," warned Zelia.

"I'll figure it out. Maybe that's a task for Tim. There, that's a task for Tim."

"Dad, how am I going to learn? We don't have a car so I don't know anything about clutches, brakes, and shifting. Things I hear my friends talk about whose parents have cars," countered Tim.

Pierre shrugged his shoulders. "I didn't put my name in, your mother did. Now we've got a tractor and nobody knows how to run it. Great!

You," as he waved his hand at his family, "figure out what we are going to do with it. Your father doesn't relish the possibility of being teased by neighbors. Getting back to this secret conversation, who is this someone and what do they want of us?"

"They want us—well, really, they want you to ask your brother if someone could work on his farm for a month while that person arranges the escape."

"Is this going to be free help? Does this person know anything about farming? This person should pay for their food. Victor doesn't have a lot of money. Although, he might be interested in pulling the wool over the Germans. They think they're so high and mighty! Damn Boche (French slang for WWI German soldier), they killed my brother."

"They will pay room and board. This person doesn't know much about farming but could work here for nothing and learn enough to be helpful to Victor."

"Doesn't know farming? Must be someone from the city. I'm not going any further with this until I know who these people are."

"This morning, I received a call from Mercedes Otto."

Pierre sat upright in his chair at the mention of an Otto. "I should have guessed. Now, they come to us for a favor."

Michele held her hand up and in a voice tinged with excitement, said, "Daddy, wait. Let Mama finish. Who is the someone, Mama?"

"Yes, Pierre, let me finish before you make up your mind." Zelia described her conversation with Mercedes. "Mercedes concluded her request, with the statement they would understand if you declined the request.

"She added they were very pleased Wolfgang

has dated Michele. She is so refined, she said. I thought that was very kind of her to say. I believe such feeling came from her heart, and not because they were asking a favor.

"Our cooperation in their request could be beneficial to us. The person who would be sent to France is Wolf. I'm sure they would agree Wolf should work here, for a month or two, to learn farming. He knows how to drive and could teach us to drive the tractor. And we need to get a car. We can afford it now. Fewer farmers today go to town by buggy."

Michele quickly added encouragement. "Papa, you'll like him, and it would be fun for Tim and I to have him work here. There's a lot we can teach a city boy!"

"If I agree, and he comes, I want this to be mostly work and little play. I'm not sending someone to my brother whose going to stand around acting dumb. He's got to be of help," Pierre said in a positive tone.

"Pierre, what will it be, yes or no? I should call Mercedes soon. Time is of the essence."

Pierre took a deep breath, looked at the expectant faces of his family and affirmed, "Yes. I'll write to Victor."

Michele jumped up, put her arms around her father, and exclaimed, "I love you!"

*   *   *

Zelia went to the phone and called Mercedes. "The answer is yes. What is the next step?"

Mercedes replied, "Thank you for discussing the matter so quickly. I'll let Henry make a suggestion."

"Henry here. Good Evening, Zelia."

"Good evening, Henry."

"May I suggest the Baron, Mercedes, Wolf, and

I come to your home at your earliest convenience to talk further."

"Tomorrow night would be fine, if you are free."

"Tomorrow night it is. Expect us at 7:30. Say hello to your family. We shall look forward to the visit. Good night."

Zelia hung the receiver on the wall phone and excitedly reported, "Four of them, the Baron, Henry, Mercedes and Wolf are coming tomorrow night to plan the mission. Henry didn't say anything more because the operator might be listening. Oh my, we must clean this house from top to bottom."

"Tomorrow is Saturday. As soon as milking is done in the morning, I can help you. This place will be spick-and-span when they arrive!" Michele assured her mother.

*   *   *

Hearing that the Laverns would host a meeting the next night, Henry relayed the good news to the Baron. The Baron immediately called Ernst Weinbaum. "Fred here. Die Wurfel sind gefallen. Schreiben Ihren Bruder schnell!"

(The hammer has fallen. Write your brother quickly.)

*   *   *

Promptly at 7:30 the next evening, a black Buick drove up the lane towards the Lavern farmhouse.

Pierre looked at the grandfather clock and muttered, "Germans and their preciseness. If they say 7:30, you can set your clock when you see them."

At the knock, Pierre opened the door. Facing him was the Baron who spoke first with an energetic, "Bonsoir, Pierre!" The Baron's swift greeting and firm handshake was so commanding that Pierre for

a moment couldn't speak. He could only wave his
hand for them to come in. As the four, the Baron,
Henry, Mercedes, and Wolfgang, walked past him,
neatly dressed and smiling, Pierre's truculent
misgivings about the Baron vanished and a sense
of pride overcame him. They had come to him for
help, and he intended this meeting would be one
of give and take. He had sold some hogs at a
good price yesterday, so he wasn't a novice at
negotiations.

The two families took places around a large
dining room table. Pierre sat across from the
Baron, Wolf next to Michele. The table was set
with cookies, and a selection of pitchers with
tasty apple juice, coffee, or water. Each made
their selection with witty passing of pitchers
and plates.

Henry began the planning session by sliding
a rolled-up map from a cylindrical tube and
spreading it over the table. With his index
finger, he circled an area. "This is a detail of
the border between Colmar and Freiburg."

Pierre scanned the map and pointed to the
corner containing symbol definitions and the map's
origin:

Map Division
State Department
FOR YOUR EYES ONLY

"Where'd this come from? I've never seen detail
like this!" He looked closer and pointed to the
symbol of a bridge. "Why, my brother wrote this
bridge was only built just a few months ago!"

"What you see here and what we will talk
about must be held secret. You must not reveal
anything, absolutely nothing about this mission,
our talk," the Baron cautioned.

The Baron described the rescue and finished by
saying, "Wolf will rent an aircraft at the Colmar

Airport." He pointed to a small airplane symbol on the map. "How far is that from your brother's farm?"

Pierre thought for a moment. "Maybe five, maybe six miles. Victor has horses and Wolf could probably ride one --attendez un instant! (wait a moment!) There's a stable not more than a half mile from the airport. He could leave the horse there while he's flying."

"I gotta learn to ride a horse?" Wolf quipped.

"Oh, and I know just the horse!" Michele quipped.

Zelia waved her hands. "Not Ginger! I'm with you on this one, Wolf. Ginger is too spirited, hardly broken in. No, Michele, you show him how to saddle Clementine."

Wolf turned to Michele in feigned surprise. "You wouldn't do that to me, would you?"

"Of course not," Michele replied with an impish grin. "I was thinking of Clementine all the time."

The Baron traced a line with a finger from Colmar to the northern coast of France. "My son, Emil, will drive the couple to Le Havre where they will board a liner for the U.S."

"May I make a few suggestions?" Zelia asked.

The Baron nodded. "Of course."

"He should drive an older car. It will be less conspicuous. They should board a liner from Cherbourg. Le Havre is very busy with commercial traffic. The French authorities keep very close records on passengers and goods. At Cherbourg, it's not as busy. French records are, shall we say, limited. A couple boarding early in the morning probably wouldn't be recorded."

The Baron agreed. "Good advice. Cherbourg it is."

"Back to Victor's farm. What does Wolfgang know about harnessing a team of horses or milking cows? If he's going to be of help, there are some skills he needs to bring with him," Pierre observed.

"I don't know horses or cows. Could I come here and learn?" Wolf asked Pierre.

"That would be the best solution. I'll teach you to milk, Michele, harnessing, and Tim, plowing. If you come in the spring, after school, there'll be plenty of plowing to be done."

Michele, looking at Mercedes, said brightly, "Horses like to push people into the sides of the stall. I'll coach-oh!, oh!-I'm his coach now!" I'll coach him to avoid such a move."

"Wolf turned to Michele with surprise. "Do they do that?" Laughter briefly interrupted the exchange.

Chuckling, Pierre said, "If you're in their stall, they like to show their authority!"

Henry turned to Michele. "If you think Wolf isn't paying full attention to your instructions, just give me a ring."

Michele smiled.

"I'll get Wolf a motorcycle so he can be early for milking. If it's okay with you, he'll come home once the afternoon milking is finished. He should learn enough in six weeks to be helpful. Afterwards, he'll board ship for France," Henry concluded.

Henry's suggestion seemed acceptable to all ending the planning session. It was nearly 9:20PM. The Otto's expressed their appreciation for the Lavern's hospitality and left.

*   *   *

Wolf's time on the farm was beneficial to both parties. In the barn, the Laverns were the instructors. Wolf learned the skills of milking, harnessing horses, and the feeding of livestock.

Wolf had been to farms before but only as a guest of a friend, never as a laborer. Wolf found working with big animals, like cows and horses, was much different than airplanes. Airplanes didn't step on one's feet or crowd in the stall. He had to learn the temperament of the animals or suffer the consequences.

Michele's appearance in the barn was a first, too. At school, she either wore a skirt and sweater or a cheerleading outfit. In the barn, because of work clothes, she didn't look much different from her brother.

She would appear on cold spring mornings with a large stocking cap pulled over her ears, a denim jacket-pants combination and knee-high rubber boots. He could only marvel at her endurance as she pitched hay, helped with the milking, and maintained the chicken coop. Now, he better understood why she seemed so strong and firm when he danced with her. Definitely a difference between city and farm girls.

The tractor was Wolf's expertise and around it, he would be the instructor. The Allis-Chalmers had been parked in the machine shed where the operations manual rested on its seat in a layer of dust. Before he left for town one night, he picked up the manual and leafed through it. He concluded there wasn't much difference between the tractor and vehicles he had serviced at Sternlicht.

While helping with the chores the next morning, he suggested they start up the tractor after lunch. Pierre stated he hoped the thing wouldn't be more bother than its worth. From that comment and other statements by Pierre, Wolf determined Tim and Michele were more excited about the tractor than their father, possibly because he did not know how to drive it. How embarrassing it would be for him if he ran it into a ditch or the side of the barn.

As the Lavern family stood around the shiny red tractor, Wolf began his instruction with a pep talk.

"Your Allis-Chalmers tractor, with those pneumatic rubber tires, is going to make your work much easier. You just wait and see. It will be easy to drive and can pull as much as your horses pull and more. I'll get it started, show you how to shift and drive it. Then each of you will steer it around the yard."

Michele and Tim nodded excitedly, Pierre, nervously, and Zelia, anxiously.

Wolf followed the manual's check list and found all in order. He climbed into the seat, pushed in the clutch, and turned the key. He had to turn the motor over several times before it started up. The poof of exhaust and loud blat-blat of the engine startled the Laverns, and for a moment, they backed away. Wolf shifted into first, and drove the tractor around the yard twice. He pulled up to the excited family, turned the motor off and asked, "Who's next?" Their son stepped forward, got into the seat, pushed in the clutch, started the engine, shifted, and drove away. Wolf couldn't help but join the Laverns in joyous laughter as Tim drove the tractor about the yard. From that moment, they were sold on the new mechanical work horse.

In the following days, Pierre was convinced gas power had replaced hay power on his farm. Wolf had taken the specifications of the hitch that would connect the tractor to Pierre's wagons and plows to Sternlicht and had the necessary parts welded and assembled. With the turn of a key, Pierre could pull anything within minutes. No more harnessing or bedding horses. "Just put in the gas and away you go!" he confidently explained to his farmer friends who weren't as fortunate.

Because of the increased work efficiency provided by the tractor, Pierre considered expanding his farm.

Working with the Laverns also brought some revelations to Wolf as well. In the past, he had spent a few evenings with Francine, the Senior class #1 snob, in Tank's opinion, and her parents, much like he now did with the Laverns. The experience with each was totally different. In both homes, he would play the piano and family members would sing along. Francine was musically talented making an evening there more like work than fun. Her parents would remind Wolf that their Francine was destined for the stage, and only the best would be suited for her. An evening with the Laverns was relaxed and memorable. Michele, too, was talented but her parents let her talent speak for itself. After a few evenings with the Laverns, Wolf began to wonder why he spent the time he did with Francine. He decided she could be fun and had a great voice but, boy, in marriage she would cost some poor guy a lot of money.

*   *   *

The night before Wolf was to board a train for the ocean liner in New York, he ate supper with the Laverns. The six weeks on the farm had gone well, and even Pierre was confident Wolf would be an asset on his brother's farm.

"I don't think you'll find Victor's farm as modern as ours. It's harder to earn a living there and the taxes remain high to pay off the World War One debts. I've tried to convince him to immigrate, but he seems satisfied with life as it is," remarked Pierre.

"Working on your farm has been an eye-opener for me," Wolf exclaimed. "I never realized how complicated farming was. I thought you plowed the ground, threw in some seed and sat back and watched it grow. Farming is hard work! It's six to six every day including Sunday when there are cows to milk. Cows should go on vacation giving you some time off."

They all laughed at the thought of cows taking leave of the farm. After dessert, Wolf said, "Wow, that was really good! It's been great being with all of you, but I should leave now. Got to do some packing."

"I'll see you to the door, Wolf. Wait there a moment.", Michele went into the adjoining sewing room.

Wolf walked to the front door and waited. He noticed the rest of the Laverns walked out of the living room leaving him alone. Michele reappeared with a small flat gift in her hand.

"Take this with you," Michele said as she handed him the neatly wrapped present. Then she put her arms tightly around him. He embraced her. They kissed. For a moment, she laid her head on his shoulder. He could have held her this way for the rest of his life. A tender moment passed, she stepped back, opened the door, placed her hand on his cheek, and softly cautioned, "Be careful!"

He replied "I'll be back," walked outside, and she closed the door behind him.

He remained on the front step, pleased she had given him something to take on the trip. If the gift was her picture, did she write "With Love" or some similar phrase of affection? He hoped so. It occurred to him they had yet to exchange the word "love." She was a beauty of contrasts, close and yet distant. The moment the latch on the door clicked, something ended that he wished could go on longer. He wanted to turn around and knock, but a command came to mind, Pflicht rufs (duty calls). The call rang clear. He must go forward. In time, he would come back, that door would reopen, and she would be there.

He tucked the gift into a side pocket on his Harley and rode back home. He parked, retrieved the package, and ran into the living room. Wolf sat down on the piano bench and carefully unwrapped a picture of her. It was a recent photo taken at Carlsons, a local professional photographer. She was looking straight ahead into his eyes with a smile on her lips. On the lower right hand corner she had written, Always, Michele.

The inscription puzzled Wolf. What did it mean? I'm yours always? This is me always? We're friends always? He would have preferred she write something more endearing like, Love.

His thoughts were interrupted when his mother's voice in the kitchen called out, "Is that you, Wolfy?"

Wishing to mask his disappointment, he handed the picture to his mother. "Michele gave me this picture with the firm instruction to carry it with me to Europe."

Mercedes studied the picture and exclaimed, "Une belle femme! Look, she is wearing the star-shaped earrings you gave her for her birthday!"

Wolf's eyes snapped to the picture. He hadn't seen them before. But now, there they were. His earrings! He held his breath as he scanned the photo for anything that might bear the name of another suitor. None! Relieved and encouraged, her picture spoke a thousand words of endearment. It would carry him through all the dangers lurking before him.

He looked at his mother, the other woman in his life, broke into a broad grin, and gave her a big hug!

CHAPTER 12

CODE "DOOR"

As Wolf walked into the living room from the kitchen, headlights flashed in the front window. He peered out and saw a black Buick pull up the driveway. The Baron and his father got out and came into the house.

The Baron motioned to Wolf to join them at the dining room table. "Sit down and we'll fill you in on the final details. I met Ernst Weinbaum again in the park this afternoon. He had just received a coded letter from his brother, David, who lives in Stuttgart. Therefore, we know Emil managed to deliver to him the package containing details of the plan and a coding wheel. David writes he was successful in convincing his boss to hold a weekend technical conference in Freiburg. It's a miracle David's superiors acted on his suggestion. He'll be expected to return to Stuttgart Sunday. Since the rescue is planned for the day before, they won't be missed until sometime Monday. By that time, they'll be lounging on deck chairs bound for the good ole' USA. If all goes according to plan, there will be no clues and they will have just disappeared.

"Ernst gave me a generous sum of francs to fund the project. Your grandmother sewed a money belt you must wear at all times. Don't leave money in your cabin. Don't take any chances with it. Pay all your expenses including room and board. Ask the French Laverns what an appropriate amount would be. When you leave for the States, give them a bonus but not so large that their purchases in town could draw attention to their sudden riches.

"Should the plan change while you're at the farm, you will need a coding wheel. Letters are preferred, but cable if urgent. The code name for this operation is "door". If you see or hear the word door in any communication after you leave here, understand that a message is encoded in the communication. To respond affirmatively, you need only say or write, "The door is open." If you cannot comply, respond with, "The door is closed."

"Time your flight to land at the designated site at 1800 hours. Take off as soon as David and his wife are strapped in the cockpit. If they are not present, remain only ten minutes. If they show, fly back to the airport. Emil will drive them to Cherbourg where they will board their liner with forged passports.

"Each time you rent a plane, convince the owner not to make a written record of the transaction. You could say, "Don't record my flight. My parents would kill me if they knew I was flying around the country." Absence of a record will short circuit any effort to spot a suspicious flight.

"We have you booked for a voyage back to the States ten days later. Enjoy the trip. When problems arise, think of several possible solutions, pick one, and go with it. We trust your judgement."

Mercedes remained in the kitchen while the three discussed the mission. She flipped through a cookbook, picked a recipe from a stained page, and selected a bowl from a cabinet. She added ingredients to the bowl and as she added milk, she realized the bowl was too small. She selected a larger bowl, wiped tears from her eyes, and poured the cake ingredients into the large bowl. It was her Wolfy that would be leaving in the morning and in her nervousness, her hearing was on high alert. The words, "when problems arise" rang so loud her ears felt pain. She wanted to run into the dining room, throw her arms around her son, and stop the whole affair. Was she the only one haunted by the thought this precarious deception might harbor an unseen critical flaw resulting in the death of her son? While mixing the ingredients of the cake, she hoped to God they knew what they were doing.

*   *   *

From the time he set foot on the ocean liner, he was determined to make this trip a memorable one. Upon boarding, Wolf walked briskly to his assigned cabin, threw the single suitcase onto the bunk, took out the picture affectionately inscribed with "Always, Michele", and placed it on the cabin desk. As he left to tour the many decks, he turned to the picture and whispered, "I'll be back."

Entering the hallway, he became a Knight of Serendipity! No strings attached, no schedule to keep. The days on ship were his to explore and relish spontaneous adventure.

With a flourish, he opened a door to a corridor that led to several lounges. One appeared to be his destination. In it, many his age were lounging about. He scouted the room for a way to make friends. A piano near the center of the room was surrounded by several new arrivals. An analysis of the playing field charged through his mind. Why wasn't someone playing it? Either no one could, or if they could, they may be intimidated by the crowd. Or worse yet, what if they played something no one liked?

For Wolf, this was opportunity knocking! No different than playing the piano on the bandstand at Sternlicht. After playing a few bars from a selection of the Top Ten, Wolf would need only ask, "How do the lyrics go?" and quickly the crowd around the piano would be singing, talking, laughing, and he'd be right in the middle. Hot dog!

To get the attention of those around the piano, Wolf bounced up and down on his chair and shouted, "Hey, it's get acquainted time! Call out your name, one at a time. I'm Wolfgang, Wolf for short. Who's next?"

"Gloria----Wilhemia----Bob, but some call me Popcorn." Wolf took special notice of Bob's face. It was a face he knew from a particularly rough football game.

"Penelope-please!—not Penny!" Names flew around the piano until all had been heard from. Wolf followed each name with a few loud notes giving everyone a chance to put a name with a face.

As soon as the introductions were over, he rose, and extended his hand to Popcorn, who in turn, expressed recognition of Wolf. As they shook hands they both said in unison, "I think I played you in football!"

"You're Popcorn Grant from Michigan, right?"

"Right, and you're Wolf from the Wolfpack of Trinity!"

"The same!"

Popcorn posed as if he was going to pass with Wolf about to tackle him. They laughed.

"We meet again but on much more amiable conditions," Wolf chortled.

"From now on, sometimes combatants, but never enemies", returned Popcorn. Leaning on the piano towards Wolf, Popcorn asked, "What brings you on this ship?"

I'm spending a few weeks on a French farm flexing my muscles in preparation for the rematch in October. Brush up on my French. And you?"

My dad plans to open a sales office in Paris. He's grooming me to run the place so I'm to make some contacts. Trust me, not all the contacts will be of the business type," Popcorn replied, winking.

Another acquaintance gained on the trip was Penelope Cunningham, daughter of Curt Cunningham, owner of the major Chicago newspaper, <u>The Chicago Daily</u>. A journalism major at Michigan University, she attended several of the same classes as Popcorn. Now acquainted, the three, several evenings, sat on deck and talked, as the liner glided over the calm Atlantic. These were unique personalities who would re-enter Wolf's life in unpredictable ways.

*   *   *

The week on the ocean liner went far too fast. For the first time, Wolf could do as he pleased. In the summer back home, he was up at 6AM practicing piano for forty-five minutes, eating breakfast and then off to Sternlicht for a day of work. At college, the routine was much the same with the exchange of classes and sports for Sternlicht. On the ocean liner, his eyes opened at 6AM but every day was his!

No longer.

The ship docked, after breakfast, in Le Havre. Wolf left the ship and entered Customs. Asked to open his suitcase, the customs official conducted a cursory search and waved him through. They would find nothing suspicious in the suitcase. Wolf had strapped the coding wheel to his inner thigh.

The railroad station was within walking distance of the dock. He bought a second class roundtrip ticket to Colmar, France, and boarded. Two transfers later he arrived in Colmar. The gravity of the mission began to work on his mind as he anxiously searched the platform crowd for Victor Lavern. Victor would be carrying a sign bearing a single name, Wolf. Wolf exited the passenger car and saw his name on a card. The man holding it could have passed for Pierre's twin brother. The combination of sign and twin resemblance was reassuring to Wolf.

Victor was larger and more weathered than Pierre. He had come to the station in a horse and buggy. The trip back to his farm took an hour passing fields lined with trees. The paucity of farms and abundance of woods offered a good sign to Wolf as it would help conceal the secret mission.

They first engaged in some small talk about the voyage, which gave way to discussion about the rescue plan. Emil had slipped an envelope to Victor when they met in Colmar several weeks before so he was well versed in 'door.'

"I will need time to rent a plane the next two Saturdays to acquaint myself with the aircraft and the terrain."

Victor slapped the reins on the horse's back. "There may be a better solution to the airplane matter. About midday November 10, 1918, a pilot flying a two-winged airplane landed on our pasture next to the barn. He came to the house and explained he was delivering this plane to the army when he hit bad weather that he couldn't cross. Nearly out of gas, he brought it down without damage. Could he leave it and return the next day or so with gas? Of course, I said, anything for the war effort. The next day was the Armistice. With all the hoopla over the end of the war, they must have forgotten the plane because they never came back for it. So, there it sat.

"A couple of days later, when it looked like rain, I hitched the horse to the back skid of the plane and pulled it into the barn. Shoved it into a corner and looked into the cockpit. The back cockpit held a large package containing operations and maintenance manuals for this plane they call the Breguet. I don't know anything about motors, but if you can get it running, you've got your plane.

"We still see some of them flying patrol around here and even across the German border. There must be some kind of agreement allowing French and German planes to fly a few miles over one another's territories. I have seen German planes over Colmar and French planes over Waldkirch where I sell produce. It should not seem unusual if you fly the Breguet across the border. You see, God smiles on you!"

Time spent on the Lavern farm in Indiana didn't fully prepare Wolf for the Lavern farm in France. As Victor guided the buggy into the farmyard, the scene looked chaotic. There was no apparent organization of equipment, animals, and buildings. All the buildings were attached to one another. Wolf couldn't tell which was the barn, the house, or the machine shed.

Chickens, geese, and cows roamed at will about the yard. A water pump sat in the middle of the yard and excess water was captured in a concrete basin that served as a drinking trough for the farm animals. If a chicken couldn't reach the water from the ledge of the basin, it jumped into the basin and drank its fill. Wolf was about to comment on this lack of sanitation, but since the cows didn't mind chickens traipsing through their water, he wasn't going to care, either. He had bigger fish to fry.

Victor seemed pleased with his holdings when he said, "Home sweet home. First, I want you to meet my wife, Gabrielle. There she is at the front door. "Gabrielle, nous sommes revenus! (We have returned!)

He introduced the new arrival. "Puis-je vous présenter Monsieur Wolfgang Otto!" (Allow me to introduce Mr. Wolfgang Otto)

Gabrielle walked into the yard drying her hands

on a large thick apron that covered most of her body. Her dress began at the ankle and rose to a row of buttons about her neck. She smiled and extended her hand.

Wolf took her hand in his, bowed and said,

"Il est un plaisir et une honneur à vous recontre, Gabrielle de Madame." (It is a pleasure and an honor to meet you, Madame Gabrielle.)

The Laverns had expected a more brash arrival from what they had heard about young Americans. This proper show of respect touched them deeply.

Victor put his hand on Wolf's shoulder and exclaimed to his wife, "Il sait parler francais!"

His ability to speak their language came as a great relief to the Laverns. As the time approached for the American to arrive, they had struggled with the dilemma that would arise if the person couldn't speak French. They knew Otto was German, but Victor only knew enough German to conduct his produce sales in the villages across the border, Waldkirch and Breisach. In the absence of a language barrier, conversation flew.

Wolfgang soon became aware that the farm clutter did not reflect the character of the Laverns. Their goals were fundamentally different from middle class Americans such as the Ottos and the Laverns. On the French farm, life was more leisurely, goals less ambitious, but spiritual life was equally important, too. Wolf applied mental brakes to avoid appearing impatient. He let their routine dictate his activities. Immersion into their way of life gave Wolf the sense he was their grown child. They had no children. Each day progressed as if he were one of them rather than a guest.

They worked hard during the day, but after supper, time was spent discussing world events, philosophy, and life in America. Wolf thanked the

Lord he had paid some attention to the courses on Aristotle and Plato in college. The Laverns usually brought some basic human dimension to the topic of the night. Wolf could at least, at an elementary level, participate in the philosophical exploration. One evening, Gabrielle asked, "Have you read 'The Diamond Necklace' by Guy de Maupassant?

"Yes, in the original. My mother emigrated from Luxembourg and treasures her French heritage. She has many books in French and that short story is in one of them. She teaches French in our high school."

"Does it not speak to accepting one's station in life—content with what we have?" questioned Gabrielle.

Wolf could not gauge whether Gabrielle was expressing acceptance of one's lot with the question. He offered a comparison.

"In America, people believe you can do anything if you have the will. Freedom to seek lofty goals is a powerful driving force. My grandfather often reminds me of the immeasurable value of freedom but the price for its protection sometimes can only be paid for with human lives."

Victor stared at the floor and lamented, "My brother and I fought in the war to end all wars. My brother never came back. Yet, our freedom to change our station in life has not happened. Those in power leave no room for newcomers. We understand Pierre and Zelia's happiness, but despite our limitations, we choose to be content."

Gabrielle disagreed. "I—we do not choose to be content. We deserve a better life. I think about visiting America."

"Yes, dear."

*   *   *

The Laverns knew Wolf's presence was not just to work the farm. They gave him as much freedom to organize his mission as he wished. Wolf first read through the Breguet manuals and wrote a time schedule of tasks that would be essential to the rescue flight. "I'll need gas, oil, and some fine sandpaper to start the engine. You don't have any gas powered equipment on the farm so I'm going to give you a present that will serve as a cover for the purchase of these items. The American brother of the man to be rescued provided a large sum of money to fund the mission, and your purchase of a gasoline- powered washing machine is essential to its success.

"Victor, I would like you and Gabrielle to go to Colmar and order such a machine. Say you have saved up these francs and its about time Gabrielle enjoys such a convenience. Have it delivered and in the meantime, I will give you what it costs."

Wolf opened his shirt and pulled out a money belt. He unbuttoned one compartment and showed them a stack of francs.

Gabrielle put her hands to her face and gave a muffled shriek! "Mon Dieu, I have seen these contraptions, and my neighbors who own them say they are just wonderful! No more scrubbing on the washboard. They have a wringer to squeeze out most of the water. Clothes dry in the sun in no time. Oh, that would be a wonderful gift!"

Victor was visibly pleased with Gabrielle's reaction. He knew her life was hard and this machine could bring her some relief. Yet he felt obliged to suggest, "Do not feel you must express your gratitude with such an expensive gift. We are doing this because it is the right thing to do."

"I want to do this because of my admiration of you two. Also, I need this machine because I don't want anyone to know what's really going on here. The purchase serves two good causes," Wolf happily concluded.

The delivery of the washing machine, gas, oil, and sandpaper brought forth a new sound to the farm, the put-put of a gasoline engine. All three read the directions for the washing machine. Gabrielle added clothes and soap. Victor poured a mixture of gas and oil into the gas tank, turned the switch on and stepped hard on the foot crank. The engine coughed but didn't start. Again he stepped hard on the foot crank, the engine coughed but began to run. Cheers erupted from all present!

The manual, which Wolf read out loud, recommended the engine should run a minute before pulling the lever to engage the agitator. Gabrielle could only wait fifty seconds before pulling the lever and then clapped her hands in joy as the agitator began briskly sloshing water and soap through the dirty clothing. The thought she could now throw that washboard as far as she could brought tears to her eyes. Only the increasingly loud mooing of cows with full udders that late afternoon reminded the three they had responsibilities other than starting a new tub of clothes. No matter where they were, the friendly put-put gave proof that another pair of hands were helping with the chores.

CHAPTER 13

A BREGUET TO THE RESCUE

With the put-put wash machine busily converting the Lavern's shabby grays to their rightful colors, Wolf turned his attention to the Breguet. He gave himself four days to prep and taxi the World War One double-wing into flying condition. If twenty years of sitting in a barn had deteriorated the aircraft beyond quick repair, he would have to hoof it to the Colmar Airport and rent a suitable plane.

He had taken a few quick peeks at the Breguet in the barn, but delayed close inspection until he had settled in and given the Laverns a hand at farming. He thanked God for the idea of the gas-powered washing machine. It served as a good cover for the purchase of gas and other essentials required in the restoration. It was an equal Godsend to Gabrielle. No longer a slave to the wash board, she now could enjoy washing clothing with superior results. In jest, she even suggested a spin through the machine might do wonders for their dog's scruffy coat!

Day one of Wolf's effort to condition the Breguet began after milking. Wolf and Victor opened the barn doors and viewed the Breguet standing in the corner.

"Gee, Victor, the airplane takes up a third of the barn floor. Why'd you ever keep a machine occupying much precious space for nineteen years that was of no use to you?"

"I don't know. Well, I do know. It gave me a sense of wealth to own something that must have cost a lot of money to make. Given the sense of expensive ownership, I took some effort to protect the airplane. For all these years, I have closed the barn to chickens and ducks to prevent them from pecking at the fabric or nesting on the wings. Do Pierre's chickens run loose?"

"Nope, he's got 'em penned."

"I let them run 'cause they pick up the corn the hogs don't digest."

For a moment, Wolf hoped such savings wouldn't end up in the taste of the chicken.

To Victor, it mattered little where the chickens foraged. He continued to relate his care of the winged treasure. "I covered the two open cockpits with tarps to protect them from the dust in the barn. I couldn't make much sense out of the manuals, but one statement printed in bold red letters caught my eye. It warned that if the plane were not flown from time to time bad things would happen to the motor if the propeller were not turned each day. After each morning milking, I turned the prop. And as I turned the prop I've always wondered why this airplane was here? Now I know."

After so many years of incarceration, Wolf expected to see a relic looking tired and forlorn. Quite the contrary. Victor's efforts at preservation paid off. Relieved of its numerous shrouds, it looked rather perky. This pleasant reversal of expectations and Victor's obvious pride in his war booty motivated Wolf to restore it to flying condition.

Wolf reviewed the manuals again and then climbed into the front cockpit. On the floor were two large foot-operated rudder controls. Victor put his feet on them and pushed one, and then the other. He whooped when they moved the rear rudder left and right. He moved the center control stick forward, backward, left, right, positioning the rear elevators and wing ailerons as designed.

"So far so good, Victor, none of the controls are stuck."

Victor's smile was one of satisfaction.

Wolf studied the contents of the cockpit. By modern standards, the instrument panel was sparse but adequate. An altimeter, gas and oil pressure gauges, and a tachometer displaying the revolutions per minute (rpm's) of the propeller. The hand brake locked and unlocked. He climbed onto the wing and removed the filler cap from the gas tank. He climbed down and opened the drain on the bottom of the gas tank, pouring out water that had condensed over the years. He repeated the same procedure with the oil pan. He filled the gas tank and replaced the oil.

The next item on his check list was the twelve-cylinder rotary motor that drove the propeller. He removed each spark plug and polished the points with fine sandpaper. Things were looking good! But as he worked, clouds accumulated and a light rain began. Because it was too wet to start up the motor outside the barn, he spent the rest of the afternoon planning test flights, and a cruise along the border to search for the landing strip inside Germany.

On day two, he rose to a clear and sunny day. "Victor, this looks like a good time to roll out the Breguet and test the motor."

After milking and a quick breakfast, Victor hitched up the team, Nellie and Napoleon, and dragged the plane out onto the pasture.

Wolf looked around and stomped on the ground. "Perfect day to put this rig to the test. The sun's warm and the ground is fairly dry. I'll need your help. This Breguet lacks a battery-energized starter. So the method of starting these motors is much like your washing machine. Instead of pushing a foot pedal on the washing machine motor, the prop has to be turned quickly by hand. While I'm in the cockpit, you'll have to spin the prop."

"How do I do that?"

"First, I call out, "Ignition switch off." You rotate the prop to a horizontal level. Grasp the left blade with both hands and spin it. I then turn the ignition switch to the "on" position, advance the throttle to the half position, and you spin the prop until the engine starts."

The checklist began in a promising way. Controls worked fine, gas tank full, prop turned. Wolf knew the next step was the crucial test. Would the motor start? Gabrielle knew the critical point was reached when she heard Wolf call out "Switch off." She came to the pasture to watch just as Victor began turning the prop.

"One more turn for good luck," Victor shouted as he grasped the prop blade for the fourth time. Looking through the windshield, Wolf nodded in agreement. Again, the prop turned, and again, the engine belched a clear blue cough out the exhaust.

Wolf cranked the ignition switch to "on" and advanced the throttle to the halfway position. "Switch on," he called out. This time, Victor grasped the prop, kicked his leg, and swung the prop with a determined grunt.

The engine belched a clear blue cough out the exhaust but didn't start.

"Try again," Wolf declared.

A kick, a swing, a blue cough. Nothing! A third spin gained the same result.

"My washing machine needs gas to run. Does this engine need gas, also?" inquired Gabrielle.

"Of course," both men replied, at the same time, in a tone giving little credence to such an elementary question.

Although Wolf was thinking more complicated thoughts regarding the reluctant engine, he again looked at the gas flow lever. It was on the "open" position. He grasped the lever and found he could move it a full quarter turn beyond "open". A

sense of joyous triumph filled Wolf. He was only
a spin away from knowing if he had found the
solution.

"Hey, I think I found the problem! Prime it
once more," Wolf shouted to Victor.

Victor waved, grasped the propeller and gave
it an enthusiastic turn.

As the propeller rocked to a stop, Wolf flicked
a switch and again called to Victor. "Try again.
Ignition 'on'."

Once more Victor threw his whole body into
spinning the prop. Spin—cough—cough—ignition!
With fuel coursing through its body, the engine
came alive. Cold, some of the cylinders fired
unevenly causing the motor to shake the whole
plane. For a minute, the aircraft trembled like
a glass during a quake while the engine warmed.
Once the engine came to operating temperature,
the motor smoothed out and the whole plane settled
down like an impatient bird preparing to leap
into flight.

The "open" label had been bolted into the
wrong position! Wolf slapped his hand on the
side of the fuselage to get Victor's attention.
He pointed at the instrument panel and gestured
turning a lever part way and then all the way.

In their triumph, the men looked to Gabrielle
for due recognition. Instead, she stood with her
hands on her hips with a face radiating a silent
'See!'

Wolf cheered, waved and threw her a kiss!

With the brakes on, Wolf studied the reaction
of the plane as he varied the foot and hand
controls. Reactions were much the same as the
grasshopper back at Sternlicht. He pulled the
throttle back to idle and slowly released the
brakes. As he advanced the throttle, the World War
One warrior came alive. Slowly the plane rolled
forward. An increase in prop rpm's increased taxi

speed. Wolf rolled to the end of the pasture. He liked the rapid reaction of the motor to changes in the throttle position. Plenty of power to take off from this pasture.

Gabrielle and Victor watched Wolf taxi back and forth over the pasture. At first, the cows and the team were startled by the engine noise and mooed and snorted their anxiety. But, soon, they acclimated to the commotion and lined up along the fence to watch the strange looking machine.

A light wind was blowing down the pasture toward the barn so Wolf taxied to the barn, swung the airplane into the wind, and advanced the throttle as far as he could. The plane leaped forward, gained speed, and with yards of pasture to spare, rose like a resolute liberator into the blue.

Sitting in the open cockpit with the wind whistling over the windshield and the plane responding to every minute change in the controls, Wolf had a sense of supreme control. This Breguet even surpassed the grasshopper in performance. Wolf's confidence he could land on a dime grew by the minute.

He could have stayed up until the tank ran dry, but he shook himself out of the exhilaration and returned to the pasture. Nellie and Napoleon dragged the plane back into the barn. Wolf thoroughly inspected the plane. Gas consumption was moderate. Wolf felt confident a full tank would be adequate for the rescue.

Gabrielle later baked an apple pie to celebrate the successful flight. At dinner she reminded them only once who had suggested a gas problem when the motor wouldn't start. Her tease brought forth laughter from all three.

Finishing the apple pie, Victor suggested Wolf accompany him to Colmar and then across the border to Breisach in the morning. "I need to sell some vegetables, and along the way we can see if anyone heard or saw the plane."

The following day, Wolf harnessed the team while Victor loaded the produce. They passed some farmers along the way. Some waved or stopped Victor briefly to talk, but no one mentioned anything about the plane. Victor surmised they thought it was just another French or German border patrol. At the border, the German guard knew Victor but asked Wolf for his passport. He looked at the picture, then at Wolf, muttered "Alles in Ordnung," (All is in order), gave the passport back, and waved them through.

Wolf sensed an immediate difference between the two neighboring countries. In France, one often saw gendarmes spending time chatting with the locals. A lone French flag flew from atop the Colmar post office flagpole. Crossing the border into Germany, Wolf couldn't begin to count the number of swastika flags, the official emblem of Germany, located on buildings, lampposts, windows, even cars. Police and Brown Shirts were everywhere. Most seemed bent on a mission, others just stood in a spot as if on guard duty. Men and women going about their business appeared happy but Wolf noted that few talked with those in uniform.

Victor guided Nellie and Napoleon to a farmer's market square in the middle of Breisach where other farmers and local merchants were selling their goods. While Victor sold his vegetables, Wolf fed the team some oats and water. The warm sun was ideal for market activity, and lulled Wolf into a drowsy state of mind. Once Nellie had eaten, her head drooped, and soon the two, one man and one horse, were leaning sleepily against one another.

In the few moments of shared body support, Wolf had missed the appearance of a squad of Brown

Shirts. They created a disturbance at the door of a shop across the street that jarred Wolf out of his brief somnolent state. Two soldiers were dragging a man out of a shop onto the street and viciously prodding him with their nightsticks. Wolf noticed someone had painted large white letters on the shop front window the word, Juden, German for Jew.

Into the melee, two more Brown Shirts emerged from the store dragging and poking a woman screaming in pain. The man between the Brown Shirts attempted to break their hold and rush to her defense. His intention enraged the Brown Shirts. They began beating the two in fits of rage.

Wolf's impulse was to try to stop the carnage. Victor sensed what Wolf was contemplating and ordered in a commanding tone—"Stay!" Wolf looked at Victor and then back at the beatings. No one was going to their aid! A few in the market crowd even surrounded the beatings and cheered them on. Many avoided watching and continued to shop. Some left the square, and as they passed Wolf, their faces were white with fear. A fear so intense, their bodies were compressed as if in a vise.

After a few minutes, the Brown Shirts tired of their fun. To finish their task, one struck the man in the head with all his might. It sounded like striking a ripe melon—a sickening bonk, and the man crumbled to the street. The woman threw up her hands, gasped, and fainted. The Brown Shirts brushed off their sleeves and left. Wolf's stomach felt like a volcano about to erupt.

As he stood between the two horses, a numbing sense of fear rose in him. He could suffer the same fate, if he ran out of gas inside the German border. This wasn't football with referees to call time-out. He was on his own.

On the way back to the farm, Victor explained his command not to intervene. "They would have killed you on the spot. That's why no one went to their rescue. Not long ago, I saw a Rabbi get the same treatment. They dragged him out of a synagogue and were beating him. A priest walking by tried to persuade the Brown Shirts to stop. A Brown Shirt hit him so hard on the side of the head he dropped to the street, flopped about and died. No one raised a finger.

"It's the Nazi's way of intimidating people. Keep to yourself, don't interfere, and you'll live a pretty good life. Get in the way, protest, and you'll get killed on the spot or disappear a day or so later. From the little the shoppers tell me, the police are usually a little more subtle. But sometimes they feel the need to be more blunt. Hence, the scene you witnessed today."

Victor's description didn't bolster Wolf's confidence.

*   *   *

That evening while milking, Victor told Gabrielle what had happened in Breisach. "I looked at the young American while he watched the beating. He looked white as snow, but I could see he was getting ready to run over to help the couple. I told him to stay. He's in the middle of it now. Up against evil in its most public presence. God help him."

After supper, Gabrielle read two verses from Psalm 26.

"The Lord is my light and my salvation, whom shall I fear?

"The Lord is the protector of my life, of whom shall I be afraid?

"Remember, Wolf, our purpose in life is to serve God. And in doing so, he will protect us and reward us with a beautiful life in Heaven. Keep these passages in mind as you face dangers in life."

Lying in bed later in the evening, Wolf felt a calming strength building in his body and soul. Closing his eyes, he drifted toward peaceful sleep. A thought came to him. 'I shall not fear.' Once again, he could feel Michele's hand on his cheek, that fragrance, those eyes, and her parting words, "Come back!" As slumber took possession of his body, he knew he must succeed.

*   *   *

The incident at Breisach heightened Wolf's attention to the details of the mission. His concern about being detected during flight was lessened somewhat by a coded message he received from his Uncle Emil in the mail.

Something big is going to happen along the eastern border of Germany. Most German military and intelligence units have been pulled from your sector so border patrols will be scant. I'll be on time.

*   *   *

The next day a storm blew in, bringing dense clouds. The wind died down resulting in a rain that lasted until evening. Once chores were finished, Wolf planned his first flight to the area of the landing site, a high plateau within the Black Forest. Cletus Bauerman had suggested this site, remote from roads, which minimized the chance picnickers or hikers might be there when Wolf landed. Located in a mountainous forest, however, the trek facing the Weinbaums would be formidable.

Knowing the map coordinates of Colmar and the

landing site, Wolf calculated the miles he would have to fly along a northeast heading to arrive at a point parallel to the landing site. With the site, being only a mile inside the German border, Wolf believed he could spot it from the French side with binoculars. Once spotted, he would fly straight to it, examine its features and return to the farm.

The next day he took off at 3 p.m. to locate the site and note any peculiarities of flying in that region shortly before sundown. German and French methods of fencing their fields were different. Wolf felt confident he could detect, at low altitude, where the border lie.

Reaching the mountain range, Wolf held the plane in a climbing mode. With one hand on the control stick, he held the binoculars with the other, scanning the German forest for a small, elongated, open patch. Judging from his distance calculations and some landmarks on the map, he finally reached the area of the site.

Despite scanning back and forth, he could only see dense forest. In less than a minute, he was well beyond the calculated site and he began to consider crossing the border to locate it. He decided he would not. A French plane flying back and forth over the border might raise suspicion.

To attempt one more scan, he stood up in the cockpit. One hand held onto the windshield, the other, the binoculars. The turbulent wind rushing off the top wing buffeted his body, shook his hands. Trees, brush, cliffs danced before his eyes. Frustration edged toward despair. He had to find it!

His eyes swept along a cliff that revealed an opening leading to a flat band of glorious green. There it was! With a sigh of relief, he banked back and spotted a country church that would serve as the landmark for the turn into Germany.

He flew to the site and noted it was surrounded by trees except for the opening on the steep side of the mountain. The length appeared adequate to land, therefore, he decided he would, on rescue day, throttle back and glide to a landing. The reconnaissance completed, he flew back to France. By the time he reached the area of the Lavern farm, dusk had fallen making it difficult to see structures below. Everything looked gray and increasingly ill-defined. Yet another trial in what he had envisaged would be just a routine flight!

Disappointed in his failure to include lights to guide him in the dark should the flight take longer than expected, he dropped to an altitude of 100 feet. He snapped his head side to side of the fuselage looking for something familiar. Then God, yet again, intervened.

"Ah, there's the steeple on the barn-and the pasture." Wolf dropped the nose and eased onto the pasture. Victor had the team ready to drag the aircraft into the barn.

"I found the site. Almost missed it flying on the French side. Finally spotted it when I looked back. It's rough terrain. I hope the Weinbaums give themselves plenty of time to reach it."

Victor figured they would be physically up to the challenge. "Germans do a lot of hiking. Die Volkswanderungen (civilian organized hikes) are very popular so it's common to see individuals, couples or groups walking everywhere—along roads, paths, through woods. God willing, they'll be there when you arrive."

"I had difficulty, I mean, the frantic kind of difficulty, finding the pasture after the sun set. When I'm about to return Saturday, would you set out laterns defining the periphery of the pasture. I'll spot the lanterns on the long end and taxi to the barn."

"D'accord." (Agreed)

Check sheet in hand, Wolf inspected the plane. All registered in the green until he put a stick into the gas tank. The hollow splash at the bottom sent a chill through the young flyer. Extra passengers equals extra weight equals extra gas consumption. And he would have to wait for them-engine running. Was the Breguet such a good idea after all? No time to rent a plane. He wouldn't share his fears with the Laverns.

*   *   *

Wolf had located the site on Thursday but decided not to fly again until the day of the rescue-two days later. In those two days, he prepped the aircraft and helped with the farming. The hay Victor had cut lay dry in the fields and Wolf spent most of the time pitching hay into the wagon or the barn. The physical labor helped work off the tension rising within him as he rehearsed the mission over and over in his mind.

*   *   *

Saturday, the sun rose into a cloudless sky and Wolf woke, heart pounding. Today, he would fly into the mouth of a dragon, and God willing, he would fly out with his human cargo. His heart and apprehension reverted to a normal pace as he spent the day milking, and feeding the livestock.

At 5 p.m., he hitched Nellie and Napoleon to the plane, and towed it onto the pasture. Wolf performed a pre-flight check and at 6:30 p.m., Victor began the process of turning the prop. Upon ignition, Wolf warmed the engine, wiped the sweat from his hands, released the brakes, and took off.

Victor and Gabrielle watched the plane disappear

into the distance as they held one another's hand. There were chores yet to be done, so Victor went back into the barn and Gabrielle into the house.

Once Wolf had occupied their small second bedroom, Gabrielle never had reason to enter it. Their visitor always left the room as neat as when he first entered it. The bed was always made, the chair snug to the desk. Clothes absent from view—probably laid out in the chest of drawers. She and Victor were so impressed with this young man who was thoughtful, helpful, God-fearing. They never had children and Wolf's presence began to demonstrate what they were missing in their life. Someone to care for, nurture, and take over the farm when they passed on. As Wolf lifted off, they had clasped hands. They were three now, not two.

As she entered the house, she felt an urge to go into his room. How would she feel standing next to the desk where he sat every evening reading manuals and pouring over maps? Would she have some sense of what it's like for a mother to stand next to her son's desk? A son she loved, admired and now in danger?

The sun lay low but enough light came through the window to illuminate the room. She walked in and stood by his desk. She felt close to him even though he was far away. On top of the desk there was a bit of clutter with books, pencil, and paper. She smiled and forgave the disarray.

She saw for the first time a framed picture on the back edge of the desk. The smiling face of a young, pretty blond woman. Somehow she looked familiar. Gabrielle picked up the picture and took it to the window and studied it in a better light. The similarity to one of Pierre's children was remarkable! She carried the picture into the dining room where a family picture hung of

the American Laverns. She compared the two girls
in each. One and the same! On the back of the
family picture were written the names, Pierre,
Zelia, Michele and Tim. On Wolf's picture was
written: 'Always, Michele.' "Pierre's daughter!
Michele is sweet with our- -our son!" Gabrielle
exclaimed.

From the time Victor shared with her the
mysterious envelope describing an episode that
was about to unfold in their lives, she felt
her life was changing. Evolving into a richer
fabric. As if someone was adding bright colors
to the gray painting of their life. Not only
was the gray being replaced, but the parallel
between the pictures spanned a great ocean for
Gabrielle. Oh Wolfy, you must return!

                    *   *   *

Pierre had informed Wolf that the French and
Germans had at least one thing in common. They
both quit early on Saturday to prepare for a day
of rest. No military aircraft were in sight as
Wolf flew to the rendezvous. He matched the prop
r.p.m.'s with his watch to arrive on time. He
hoped they would, too.

Passing over the country church, he turned
and crossed the border. His body's response to
the turn into Germany and its Brown Shirts was
immediate. His heart thumped, his palms sweaty.
Baron's words, Stay calm, make decisions when you
need to, we trust in your judgement, strengthened
his resolve. Once the opening to the plateau was
in sight, his attention to the task of landing
erased his apprehension.

He lined up to a straight approach and pulled
back the throttle. The plane slowed and glided to
the edge of the site. The wheels met the ground,
the plane bounced, hit, rolled to the far tree

line and stopped. Wolf set the brake on one wheel, revved the engine, and the plane turned on the free wheel to face the open end. He set the other brake, adjusted the throttle to idle and looked around for his passengers. They were no where to be seen. He clenched his teeth.

He looked at his watch. 7:01 p.m. They had ten minutes to appear. In the meantime, gas was being consumed. Wolf climbed up, and stood on the edges of the cockpit. His head elevated above the upper wing allowed him to scan in all directions.

No one.

Maybe they were caught. He dreaded the thought.

7:06 p.m.

No one.

He couldn't turn the engine off. The husband of the couple may not have the strength to turn the prop. Even in idle, the engine sounded too loud for comfort.

A crow cawed, a sparrow chirped. A groundhog poked his head out of a burrow. Still not the life Wolf yearned for.

A world away, he would have enjoyed participating in a scene unfolding.

*   *   *

Michele, her friends, Cori, Lori the redhead, and Jennifer, sat in a Booth at the High Top Café, Northern Bend.

"What will it be, girls? Can I start with you?" the waitress asked.

"Oh, I'm not sure. Ask her," Cori replied, pointing to the red head across the table engrossed in the menu.

"Well, okay, I'll start. I'd like a hamburger." Lori pointed with a slender finger to an item on the menu, "No cheese, yes, fries—no—change that, an Indiana hot dog with chili—no—"

"Hmmm, let's start with something easier. What would you like to drink?"

"A coke," Lori said with a smile and then turned to Cori.

Cori, busily scraping remnants of red fingernail polish from her thumb, ignored her turn until Michele elbowed her in the ribs.

Startled out of an essential duty, she sputtered, "A coke, too."

"Orange fizzy, please," responded Jennifer.

"A beer?" asked the red head.

Giggles.

The waitress smiled as she tapped a pencil on her order pad.

"No, just joking. A lemonade, please."

"I'll be back with your drinks. Try real hard to reach some conclusion about what you want to eat."

A few minutes later the waitress returned with the drinks and left with the rest of their orders.

"I bought a Les Brown record yesterday at the Platter. Listened to it a million times. Daddy holds his ears but Mom likes it!" the red head ended on a high note.

"Why does Mr. Wilson give such hard history exams?" Cori exclaimed. "What earthly good are all those dates? They mess up my notes!"

"To Carlos?"

"Not to Carlos! My class--oh, I get so bored. Carlos' little jokes he sends back are the only thing that keep me awake."

The redhead agreed. "When I say anything to my mom or dad about all that ancient history stuff they always say, 'That's part of your education. You must be well educated to get ahead in this world.' She raised her eyes in disdain. Pointed to the ceiling, she said, ribbingly, "But if Mr. Wilson were to ask how many times Wolfy fon Schm0tto danced with Michele de La'vern at homecoming, I'd immediately know the answer!"

Laughter.

Eyebrows lifted, Cori asked, "Michele, what was it like to have Mr. Atlas at your farm all day?"

"Kinda fun. Like teaching him to harness a team. Those Belgians had him pretty edgy at first. They would stomp to shake off flies and he'd jump a foot. But he got pretty good at it. Dad thinks he's a good worker. Mom thinks he's funny. I like him, I admit, but we aren't steady or anything."

"Has he kissed you?"

"Twice."

"Oh, my!"

"Oh, my, is right! If dad had caught us--he'd be shocked and I totally embarrassed!"

The quiet member in the booth shifted uneasily and softly shared a concern. "I wonder what my father would say. Not likely I'll ever know. He's never home at night. Comes in from work, eats supper all quiet and then leaves." Jennifer stared into her Orange Fizzy and continued in a soft, wavering voice. "Mom doesn't ask him any more where he's going or when he'll be back. I think she's afraid to. I love daddy but he's mean to Mom." She began to cry.

Silence and wide eyes were the initial reaction to such alarming news. Then emotional responses.

"Why would he do that to your mom, and you?" Cori demanded.

The redhead slapped her hand on the table. "I thank God my dad is home at night. If not, mom would probably hit him with the frying pan."

"Jennifer, we really don't know what its like to be in your shoes," Michele added in a calm voice. "But we love you and want to help anyway we can. I think the best thing you can do is stick with and support your mom. Maybe even you don't know what she's going through. Together you'll make it and hopefully your dad will change."

"What I said was uncaring," the redhead nodded. "Michele, always the sensible one, is right. Stay close to your mom."

*   *   *

7:09 p.m.

"Here ve are! Here ve are!" heavily accented cries came from the edge of the trees. Wolf turned to see a couple coming towards the plane. The man was helping a woman cover the last few yards to freedom. As they approached, she appeared exhausted and began to stumble.

"Eilig! Eilig!" (Hurry! Hurry!) Wolf encouraged.

The man looked up at Wolf and stopped. His mind raced with fear. The pilot looked and spoke like a German. Was it a trap? If they climbed into the plane, no one would believe they were just taking a stroll in the woods. To disappear into a German prison would be a fate worse than death. He was about to turn back, when Wolf realized they might have expected the American to speak English so he yelled, "I'm an American, hurry up!"

The man's confidence returned with the English words. Foot-weary, they stumbled the final yards to the plane.

"What's the code word?" Wolf asked.

"Door! Door!" the man blurted.

"Good. You must be the Weinbaum's." Wolf leaned out of the cockpit and shook hands with both.

The woman collapsed into her husband's arms. Wolf told the husband to climb into the back cockpit and he would lift his wife up. As Wolf put his hands under her arms and lifted, he was surprised at how light she was. He could easily feel her ribs. With some struggle, the two men managed to get her into the cockpit. She sat on her husband's lap, limp, panting, but smiling.

Wolf smiled back and patted a welcome on the man's shoulder. "There are sandwiches and water on the floor. Eat if you can. The ship is still a long distance away."

Once they were securely belted into the seat, Wolf released the brakes, pushed the throttle to its maximum and the plane lumbered forward. It had not yet gained flying speed when it rolled off the plateau and began to fall along the mountainside. The precipitous drop frightened his passengers and he could hear their cries of despair. But Wolf knew that flying speed would soon be regained by the fall and set a course to freedom. Fuel allowing.

*   *   *

At 7:15 p.m., a black sedan drove up the road to the farm but parked some 100 yards short of the house. Victor had never seen Emil's face when the mission envelope was passed to him at the Colmar market. He only felt a bump on his shoulder, then someone whispered, "Door" and an envelope was thrust under his arm. Victor had been instructed in a letter from Pierre not to look at Emil's face. In the event Victor was forced to identify Emil in a line-up, he could not show recognition.

Victor saw the car approach and stop. No one got out. Victor understood. He knew that when Wolf accompanied the rescued couple to the car, he would know the driver. Still, the black car sitting there, with engine running and driver's window down several centimeters was unnerving.

Everyone just waited. The Laverns were silent. Only the usual farm animal sounds disturbed the quiet. All waited for the sound of an approaching airplane. Victor left Gabrielle to first light the lantern near the barn and then the two at the other end of the pasture. He returned to Gabrielle. His watch read 7:30. "He's late," Victor sighed nervously. Each new minute without sight of the Breguet increased their anxiety.

No one stirred in the black car.

The sound of an airplane barely audible at first, then increasing in volume brought smiles back to the Laverns. Wolf held the plane at 1000 feet up to a quarter mile of the grassy runway.

Trouble, never far away, took a punch at the antique plane. The motor gasped for gas. The nose dropped and skimmed to tree height. Loud, anguished cries emerged from the rear cockpit.

Trouble, touched by the laminations, backed off. The spent engine and its cargo plopped onto the pasture. While Victor hitched the team to the plane, Wolf helped the Weinbaum's onto the ground. Both were trembling from the ordeal but appeared refreshed from the sandwiches and water.

"You must get into the car. You will be driven to an ocean liner scheduled to sail to America," Wolf explained.

Mr. Weinbaum, in some distress, spoke. "I apologize but ve must use die toilette first!"

Gabrielle stepped up and said, "Come with me." She led them to an outhouse. Mrs. Weinbaum entered first, then Mr. Weinbaum. As he stepped out, he bowed and kissed Gabrielle's hand. "Ve cannot thank you enough. Gott loves you!"

Wolf led them the one hundred yards to the car. The driver emerged.

"Uncle Emil!"

"Wolf!"

For a moment, they held one another tight.

"Good to see you, kid," Emil exclaimed. He stepped back. "Hey, you look good in that country outfit!"

"Oh, Uncle," Wolf chuckled, "only you would think to say that at a time like this!"

Emil introduced himself to the Weinbaum's and handed each their new passport. "To circumvent immigration laws in the U.S. your first names, David and Sylvia, remain the same, but your last name is now Haberstein. If asked by anyone, you were only visiting in France. You live in Northern Bend, Indiana, U.S.A. What city in France are you familiar with?"

"In der 20's ve vacationed in Istres, a small Mediterranean fishing village. Loved it didn't ve Sylvia? Peaceful. Fresh fish."

"Great," exclaimed Emil. "That's where you just vacationed. Try to steer away from any conversation about yourself. The less attention you draw, the better. We have a long drive ahead of us. Let Mrs. Wein…ah, Haberstein sleep in the back seat, and you, Mr. Haberstein can sit up front with me. We must reach Cherbourg by 11:00 a.m. tomorrow when your ship will anchor up."

As the Habersteins climbed into the car, Emil turned, placed both hands on Wolf's shoulders and looked straight into his eyes. "German intelligence knows you're here. They spotted Otto on the ship's registry and noted your crossing the border at Colmar. Herman Schroeder, the big shot I'm dealing with, hopes the scene you observed in Breisach didn't give you the wrong impression about German authorities. Ya, as if we can just forget beatings.

"Anyway, they are still bent on learning how we stabilize the 37mm cannon in the fuselage. They have yet to beat the vibration problem. If the firing mechanism is shaken loose from the barrel, it sends shells right into the cockpit. It's a nail-biter for Luftwaffe pilots. Has anybody been here yet?"

"No."

"I'll wager they will drive here and invite you to visit an aircraft assembly plant, chat, but make sure they don't get a clue out of you. They must know your departure date. They'll come a few days before that. When do you leave?"

"Next Friday."

"If they ask you, go along with them. My contacts haven't said a word about the mission, so you're home free. If they persist about their 37mm cannon issue, suggest a spring anchor. Then you ask about the composition of the motor block alloy. That question will put them all in a dither because they will then realize you ain't just their version of the typical American loafer. Don't worry, they can't afford to harm an Otto-not when there is important information to be gained. They may be ruthless but they ain't stupid. How's everybody at home?"

"They worry about you. Everybody does. Grossmutter a lot. I'm to tell you not to deal with the Germans anymore. Dad says if they believe you're spying, you could just end up missing."

"Tell 'em to stop worrying. Nothing is going to happen to me. Once I wrap up this contract for instrument panels with the French aircraft company, I'll come home. Hey, living in France is like one long vacation. Dealing with Fritz is just part of the game. It's poker at its best. On second thought, don't tell them that last part. That's just between you and me, okay? In a few weeks, I'll be back—or maybe England. They're revving up their aircraft industry so there's a market we could tap into. I got to go. You been to Paris yet?"

"No, that's not part of the plan."

"Just as well. If you parle vous you're one of theirs. It's a tough city to leave. So 'bye."

"Au revoir, Uncle."

Emil climbed into the driver's seat, started the motor, waved a farewell, and sped into the night.

Wolf returned to the house and described the flight. Exhaustion taking its toll, he excused himself and went to his room. He changed into pajamas, read the inscription on the picture, and fell into bed with a comforting sense of accomplishment.

*   *   *

As the sun peeked over the horizon, Kaiser, the rooster, puffed up, surveyed his domain, and crowed the arrival of a new day. The raspy cackle broke Wolf's slumber. His first thought was troubling. What if the Germans showed up knowing his role in the escape and lured him across the border into prison? His uncle's assurances did little to modify his concern.

Worry didn't do chores, so Wolf dressed and entered into the usual events of the day. But, as Emil predicted, an open touring car with a sole passenger in the back seat drove up the lane at 9:30AM. The driver, graying at the temples, was dressed in a military uniform the other in a black suit. The passenger got out and walked into the courtyard. Both Wolf and Victor saw the car approach. A formal German visit the day after the rescue didn't look good.

"It's der Boche!" whispered Victor. "We'll both walk out of the barn. You'll have to speak with him. My German's inadequate for what he may want to talk about."

Wolf stepped forward with, "Kann Ich Sie helfen?" (May I help you?)

"Sind Sie Herr Wolfgang Otto?" (Are you Mr. Wolfgang Otto?)

"Yawohl!" (Yes!)

"Sie müssen mit mir kommen!" (You must come with me!)

*   *   *

Meanwhile, an aviatrix is discovered. The revelation began with a telephone call.

"Pierre," she said holding her hand over the transmitter, "it's the Baron. He wishes to talk with you!"

"What about?" Pierre asked with a puzzled look.

"He didn't say, but his voice was pleasant. Hurry!" She thrust the receiver toward him.

Pierre edged up to the wall phone, took the receiver from his wife, eyes blinking, as he tried to imagine what the Baron wanted to talk about. Was it about his brother? What would he say?

"Hello, this is Pierre."

"Pierre, I'm pleased to reach you. Do you have a moment?"

"Yes."

"I read in the paper today that the Farmer's Union is holding their annual convention in Evanston, Illinois, this year. The article states that they plan numerous talks and demonstrations. The convention is Friday, and on that day I have to fly to Chicago for a meeting. If you can spare the time, would you, Zelia, and the children like to go with me? I'll fly you to Evanston. I'm sure they will have buses meeting convention-goers and equipment representatives arriving on the different airline flights. You can go with them and return at about 5PM. I'll fly there from my meeting and we'll be home by 7PM."

Pierre's pulse quickened. He had never flown before. Soon he could go like some of those company presidents he'd read about. "I am a member of the Farmer's Union. I hadn't planned to go, but if it isn't a great inconvenience for you, I'd like to accept."

"Accept what?" Michele asked excitedly.

Pierre put his finger to his mouth and concentrated on the caller.

"Excellent. Henry will pick you up at 730 a.m. on his way to Sternlicht. We'll fly from there. Cletus Bauerman and I will pilot. Have a nice day."

As if out of breath, Pierre reached for a chair to sit down. "To fly all of us to the Farmer's Union Convention in Evanston, Illinois, Friday!"

"Can I go? Can I really go?" Michele pleaded. "He said—I heard him say it-you and your family!"

"You all go, I'll watch the farm," Tim offered with a grin. "I'll sacrifice!"

"Oh, Timmy, you are the sweetest brother!"

*   *   *

Friday morning, Pierre reset the time on his watch from 7:26 a.m. to 7:30 a.m. when he saw the black sedan appear on his driveway.

Inside the plane, the family was delightfully amazed at the luxurious furnishings present in the cabin of the Executive Suite in the Sky. The passengers could see into the forward cockpit because the curtain usually separating the two compartments had been pulled aside. They watched in awe as the two pilots checked instruments in preparation for take-off.

The Baron spoke into a microphone. "All passengers please fasten your seatbelts. This is a precaution should we encounter choppy weather that could cause the plane to bounce around a bit."

The passengers, at first, cast fearful eyes at one another at the words 'bounce around.' Zestily, they located and connected their seat belts.

Within minutes the airplane was in the air

cruising toward Evanston.

Cletus Bauerman unbuckled his seatbelt and went into the cabin. "The Baron invites Michele to come into the cockpit and sit in the copilot's chair."

Michele looked at Cletus wide-eyed. "You sure he meant me?"

Cletus laughed. "He said, Michele."

She went into the forward compartment and due to the low ceiling, stood slightly crouched.

The Baron pointed to the copilot seat on the right. "Sit down." She climbed into the seat.

"Fasten your seatbelt."

She did.

"These sunglasses and cap will eliminate the glare." She put them on, turned to the Baron and smiled.

The Baron mused. Why do sunglasses make some women even more glamorous.

"Wolf tells me you took to the tractor as if you had driven that sort of thing before."

"My girlfriend let me drive her parent's car. Oh, don't tell mom or dad that!"

The Baron detected a twinkle in her eyes. "That's a secret that shall never pass my lips."

They laughed.

"Like a flying lesson?" the Baron asked.

"I'm taking a preflight course, but I've never been in a cockpit before, much less an airplane. But sure!"

"I'm going to let you fly, but if a problem occurs, I don't want you to panic and fight the controls with me."

"Baron—may I call you Baron?"

"Yes, of course."

"I don't panic. You can't panic when you've got the reins of a runaway team."

"Good." The Baron liked her confident response.

"Put your hands on the wheel which controls

flying to the left or right like your friend's car," the Baron instructed, raising one eyebrow in a slight hint of tease as he looked at Michele. She giggled and gripped the wheel.

"Put your feet on those rudders controls. They control like the wheel. Push on the left one and you bank left. Push on the right one and you bank right.

"Increase altitude by pulling the wheel toward you and decrease by pushing it forward. We are following a heading of 315°. Fly the arrow to that heading," he said, pointing to a compass. Then pointing to a gyroscope, "You maintain altitude by flying to the horizon. These two levers between us are the throttles to the two engines. I've matched their power by the bar across them. If you lose altitude, edge them forward to increase power. There you have it, your task is to coordinate these different functions. Now fly."

With that charge, he let go of the controls. She was the pilot! She reacted as the controls tugged at her hands and feet. A little push here, a little pull there, and the plane responded like an obedient horse. Her wish was its very command. Secure in the seat, visibility unlimited, awesome power, and control at her fingertips. For Michele, this was Mount Everest!

She tested the Baron's explanation of the throttles. She inched them forward, and thrilled at the effect of acceleration pressing her body back into her seat. The airspeed increased from 300 mph to 340 mph, as quick as she advanced the throttles forward. Instant reaction. The tractor reacted faster than the horses, but this machine reacted *now*!

While checking his flight plan, the Baron could sense the steady course she maintained. The brain, eyes, hand and foot coordination that he looked for in a fledgling pilot were there, even earlier than most. She could be a natural in the cockpit like Wolf.

The Baron busied himself with maps and radio communication in preparation for landing in Evanston. Meanwhile, Michele could feel herself relax to that level of tension only necessary to maintain control of flight.

Soon the Baron continued instruction. "As we near Evanston Airport, I'll guide you through the necessary banks. As you bank, the plane will lose speed so you may have to increase power. When we are in the final approach to the landing strip, release all controls to me, but I want you to call out our altitude so I can best judge our angle of descent."

With the cockpit curtains still tucked to the side, Michele's parents could watch the interaction between the Baron and their daughter. It became evident the Baron was confident in her performance as he gave instructions and then occupied himself with other duties. He even got out of his seat once to check some instruments in a cabinet behind his seat. He smiled at the Laverns and nodded his head as if to say, she's good!

Cletus and the Laverns carried on a conversation as the plane soared through the cloudless sky. But as the plane began to descend toward the airport, Pierre said, "Shouldn't Michele return to her seat here?"

"She's doing just fine. I can feel her control of the plane. She has a natural ability," was Cletus' assessment of the situation.

The Laverns were proud of their daughter's achievement, and knew she would leave the farm for good. Their little girl had grown up. Pierre grasped Viola's hand and squeezed it. Their thoughts were one.

CHAPTER 14

HE HELD THE METAL SHAVINGS AS IF THEY WERE GOLD

"I am Willi Reinstein, First Assistant to Dr. Herman Schroeder, Director of Aeronautical Development of the National Aeronautical Department in Berlin. Your uncle, Herr Emil Otto, informed Dr. Schroeder that you were working on this farm for the summer."

"Well, actually only until Friday."

"Then my timing is fortunate. I represent The National Aeronautical Department on behalf of Dr. Schroeder. We understand you fly the Airacuda manufactured by your Grossvater, the Baron Frederick Otto."

"That's true. It's great to fly."

"If you could be spared the day, Dr. Schroeder would like you to visit our aircraft factory in Freiburg. Possibly fly a Heinkel 111 and give us a comparison to the Airacuda. Would you like to do that?"

"Of course. However, I need to obtain permission from Monsieur Lavern."

Speaking to Victor in French, "Could I spend the day with Herr Reinstein in Freiburg?"

"Yes. I can handle the chores. Be back by evening milking."

During this brief exchange, Wolf faced Victor, but out of the corner of his eye, watched Willi's reaction to this conversation in French. In his attempt to interpret, the perceptible movement of Willi's lips and furrowed brow amused Wolf.

Wolf knew such effort had failed when Willi asked, "What did the farmer say?"

By this point in Wolf's conversation with Willi, Wolf had the impression this intermediate was short on brains and long on pomposity. "Monsieur

Lavern requests I return by evening milking."

"Tell the farmer, ah, Monsieur Lavern, I'll have you back by 1800 hours."

They both entered the back seat. Willi tapped the driver on the shoulder, and off they went. Approaching the border guard, Willi stated, as he performed a straight arm salute with such vigor his hat shifted slightly, "You need not show your passport. They will recognize me."

Passing through the gate, the German border guard returned the salute but Wolf got the feeling the guard wasn't impressed with the occupants of the car. Probably thinks he's just another stuffed shirt.

Once in Germany, Willi took every opportunity to point out the contrasts between the two adjacent countries. True, the quality of the roads was better in Germany, more farm equipment in the fields, and more cars on the roads. But Wolf never saw a beating, armed police, or frightened faces in France.

Wolf noted that the touring car was well made with a loaded gun rack on the back of the front seat. He quickly erased the thought one of them could be used to march him into a prison.

Willi outlined the schedule of the day. "We have an appointment to meet Dr. Schroeder and some engineers after we have toured the factory. Dr. Schroeder is aware of the performance statistics of the Airacuda. He thought a chat about comparisons between the Heinkel 111 and the Airacuda might be beneficial to both sides. Not to offend you, but Dr. Schroeder has been disappointed in the progress of technical talks with your uncle, Emil. We would hope for more exchange. After all, we are all Germans! Finally if there is time, you may have the opportunity to fly a Heinkel 111. Today could be quite exciting!"

Freiburg was a beautiful city. They drove

through a business district lined with small and large shops. Wolf saw a small shop with "Juden" painted on its display window. No one appeared to be going in or out of the shop. Pointing to the sign, he asked Willi the reason. "Why them?" Willi looked straight ahead, teeth clenched. The question went unanswered.

Entering an industrial area, Willi cheerfully announced they had arrived at their destination. The title of the aircraft factory appeared on a sign attached to an arch over the front gate. In letters twice the size of any other word on the sign was the name, Heinkel.

"Professor Heinkel is an outstanding aircraft designer! He has and will astound the world with his innovative approaches to speed," Willi proclaimed with obvious pride.

The door to secrets was opened, and Wolf stuck his foot in with a question. "Is the speed tied to the alloy of the engine block?"

"Ah, you are informed. I can say no more. A secret. The world will see," Willi responded with a momentary sneer.

Again, the exchange of salutes at the gate. The driver parked and both got out. Thinking they would enter through the main door, Wolf began to walk in that direction.

"No, not that way, we will enter through this side door," Willi directed as he tugged on Wolf's sleeve. "We are having a very important visitor this morning who you may meet in the course of this afternoon's activities. My assistant, Hector Eisen, will be guiding Field Marshal and Commander-in-Chief of the Luftwaffe Herman Goering, Professor Heinkel, and an entourage through the plant."

They entered into a huge section of the plant where workers on several production lines were assembling engines. It was noisy, and Willi had to shout as they stopped at different points along a line close to the wall. "First, I want to show you where we build aircraft motors and when you fly the Heinkel 111 you'll have to agree they're the best in the world!"

During the tour, Willi would glance at the door leading to the front of the building and then at his watch. Wolf saw a large clock on the wall and it was a few minutes to 11. He guessed Field Marshal would walk through that door at 11.

Promptly at 11 a.m. the door opened and a portly man in a white uniform surrounded by a group of military and civilians entered the plant. Willi smiled as he saw the group and shouted with pride, "The man in white is Field Marshal Herman Goering." Then Willi turned pale. "Where's Hector?" he cried as he frantically searched for his assistant. The group standing at the door began to look impatient.

Willi, twitching like a hooked fish, looked, wide-eyed, at Wolf. "I must conduct the tour myself. I'll be back or someone will," he blurted over his shoulder as he rushed to the group.

Left alone, Wolf didn't know quite what to do. So he just stood where Willi left him and watched the group. Willi directed most of his comments to the Field Marshal who appeared overweight, and obviously, the one in control. Whenever the Field Marshal spoke, everyone in the group would lean towards him to hear what he had to say.

Since the group moved at a protracted pace toward the opposite side of the building, Wolf knew he was in for an extended wait. Looking around the huge room, he noted a slightly ajar door a few feet away. Since all eyes in the room were riveted to the group, Wolf slowly walked to the door and looked in.

What he saw stunned him. The room was filled with huge machines drilling out cylinders in motor blocks. An operator was chained to each machine. These men were dressed in a different overall than the men in the plant and appeared thin, almost emaciated.

Wolf's eyes met the intent stare of an operator nearby. The man would glare at Wolf and then look down to a pile of metal shavings beneath his drill. Wolf interpreted the back and forth stares to mean he should take a sample of the drill waste. This frantic pantomime didn't make sense until it dawned on Wolf that these shavings might be from motor blocks cast from the secret alloy! This operator was encouraging Wolf to take a sample back to the free world.

With all attention still focused on the group harvesting every utterance of the Field Marshal, Wolf stepped to the drill, caught a handful of shavings as they fell from the drill, stuck them in his pocket and walked back to the site where Willi had left him. The prospect he may have the solution to improving the Airacuda's engine performance in his pocket made him feel giddy. Wolf gritted his teeth to avoid showing any appearance of having pocketed something of great importance. So he stood with hands behind his back, looking a bit bored by it all.

Willi, shouting over the noise, disappeared with the group through a door on the far side of the building. Wolf watched Willi and the opportunity to fly a Heinkel 111 evaporate. Willi gone, what was he to do?

He didn't have to wonder long.

The uniformed driver of the touring car came through the door which Willi and the swarm had just exited. He came at a rather leisurely pace, straight to Wolf. "Mr. Reinstein didn't introduce me. I am Sergeant Arno Külz. He begs your forgiveness for abandoning you. Seems his assistant took ill at the last minute so Wil—ah—

Mr. Reinstein has to conduct the tour himself. He'll be at that all day. He suggests I take you back to the farm."

"Tell Mr. Reinstein I fully understand and accept his apology. I don't see an opportunity for a return visit before I depart, but I hope to visit France again. We may be able to arrange a time then."

The driver nodded. They walked to the touring car. "Would you like to sit in the front seat?" Arno asked.

"Sure."

Leaving the plant, the driver took a path different than the one on which they arrived.

"Do you mind if I take a little longer route? I get bored driving the same way all the time."

"Only need to get back for milking," said Wolf.

Beyond the factory was a line of hangars facing a flight line. Parked outside the hangars were a variety of aircraft. Wolf studied each as they drove by. Trucks, aircraft, and parts everywhere could only be passed at slow speed. The driver came to one plane and slowed even further as if to suggest that Wolf examine it in detail. He did, and to his surprise the plane had no propeller but rather a large hole in the front and another hole at the back of the fuselage. The openings were rounded on their edges, not the usual fittings for a piston motor.

"That plane doesn't have a motor," Wolf remarked.

"I know nothing about airplanes," the driver replied. "I'm just a driver, nothing more."

Leaving the odd looking aircraft, the driver went back onto a main road leading to the border. The mid- afternoon sun was warm, and the two exchanged comments about their home life. Wolf sensed the driver wasn't too thrilled with the military build-up occurring in his country.

"I'm a holdover from the past war. The pay isn't much, but we make do. Just when I thought I could finish my military time driving people here and there, they assign me to a unit training to drive a tank._They're hot, stinky, and not my idea of where I want to be if there is a war. Judging from the last one, wars only serve up a lot of grief."

They arrived back at the farm just as Victor was walking to the barn to milk. Wolf thanked the driver for the trip. The driver saluted, turned the car around and left at a very leisurely pace.

*   *   *

Wolf wrestled with mixed emotions as he packed his single suitcase for the trip back to the States. Life on the farm was arduous but appealed to his youthful energy and zest for the outdoors. He had mastered the art of harnessing and driving Nelli and Napoleon. Plowing was easy sitting on a tractor. He even began to comprehend the complexities of sowing, harvesting, animal husbandry, and farm finances. He could be a farmer and probably a pretty good one. But Sternlicht was his soil and from whence he would grow. So with some reluctance, but great expectations of things yet to come in his life, he said goodbye to the Laverns and climbed aboard the train to Cherbourg.

The voyage back to the USA was in sharp contrast to the one to France. Wolf realized how tired he was when he entered his assigned cabin on board ship. A gentle, cool breeze wafting through an open porthole brushed across his face. He left the light off, set his suitcase on the floor, and intended to lie down just for a few minutes in preparation for a tour of this ocean liner. Hours later he awoke. The hum of the ship's motors and the rolling motion told him they were in open waters. As yet, hunger was not an issue so he pulled a blanket over himself and entered into dreamland.

The night passed with a mixture of troubling and soothing images. Men were beating on a figure. Wolf began to move in the direction of the cries of anguish but couldn't. Some invisible force held him back. A face grotesque with fear rushes by. A pause, then darkness. A fragrance. A young woman standing on a hill, then sitting on tractor. Turns her head—it's Michele smiling. She beckons to him. He begins to move in her direction but can't. His shoes are too heavy to drag. A sense of impending loss. Michele is close to him, placing her hand on his cheek. Darkness, sleep.

He awakened to a changed ocean. The ship had entered into a storm that rocked the vessel ponderously in all directions. Flying in rough weather conditioned Wolf to these gyrations. Hunger uppermost in his mind, he swayed along the passageways to the dining room. Few travelers were present.

A waiter led him to a table and asked with a shrug, "Are you here for breakfast, Dramamine or a puke bucket?"

As he tucked a napkin around his waist, Wolf chuckled. "I'm here for your first offer. I feel fine and hungry as a bear! What's on the menu?"

"Finally a passenger seaworthy enough to enjoy the preparations from the kitchen. You name it. The cooks haven't much to do since few are in the mood to eat. They'd rather be doing something than just sitting around. How about I start you out with a whole grapefruit, followed by steak, eggs, muffins and a pot of coffee? If that doesn't fill you up, they'll cook up the thing that laid the eggs."

"Well, then we'll never know which came first. Let's just work with everything up to and including the coffee."

The prolonged sleep and hearty breakfast infused renewed strength into Wolf. After the third cup of coffee, Wolf swayed his way past other swaying passengers, some looking a vile shade of green and carrying a bucket, until he reached the top deck. Going fore and then aft, he discovered a covered area in the stern sheltered from the wind and rain where he could recline in a deck chair, cover up to his nose with a blanket and ponder the past, present, and future.

The travel conditions proved fortuitous. Days of eating, sleeping, and reclining charged Wolf physically and mentally. Two months away from Sternlicht gave him new insights into the benefits of being the grandson of Baron Frederick Otto. Such reflection never occurred to him before. Always busy with this or that, this was the first time his life was void of schedules and orders. He was totally by himself with his thoughts. People, places, and things bounced back and forth in his mind as he sat in the recliner.

Mountainous waves rolling by playfully cast spray at Wolf. The drops of water splashing on his face reminded him of his sister, Jacqueline, doing the same thing when they swam in Lake Michigan. What fun.

He felt a kinship to the ship as it charged through the storm and rolled with the punches. Despite the efforts of the waves breaking across the bow, the ship never wavered from its course. Wolf hoped that this had been the pattern of his life and he vowed to intensify that commitment in the future.

An announcement by the ship's captain startled Wolf out of his daydreams. "We're but one day away from New York and I'm happy to report that calm waters are just ahead. I hope the pleasant weather will settle any upset stomachs."

Home soon. Wolf needed to plan how he would put his promises into action. Less than a week back home, he would be off to Trinity University for football practice. He looked forward to the surprise in the brown envelope he had for the Baron and his dad and hoped it would answer their quest for the desired alloy. Not all he thought about, however, was easy to define and forecast.

Michele. Still a mystery. A very pleasant mystery, but a mystery. Her kind wasn't easy to define and forecast. Wolf, at this point in his life, didn't expect any firm commitment from her. Yet some deeper expression of her affection for him, beyond the photo, would be appreciated.

The next morning after another steak and eggs breakfast, the ship docked in the New York harbor. Wolf gathered his belongings into the suitcase and left the ship in the direction of Grand Central Station. As his foot touched the pier he heard a voice shout, "Wolfy, over here!" He turned and saw his mother running toward him. They met, hugged, kissed, and hugged.

"Mom, I'm so happy to be home!"

"We missed you, we prayed for you and you are back!"

His dad and grandparents rushed to Wolf and his mom, and all clutched in one solid hug of gratitude. "We couldn't wait for the train," Henry explained. "When we read the telegram you sent from Cherbourg, I called the Baron and said, "Roll out Executive 4. We've got to meet that ship." So here we are. We'll take a cab to the airport and on the way you can tell us about the voyage back. We know you went through a storm. In the plane you can tell us about your vacation in France."

Cletus Bauerman greeted Wolf when they arrived

at the Executive 4 aircraft. "Well done, Wolfgang."

Wolf knew Cletus was sincere but also knew Cletus had begged the Baron to let him carry out the mission. The Baron had declined because he feared Cletus, still troubled by the mayor's accusation, might attempt something brash to balance his record.

The Baron and Cletus set a course home and then the Baron walked back to the passenger cabin to join the family discussion. Wolf described his experiences. When he told of the beatings he observed in Breisach, his grandmother exclaimed, "Why does Emil play with fire? He should come back to the U.S. There have to be plenty of business opportunities on this continent. Sometimes I think he likes to worry his mother. Why doesn't he come home, meet a nice girl, get married, and have a family like you, Henry?"

"Mom, it's in his nature." Henry held his mother's hands. "He likes Europe, he likes Paris and he gets us business. He's a good guy, Mom, and I know he doesn't want either you or Dad to worry. He just likes the challenge there. What did he say to you, Wolf?"

"The same thing, Dad. He did say he was wrapping up the contract with some French firm and then thought he would go to England. He thinks the Germans are up to something on their eastern borders. Maybe by going to England he can distance himself from trouble. He said to tell everybody not to worry; he's in control."

The Baron reacted to the news about German troop reassignment. "Movement to the east can only mean Poland. Hitler marched into the Rhineland, then Austria and Czechoslovakia and nobody raised a finger. He'll get some resistance from the Poles, but Lebensraum is his goal and Blitzkrieg is his method. Until he encounters an opponent with superior weaponry and the will to

fight, he's going to conquer all of Europe. The
U.S. will be back to where it was in 1917. Long
on patriotism, and short on modern equipment.
If the U.S. declares war, we still don't have
a fighter-bomber superior to the Heinkel 111.
That motor problem still dogs us," he declared
dejectedly.

"Oh, Fred, you'll figure it out! Right now,
let's leave work behind. Wolfy, tell us about the
Laverns," Annie suggested.

"I will, Oma, in just a moment." Wolf leaned
forward in his seat and pulled his suitcase up
to his knees. "I've got something here that just
might interest you, Opa." Wolf retrieved the
brown envelope and began to open it. He told how
he entered the machine shop and was encouraged
by the chained operator to pick up some of the
filings. Filings from the bores of an aircraft
engine.

The mere mention of filings and motor blocks
brought the Baron and Henry as close to the
edge of their seats as their seatbelts would
allow. Wolf handed the envelope to the Baron who
carefully withdrew some of the contents. He held
the metal shavings as if they were milled from
gold.

The Baron's hands trembled. "These are scraps
from the motor block? Might they have been from
another source?"

"Nope, he was drilling a block and I caught
these filings as they fell."

Holding the filings so all could see them, the
Baron exclaimed, "If this is a sample of the
alloy we seek, I hold the advantage in my hand.
Wolf, you are a genius!"

Mercedes took Wolf's hand in hers. "Didn't you
place yourself in jeopardy by going with that
official? If they knew you had flown the Weinbaums
to France that could have been a ruse just to

get you across the border and into one of their prisons."

"Mom, Emil told me they knew I was in France. He said it was only a matter of time before they came to the farm to see if they could, through conversation, get me to reveal desired technical information. An attempt to avoid them would have cast suspicion on me and making a connection to the disappearance of the Weinbaums. If their intent was to punish me for the disappearance of the Weinbaums, they wouldn't have sent weasel Willi to fetch me. I went along and came back with the catch of the day!"

At this moment, the Baron and Henry began a discussion about getting the shavings to the Weinbaums for analysis. Wolf touched the Baron's arm. "Opa, one more thing. I saw a weird looking airplane at the Heinkel factory."

The Baron folded the envelope and placed it in his briefcase. "What was weird about it?"

"Well, it had a big hole in the front where the propeller should go, but there was no mounting for the motor. It was just a big hole with rounded sides. And it had a smaller hole in the back that had rounded sides. Really strange. I think the driver meant to drive me by it. Went out of his way, in fact."

The Baron sat back in his seat, pursed his lips, and shook a finger in the air. "They're still one step ahead of us. We may have the alloy for a better engine, but they're already working on a new form of propulsion! The holes in the fuselage now gives credence to some of these decodes I've read at IDC. Emil-"

"Fred, don't you give one more assignment to Emil! Don't you dare! I want him back here!" Annie demanded as she glared at the Baron.

Following the outburst from someone who seldom lost her temper, the only sound heard in the cabin was that of the motors. Everyone knew Emil's work in Europe was a point of contention between Frederick and Annie.

Frederick took Annie's hand. She first attempted to free it but then relaxed. "Annie, please. I will not, I promise, I will not ask Emil to investigate. I'll wire him tonight to come home. Please believe me."

"Fred, I believe you. I trust you." She drew her hand back. "But I'll believe you more when Emil walks through our front door."

"Tonight I'll wire him."

"Yes, yes," she sighed. "Talk to Henry, our son here," patting Henry on the arm, "about those shavings." She relaxed back in her seat nodding to all and saying, "Talk, talk."

The sound of the motors prevailed for several seconds until the Baron cleared his throat, wiped his brow, and said to Henry, "I'll take these shaving to Weinbaum tonight."

Once the silence was broken, Wolf took his grandmother's hand in his. "Oma, just one more thing before I tell you about the Laverns. Looking at his mother, he said, "Did I hear anything from Michele?"

His mother handed him a letter. "You received this."

Wolf opened the letter, read it silently and then out loud.

Dear Wolf,
    "I'm sorry I won't be home when you return. I had to go to freshman orientation at St.
    Benedict's. When you arrive at Trinity please give me a call. I am anxious to hear about your vacation in France.

    Always,
    Michele

"A call. I hope that means to come over. Always distant. It's the story of my life with this woman! Mom, I've got to talk with you about her."

His mother lifted her eyebrows. "So?"

"I really like her and I think she likes me, but she never says so."

"What have you said to her?" Annie asked.

"Well, nothing—but can't the girl say so first?"

Mercedes shrugged her shoulders. "She gave you her picture. Have you given her one of yours?"

"No."

"A girl is saying a lot when she gives a boy her picture. Has she given her picture to anyone else?"

"I don't think so. Maybe I'll ask Tank's sister, Sandy. She's friends with Michele and can keep secrets. I wouldn't want Michele to know that I asked. She arranged that chance meeting with Michele at the Big Top Café. I don't think Michele suspected.

"Remember the time I went to the Lavern family picnic? As soon as we arrived and those people were standing around, she took my hand and said, 'I want to introduce you to everyone.'

When she took my hand I felt like a king! We walked, she talked. She knew everybody and everybody enjoyed talking with the both of us. She's so good at that. I could have given her a big hug!"

"Sounds like you'll have to take a patient approach with her, Wolfy."

"Mom, I swear, it's never been more than a kiss and a hug. Everything too brief. Once, I told her I could hold her forever. But when we hug, it's for a second or two because I can sense she wants to step away. I quickly release her. I never want to see hurt in her face."

"I believe you, Wolfy. That's what I mean by patience. There's a lot of future ahead for both of you. I think she's very fond of you. I get the same impression from her mother. Restraint is the best course of action now.

"Your grandfather will have to tell of his recent experience with the Laverns. He doesn't miss an opportunity to turn a negative into a positive. Ever since that night we all went to the Laverns, you'd think Pierre and the Baron had been friends all these years!"

"Opa, what's with you and the Laverns while I'm away pitching hay?" Wolf said tapping his grandfather on the shoulder for attention.

The Baron turned, and described the trip to Evanston.

"Frank Hastings, at the airport, told me, while you were gone, Michele was taking instrument and navigation classes and soon should be into her flying lessons. On the way to and from Evanston, I let her take the controls. It was her first time, and I was impressed. She didn't hesitate to make flight adjustments and did it very smoothly. If she gets her license, both your dad and I would like to hire her as a copilot on the charter flights. More women are chartering flights now, so she would be good for our image."

The Baron stopped talking, raised, and shook his finger toward the ceiling to give his mind time to organize a new thought that just popped into his mind.

"There's a business angle to her, too. She speaks fluent French and the Laverns entered the U.S. through Quebec. With Europe becoming engulfed in war, it's time that our charter business looked to the north. Trade with Canada is on the increase, and executives will have to fly in both directions."

"Are you going to hire her?" Wolf asked with hope written on his face.

Henry raised his hand as if to signal not so

fast.

"She just started taken flying lessons at the airport. But if dad says she's a natural and earns a license, we will. I want her to ask for the job. To want it as a goal. We have better employees if they do the asking because they view it as an accomplishment. If given to them, Sternlicht may not have been their first choice and they use us as a springboard to something they think is better. I told Frank that once she is a registered pilot, to suggest she see us about a job as a pilot. If she wants us, she'll come to us. If we approach her with an offer, it may look as if you engineered it and then she won't feel as if she got the job on the basis of her own abilities."

"Okay, Dad." Wolf turned to his grandmother and wrinkled his nose. "Now there are two of us that are supposed to be patient! Anyway, you should have seen the Lavern farm. Chickens walk in the water trough and-"

*   *   *

Summer Became Fall

Football and classes at Trinity had occupied most of his time, but now it was time to call Michele for a date. Knowing the rigors of freshman orientation at St. Benedict's, he waited until their classes were underway. He knew the nuns were strict with those living on campus. That was okay. He just wanted to see her, be with her.

Wolfgang walked resolutely toward the pay phone at the end of the hallway. Single-mindedly focused, he gave only cursory greetings to others milling around. He entered the phone booth, plunked in a coin and dialed a number.

The phone rang once, twice. He drummed his fingers on the dial. A third time.

"Third floor Bentley!"

He closed the phone booth door. "This is Wolfgang Otto. May I speak to Michele Lavern?"

"Wolfgang, oh," (flustered) "you're the foot— Just a minute—(a rustle of papers)-"room 342. Hold the phone. I'll get her."

Wolf could hear scuf-scuf-scuf as the person on the other end hurried down the hall. Must be wearing slippers. He held the phone close to his ear and could hear voices in the distance. Then a double scuf-scuf-scuf coming back. Both wearing slippers. His heart pounded as he waited for her voice.

"Wolfy!"

"Hi, Michele!"

"I'm so glad your back. Sorry I had to leave before you returned."

"Hey, that's okay. When can I come over?"

"We're having a Bene hop this Saturday night from seven to ten thirty. Can you come then?"

"Great. I--"

"Can you bring a date for my roommate? Her name is Jeanne Dupuis. She's really nice and comes from Montreal, Canada."

"I'll do my best. Don't think my roommate is doing anything. He's Wally Kiznetski, and come to think of it, he's from Buffalo, New York. That's close to Canada so they'd have something in common to talk about already."

"Oh, she'd really like that. She loves to dance."

"Good. I--"

"I have to say goodbye. Sister doesn't like it if we tie up the phone. À bientôt!" (Soon!)

"Salut, Michele." (So Long!)

As Wolf, smiling, walked back to his room, he knew what to expect when he arrived at St. Benedict's College. It had a reputation for high scholastic standards. Wolf had attended these hops in his freshman year and heard first hand the groans of frustration. At exam times, rumors ran rampant that both institutions were conspiratorial in their demands on those enrolled. But the administrators held firm to their claim that they were preparing their charges for a world expanding in opportunity and shrinking in the eyes of ambitious dictators. A time of opportunity surrounded by a ring of peril, they would say.

Bene dances were held in their gymnasium. Card tables lined the walls and music issued forth from 45 r.p.m. records. The stylus hit the first record promptly at seven and went round and round until ten-thirty. Then the lights went up and everyone went back to their respective dorms. Any drink could be ordered from the temporary bar as long as it was lemonade.

Some Trinity daredevils would smuggle in a flask of whiskey to freshen their drinks. Such tactics were disastrous if Sister Mary Clemens, guardian of the evening's activities, discovered its illegal and immoral use. As a lesson to all, the transgressor would be immediately evicted with an embarrassing ceremony. Worse, the evictee was banished from all Bene socials for the remainder of the year. Overt displays of affection on or off the dance floor were also discouraged. But even Sr. Mary was sympathetic to the romance of the slow dance and allowed the lights to be dimmed a bit when they were played.

Saturday evening, Wolf and Wally took a bus to St. Benedict's and called for their dates at the reception desk. The men nervously waited in the lounge for their appearance. Several table lamps illuminated an assortment of couches, coffee tables, and upholstered chairs. The women lived in the dorm above and would enter the lounge through a door from a hallway.

Dates came in groups of twos and threes so all the men present would stand when the sounds of chatter and laughter were approaching. Two groups came, but Michele was in neither. Wolf and Wally sat down for the third time. Waiting was gnawing at their nerves.

"This is the part I don't like," Wolf lamented.

"What have I done to deserve this? Powder your nose and get down here," Wally added.

Wolf confided a nagging doubt. "I sure wish I knew how Michele feels about me. I'm corn'foosed."

"Tell her to date others," Wally suggested.

"Are you crazy? I got enough competition back home."

 Tell her you're gonna be gone a lot, football and stuff, and maybe she'd like to see others. There'll be a reaction. Count on it. Then you'll know which side of her fence you're on."

"Uh, sounds like shooting myself in the foot. I need some solid evidence from that corpus delightful." Wolf pleaded.

A familiar voice behind the door prompted Wolf to stand and assert, "Hey, it's them!"

"Wolf, what's my blind date's name, again?"

"Jeanne, Jeanne Dupuis. Write it on the back of your hand! Michele's gonna think I didn't take her request seriously."

Two women entered the lounge. Wolf walked to Michele and took her hands. Warm, dry. He marveled at her composure. With her hair swept up and wearing a light blue dress, she was everything Wolf remembered and could ask for.

Once Wally was introduced to Jeanne, the four noisily mingled their way toward the faint sounds of Harry James. As the music drew them closer, the two pairs broke into a quick step as they passed through the door into the gym. The desire to dance was epidemic and the floor was crowded. No wall flowers this night. The Lindy was the beat that erased the tensions of meeting for the first time or after a long time.

The song ended and as they stood waiting for the next number, Michele spoke of her new classmates. "There are girls from everywhere. They're from Georgia, New York. Jeanne, Canada. Her French, right now, is better than her English so they put us together. Her father is in the Canadian Air Force somewhere in England."

"Her mom is in their state department. They thought now would be a good time for Jeanne to get an education in another country. They would have preferred France but because of the war, they picked the U.S. It's all so exciting. These nuns are quite strict, but the girls are such fun. World Lit is boring, but the history professor brings every page alive. How's your life?"

"Couldn't be better," as he squeezed her hand and smiled.

Michele laughed. "My thoughts, too!" The student playing the records was still looking for a requested number to spin. "For exercise and fresh air, I've taken up tennis. Do you play tennis?"

"How do you spell it?"

"Oh, oh, it's the beginner's circle for you, too!"

"You learn and teach me."

"The school has clay courts and we have to maintain them. To smooth the surface, they pull a water-filled barrel with a small tractor. When they asked if any of the freshmen could drive it, guess who stepped forward?"

Wolf held her hand up in the air. "Without hesitation, you!" He edged closer to Michele and spoke in a low, serious voice. "I don't want to say this, but I must. I don't want you to think I'm going to dominate your time here. I'd like to, I really would. However, you should feel free to date others."

Frowning, Michele shook her head in the negative. Wolf continued a bit less persuasively. "Some weekends after the games, I'll have to fly back to Sternlicht."

Michele put her finger on his lips and picked an imaginary hair from his collar. She looked around teasingly and whispered, "You'll do just fine. Here's a Lindy. Let's dance the whole night through!"

CHAPTER 15

THE PEOPLE DECIDE

Early December, 1941

Once again, Mayor Renford was met at the front door by his wife waving the evening Northern Inquirer. "What's the matter now?" he growled.

"Have you seen the headline?"

"No, I just got home!" He grabbed the paper and read the front page outloud.

TAX WINDFALL HINGES ON MAYORAL ELECTION.

Karl Pletz, candidate for mayor, commented on the impact of the proposed future location of Sternlicht's aircraft factory on the city's tax revenue. Mr. Pletz made it clear that if Sternlicht selected a site at the airport within the city limits, he would not make an issue of armed aircraft present on the airport property. He stressed his position because if the plant is located outside the city limits, the property tax would fall to the county. "If elected, I would put those additional revenues to good use to repair the 10th Street Bridge, upgrade the park playground and expand the convention center. I have great plans to attract outside businesses."

Clifford began walking circles in the living room. "Hey, I've got great plans, too. What's this talk about property taxes and armed aircraft? I can make exceptions! Did Manning call me for an interview about this?"

"Call here?"

"Yes, here!"

"No, why should he? Wouldn't he call you at the office?"

"I was out, and maybe he thought I'd be home."

"Well, you didn't get any calls."

"He's trying to twist my good intentions!"

The Grandmother clock in the dining room began to solemnly toll the hour. "Bong-bong-bong-bong-bong."

Clifford scowled silently waiting for the clock to conclude its business.

To emphasize his exasperation, he dragged out his first word. "W--h--y does your clock always interrupt me when I'm about to make an important statement?" He angrily slapped the headline. "And on the front page. It's a conspiracy. That Pletz. He runs a little machine shop on the south side. What would he know about running a city? Ten to one he does business with that Otto crowd. Both krauts. Dangerous. Doesn't anybody see the connection? That's it. They're all in it together!"

"Before you make any public statements about something that is only a figment of your imagination, you better get the facts first."

"All right, I'll call Manning right now. At home. What's his number? Look it up."

Dorothy sighed, wearily picked up the telephone book, found Howard Manning's number and pointed to it. Clifford mumbled the digits as he dialed.

A man's voice answered. "Manning residence."

"Howard?"

"Yes."

"This is Clifford. Howard, I was disappointed to read the lead article about the airport in the paper this evening. Had you consulted in this matter, my opinion could be included. You didn't have the whole story!"

"I called your office immediately after my reporter brought me the interview with Pletz. Your secretary didn't know where you were."

"I had important business out of town. Anyway, you could have postponed the article until tomorrow!"

"When I have a lead story, I run with it. I'm

not about to be scooped. Give me your statement in the morning. I'll print it in tomorrow evening's edition."

"You'll run it on the front page?"

"I'll run it where it fits."

"My secretary will bring it in the morning. Goodnight."

"Goodnight."

Clifford hung up the phone and walked into the kitchen.

"You didn't say anything about being out of town today."

"I got a call from Traski's Lakeview Resort. They wanted some expert opinion on expansion, so I drove out there. Remember, I attended their dedication."

"Didn't the husband die recently?"

"Yes, but several people work there and I gave them some good tips. They thanked me a lot." Clifford entered the kitchen, took a bottle of Scotch from a cabinet, and poured himself a drink.

Dorothy pondered her husband's reactions as she watched him drink it straight without the usual splash of water.

*   *   *

Evening, Community auditorium, Northern Bend

The boisterous crowd exploded into a resounding cheer when the Chairman of the Election Committee appeared on the stage.

"Results! Results!" several shouted.

"Results I have," answered the chairman. His words silenced the room as everyone wanted to hear the long awaited tabulations.

This was the first election announcement where Renford stood alone in the hall. His campaign had tripped on the debate over the location of the Sternlicht plant. Each day, thereafter, his office seemed less and less spirited. Despite alternating encouragement and threats, his re-election effort ran out of steam. As if in solitary confinement, he stood in the back of the huge room. He even edged toward the back door in preparation for bad news.

His eyes darted about the room for staff, family or anyone that could stand beside him as a sign of support. Where was everyone? He never understood why he had to remind them each election to be with him when they read the results!

The chairman shuffled a sheath of papers at the podium in preparation for his delivery. The cumulative nervous anticipation broke through the silence as different groups, about the hall, began to release their emotions by clapping, raising placards and stomping feet.

"Good afternoon, ladies and gentlemen. As you know the tabulation of absentee ballots has delayed the announcements of the results until today. Now I'm pleased to read the final computations. I begin with the Mayor's office."

A cheer arose from a large gathering near the stage. A sign reading PLETZ WILL LEAD! bobbed up and down from within them.

Clifford, the incumbent, drew a deep breath and crossed sweaty fingers behind his back.

"For mayor and we have accounted for all precincts: John Pletz, 76,481!"

The room erupted in cheers! Several groups began to dance about the floor waving banners.

Clifford's heart sank as his mind calculated the loss. There were only 120,000 voters in the whole city.

"Clifford Renford, 32,552 votes." A few groans of disappointment accompanied the obvious loss.

"Paul Weston, a write-in, 13,498." A group clapped vigorously and pointed to their up-and-coming candidate.   "The winner and your new mayor is Karl A. Pletz!"

The room responded with shouts of approval. Paper, hats, banners flew into the air.

No eyes looked to the back of the room. All eyes glistened as they looked forward.

Clifford, humiliated by such a margin, slipped unnoticed through the door and into the hallway. He hurried past several doors to his campaign headquarters. Empty. Until his staff would filter back, his mind was at work formulating his comments to them. He'd tell them how disappointed he was with their efforts. Lack of conviction and resolve. That's it—no energy! No, maybe he should skip the reprimand, and concentrate on developing a plan for the future. President Roosevelt's New Deal should hold some opportunity for—ah--. He drummed his fingers on the back of a chair. Ah--. His imagination came up wanting.

Minutes went by. No one came. Only the tick of the wall clock gave witness to another presence. The nerve of them!

Quick steps outside the door. Finally!

Chester Patterson, his city attorney, entered the room and closed the door.

"Chester, where is everyone?" Clifford demanded.

"There is no everyone. Your everyone has flown the coop. On to other things. Better things, I happily add."

"Don't get insolent, Chester. We've got a lot of good planning to do."

Chester threw his head back in a burst of delirious laughter. He raised his hands in joy and jumped in circles shouting in glee. "We've got? You 'ole goat. That's your problem! You've never had a good idea. The good ideas came from your staff. From you, threats. You're on your own now."

Clifford, against all his principles, began to

plead. "But you're here, Chester."

"Only to tell you, after the meeting this morning, I went down to the army recruitment office and received a direct commission as a Captain! I'm a Captain in the army! Now, as I stand here. I'm free, free at last! Free from your insane tirades."

"Chester, I was thinking of doubling your salary!"

"You thinking? When I walk out that door, I no longer have to give one twit about your thinking or it's consequences. You've made your bed. Now sleep in it!" Chester stopped for a moment of reflection. "Now, I can be myself." Without wasting a good-bye, Chester left the office, closing the door resolutely behind him.

Clifford, through the office window, watched him walk down the hallway waving and speaking to people as he passed them.

Again, only the clock gave proof of another presence. Down but not out, his mind began churning once more. Options? Politics was his game but where's the field? Again, he drew a blank. His attitude perked up when it occurred to him that a suppertime discussion with the family might highlight choices for him. They never seemed to be at a loss for words when he shared his ingenious inspirations.

With the absence of well wishers, he left the community hall and was soon home. The house was dark. Intense darkness. He opened the front door, flicked on a hall light and called, "Dorothy?"

No answer.

Walking past the mirror on the coat rack, the image startled him. His suitcoat open, his shirt buttons at his stomach strained to hold on as his shirt gaped. He sucked in his breath to close the gap. He walked from the hall into the living room and let his breath out. His stomach and shirt regained their previous pudgy appearances. It pained him that she always bought his shirts too small.

He looked about and listened. Again, only a clock in the hallway gave evidence of another presence. Tick, tick, tick. His eyes noticed two slips of paper on the dining room table. He never liked slips of paper on the dining room table. It always meant someone was away. He turned on the chandelier over the table, picked up a note and read it aloud.

"Dad, Hired at Sternlicht as an engineer. Started today second shift, four to midnight. Am excited. Assigned to a secret project. Allen."

Clifford marveled at some people's luck. He had come up the hard way. Too poor for college. He fought his way to the top. For Allen, to wave a diploma and get hired, was evidence enough to demonstrate how hard Clifford has worked to make things better for others.

One down and one to go. Cliff hesitated to read the second one. She won't be here either. At this time in his life, this wasn't going to be good. As he reached for the note, the Grandmother clock continues ticking in the hallway. He dropped his son's note and picked up his wife's.

Cliff, I'm so proud of Allen. I know he will succeed at Sternlicht. When Allen told me, I marched right down to Weinbaum's Motor Works because I heard they were hiring. They just got a big government contract and want me in their public relations office. Finally someone has recognized my writing talent. Will be working late tonight. Made a dish in the frig. Just heat 10 min at 300 in stove.

Sorry about the election. In time, you'll do

the right thing.

Love, Dorothy

Clifford slumped into a chair. For the first time in as long as he could remember, every chair at the supper table was empty. Her words echoed back and forth in his brain. The right thing? Not a glimmer of an idea came to his mind. His thoughts were as empty as the chairs before him. He looked at the four walls. Silence. No voices. No one to explore with, make plans. Chewing on a fingernail while thinking of her note, her words of confidence were followed by a disturbing thought. How would he know the right thing?

The deposed mayor was startled when the Grandfather clock loudly tolled—echoed, bong-bong-bong-bong-bong!

This time, no important statement. Just prolonged, agonizing silence.

CHAPTER 16

MICHELE'S FORAY INTO THE WORLD

As Pierre sat down to a long anticipated hot supper, the phone rang. "Why does that phone always ring just as I sit down? It's a conspiracy," he grumbled.

"No conspiracy. It's your children who have friends that don't milk, have had their suppers, and love to talk on the phone," Zelia clarified, picking the receiver off the wall phone.

Zelia raised her head to the speaker and announced in a clear, proud voice, "The Lavern residence." Her eyebrows arched as a distant voice asked, "This is a pre-paid long distance call for a Michele Lavern. Can she take the phone?"

Zelia covered the speaker, turned to her husband with, "It's long distance for Michele!"

"Long distance? Has she said she was expecting someone from out of town to call?"

"No."

"Maybe it's a trick. Ask who's calling."

"A trick? They pay." Zelia uncovered the speaker. "Who is calling, please?"

"Jeanne Dupuis from Montreal," the operator replied.

Again turning to her husband, "It's her roommate from college." Zelia walked to the stairway and called, "Michele, Jeanne Dupuis is on the phone from Montreal. Hurry, it's prepaid."

Michele flew down the stairs and pressed the receiver to her ear. "Jeanne, oh, I'm so happy you called. Are you coming?"

"No, I'm not coming, but, I've got something absolutely dashing to ask you and I hope you will say yes!"

"You sound excited. I hope I can."

"A big, big Canadian-United States conference will be held in Ogdensburg, your state of New York. It's on the Saint Lawrence River just south of Ottawa, our capitol. Mother is in the Canadian State Department and is in charge of naming the Canadian delegation. Furthermore, she can recommend to your state department American citizens she knows who are fluent in French to serve as interpreters. Some of our delegates are French-Canadians who prefer to speak only French. If you can go, Mother will recommend your name. Isn't that super? Just think, we'd sit on either side of a conference table and so much would depend on us. We'd be so important. Oh, I can't wait. Do say you'll come. Michele, all our expenses are paid, and we will receive $1.75 an hour for doing what just comes natural. Say yes!"

"I want to. Give me a moment to speak with my parents." Michele placed her had over the speaker. In a trembling voice, "Mom and dad, Jeanne wants me to come to a conference in New York and work as an interpreter. I'll get $1.75 an hour to do what comes natural—those are Jeanne's words—and all expenses are paid. Can I go? Please!"

Pierre sat back in his chair, eyes blinking, replied, "You just got back from college and we haven't had a chance to talk about your studies and such things."

"Pierre, she doesn't have time to discuss your plans for the summer. Yes, Michele, you can go!"

"Jeanne, the answer is yes, yes!"

"Great. Expect a call in a day or two from your State Department in Washington. They'll give you the particulars. See you!"

"Au revoir!' (Good bye!)

"À bientôt! (See you later!)

10 a.m., three days later
"Michele, would you answer the phone, please."

"Yes, mama. Good morning, this is the Lavern residence."

"Good morning, may I speak to Miss Michele Lavern?"

"Speaking."

"This is Preston Negley, Undersecretary for Canadian Affairs of the U. S. State Department in Washington, D.C. Your name has been given to us from our Canadian counterpart. Do you speak French?"

"Oui, monsieur, je parle francais! J'aime beaucoup la langue francaise et je l'etudie avec plaisir. Parlez-vous francais, monsieur?" (Yes, sir, I speak French! I love the French language very much and study it with pleasure. Do you speak French?)

Silence.

Michele, thinking he might be upset with her response, clarified. "I said I do and asked if you did, too."

"Ah, no. That's why I didn't say anything. Our Canadian contact said you spoke French and I just wanted to hear you speak. Sounds like you do. As a rule, we assign our own interpreters, but they all are on other projects. Therefore, we will be counting on you. I understand your roommate in college is a Canadian girl from Montreal."

"Yes, sir. Her name is Jeanne Dupuis."

"Yes, I know the name. As soon as I received your name, I contacted the FBI and they conducted a quick background check so that you could be cleared for Secret classification."

"What does that mean?"

"We are inviting you to participate in secret meetings between military and diplomatic representatives from Canada and the United States. Therefore, we had to ascertain your loyalty to the U.S. You passed the test without reservation. What you hear and see must be kept secret-even from members of your family. Can you accept that demand?"

"Can I tell my parents where I will be going and can I write or call them to assure them that I'm okay?"

"Yes, of course."

"Then I can comply with your demand for secrecy. What am I to do?"

"I am requesting you to participate, expenses paid, as an interpreter in a conference to be held in Ogdensburg, New York that will begin in three days. When you leave, you can pick up your round trip train tickets at the railroad station the day after tomorrow. This way, you will arrive on the eve of the conference. A room has been reserved in your name at the Hotel McConville. You will be met at the station by a driver who will hand you an envelope of documents providing background to the conference. Given all of this, are you prepared to serve?"

"Yes, sir."

"Good, I'll see you in Ogdensburg. Good Day."

"Au revoir, Monsieur Negley!"

"Ah? yes, goodbye."

Michele's hand shook with excitement as she hung up the phone. "Mama, mama, I'm to leave for Ogdensburg, New York, the day after tomorrow!"

Zelia hugged her daughter with zestful admiration. Yet, deep in Zelia's heart, there was a twinge of envy. Her wish would be to go with her. If only someone in Canada had mentioned her name, too. Still, maybe someday.

Northern Bend Railroad Station

"All aboard!"

"Goodbye, Mom and Dad! Don't you worry about me. I'll write you every day. I'll be home soon and then we can do things together the rest of the summer." Michele kissed her parents and walked up the steps into the passenger car. The porter followed behind, and heaving the portable step into the passageway, the train began its journey east.

Pierre and Zelia watched the train disappear from Northern Bend. Pierre took Zelia's hand and lamented, "Something tells me this scene is going to repeat itself many times from now on-watching Michele leave for somewhere. I truly missed her when she was at college. When she was growing up and in high school, she was always around and I don't think I fully appreciated those times. Now she's gone, soon for good and I want her back."

"She's not gone, she's away. She'll be back. She loves us but she wants to explore the world and we must not hold her back. She will write and she will return. And then we can share in her experiences and be proud she is our daughter.

"Pierre, we must not forget, we still have Tim with us and he's a dear. We mustn't push him to stay on the farm. That should be his decision. Yet I pray he will remain."

Pierre stopped, searched the empty tracks, wiped his eyes with a handkerchief. "I hope so."

Ogdensburg, New York, the next day
The train slowed to a stop in the Ogdensburg station. Michele gathered her belongings and stepped down the stairs to the station platform. A few feet away, she saw a young man holding a sign with the name, Michele Lavern, printed in large letters. In smaller letters below was printed, State Dept. For a moment she paused on the steps to savor the significance of the sign. Her friend had made her somebody, and now, she vowed to prove her right.

"Hi, I'm Michele."

"Hi, great. I wasn't sure which car would be yours. I'm Charles Burns, Ensign Charles Burns,

but just call me Charley. I'm to pick you up and
take you to the Hotel McConville. Not the Waldorf
but nice." The ensign pointed to a sedan. "Some
of the big shots are there already and I-hey, not
to imply you aren't a big shot but you know what
I mean. Say, you look pretty young to be at this
meeting. What's your angle?"

"I'm to be an interpreter. I'm fluent in French.
What's yours?"

"Wow, French! I had two years in college and
still can't parly poo. I'm in naval intelligence.
Charley is my name and intelligence is my game!"

Michele waved her hand quizzically at his
civilian clothes.

"I wear my uniform at the meetings." Charley
held the front passenger door open. "Hop in.
You're the only one I'm picking up at this train.
You meeting anyone for supper tonight?"

"I believe my friend from the Canadian group
will be at the hotel so I want to talk with her
before I make any further plans, but thanks!"

"You're friends with a Canuck? That's something
else! If she tells you any secrets, I'd give my
right arm to know them first. Some of those big
shots are so pompous when they know something
they think no one else does."

"You'll be the first to know."

"I'm serious. It'd be great if we peons were—
not that you're a peon-but you know what I mean—
young people—were instrumental in designing the
cooperative agreement."

This was the first time Michele had any inkling
about the purpose of this international meeting,
but she choose not to reveal her ignorance. Thus,
she asked, "When will I see the agenda for the
meeting?"

Charles handed her an envelope. "Here's all
the dope. Things will go into high gear at
0800 tomorrow when the delegations will meet

to establish objectives. The big shots like to do all the talking so we need to get our oar in the water early, lest they think we're know-nothings."

"What do you do if they ask about navy things? Is it all in your head or did you bring a lot of books?"

"I," he exclaimed pointing to himself with a flourish, "have a phone line direct to naval headquarters in Washington. If I'm handed a chestnut I can't crack, I get on the horn to my contacts and they come up with the answer."

"Just like that?"

"You bet, just like that. What will you do if someone says something in French you've never heard before, huh? huh?"

"I brought a dictionary just in case."

"In case your dictionary comes up wanting, what will you do?"

"I'll borrow your horn."

"Only if you'll have dinner with me tonight."

"I sure hope they have pay phones in the inn."

"As my mother once said, If at first you don't succeed, try, try, again. There will be more suppers to come."

Michele, teasing, waved her finger at him. "That's a good boy,".

"Nice town, Ogdensburg. Been here two days collecting intelligence."

"I thought intelligence was collected on foreign countries."

"The big shots got to know where to stay and eat. I was sent ahead to map it all out."

"They're so trusting."

"And rightly so. A few top drawers have congratulated me on my fine taste."

"I'm in suspense. What did you select for us peons?"

"Same place, of course and here we are," he

replied pulling up to a multi-storied building. "Hotel McConville, 101 Ford Street. This one, closest to the train station, edged out two others. Better yet, it's only five minutes to the ferry to Canada. That ferry puts Ogdensburg square on the international map. We're in the middle of the world, center of attention."

"I sure hope this conference doesn't end up a disappointment to you. If it does, I pity your mother!"

"Nah, I'll make the most of it, one way or another. Like dinner with you."

Michele laughed. "If at first you don't succeed-" She paused to let him finish the phrase. "Try, try again. I know!"

"See you at 8 a.m." Michele carried her suitcase to the front desk and addressed the clerk, "Hello, I'm Miss Lavern, I believe I have a reservation?"

"Good afternoon, Miss Lavern. Just a moment. Ah, yes, your room number is 404. This is the key, and I have a message for you." The clerk handed her a small envelope. Michele read her name on the envelope and recognized the penmanship as that of Jeanne's. Michele smiled, put the envelope into her jacket pocket, and picked up her suitcase. Walking to the elevator, she knew, the moment she contacted Jeanne, she would be swept into exciting but uncharted, unfamiliar waters of international diplomacy. She had read, and heard over the radio, the bad news from Europe. Now she would be a part of it. Maybe only a very small part, but that would be enough for now.

CHAPTER 17

BEING AN AMERICAN

Room 404, Hotel McConville
Michele had never been in a hotel room before.
She didn't know what to expect. What she saw
when she opened the door delighted her. At the
opposite wall was a large window overlooking the
St. Lawrence River in the distance. She could
just make out a tugboat pushing several barges.
What a view! The room was furnished with a bed, a
writing desk, a wall telephone, a lounge chair, a
dresser with an oval mirror, and her own private
bathroom. All the comforts of home. She put some
of her belongings into the dresser and hung the
rest in the closet. Thus organized, she sat in
the lounge near the large window, gazing for
a moment, at the busy streets below. She then
opened the message and read,

Michele,
Welcome to the edge of the Canadian border!
Ring me at 307 as soon as you arrive,
Jeanne.

Michele picked up the phone and dialed 307.
"Jeanne here."
"Jeanne, this is Michele."
"Michele, it's so good that you're here. Are
you free now?"
"Sure."
"Let's meet in the dining room. We can have
coffee and talk."
"See you in fifteen!"
Michele freshened up in the bathroom and
hurried to the elevator. She strolled through the
lobby into what appeared to be a newly decorated
dinning facility. Sunlight, beaming through large

windows, illuminated numerous tables. Though
several tables were occupied, she soon spotted
Jeanne, in a large brim hat, looking toward the
lobby door. She ran to her, they hugged briefly,
and then sat down at her table.

"Michele, it's so good to see you. I hope
you had a pleasant train ride. I like your hair
style. Who does it for you?"

"I had a fun train ride. Ate lunch in the diner.
That is so neat." Michele touched her up-sweep.
"My mom cuts it. We look through Life Magazine
for the style we like and she just copies it.
Daddy thinks it's too bold, but I received a
compliment on the train so I know it's right. By
the way, what do you hear from your dad. I hope
he's all right."

The moment Michele mentioned Jeanne's father,
Jeanne's eyes filled with tears and she quickly
pressed a handkerchief to her face.

"I'm sorry, Jeanne. I didn't mean to upset
you."

"That's all right, Michele. I wish I didn't
get so emotional when I think about my dad.
He flies with the Royal Air Force and when the
Germans invaded France he flew there to fight. Mom
and I worried so when France surrendered, but he
had escaped back to England. Things are terrible
over there. The Germans have many more planes
than we do, and really, we wish Daddy would come
back to Canada."

"I can't think of anybody at home who wants
war. Daddy doesn't." Michele cast her eyes down
to her plate. "I guess Tim would have to go.
I can't imagine what we would do if Tim were
killed. We would be crushed."

Michele's body shook as if to cast off such
dreadful thoughts. She broke into a bright smile
and suggested, "On a brighter note, I want to
thank you for asking your mother to invite me to

this meeting."

"I thought of you right away when Mother mentioned that the Americans would need a French interpreter."

"So here we are and given the circumstances, I wouldn't want to be anywhere else," Michele resolved.

"We're here and we'll do what we can. The ferry ride across the St. Lawrence was great. I stood out on the deck with the wind in my hair the whole way across. I think the best part of a boat trip is approaching the port where you can see the city skyline and watch the activity along the harbor. Ogdensburg is such a pretty community and this hotel is adorable! I hope to see the Prime Minister when he comes over. So exciting! What do you plan to wear tomorrow?" Jeanne asked. "Our colors are red and blue so I'll wear a red skirt and a blue blouse."

"We're red, blue, and white, so I'm planning a red jacket, blue skirt, and white blouse."

"We'll be spectacular-you just wait and see. Oh, suddenly I'm famished. Let's eat!"

Michele smiled, and looking about for the waitress, she saw Charles walking toward their table. He waved and hopefully asked, "Hi, Michele, can I join you two for dinner? Is this your friend from Canada? I don't want to interfere, but I'd like to meet someone from the Canadian side."

"Yes, of course you can join us. Jeanne, may I introduce Charles. Jeanne Dupuis, Ensign Charles Burns," Michele added last names pointing at one and then the other. "He prefers Charley. Actually, I think it fits."

"Hi, Charles—ah, Charley. Are you with the U.S. delegation?" Jeanne inquired.

"Yup, I'm in naval intelligence. Boy, you two are pretty young to be involved in this high level stuff. What's your angle, Jeanne, are you an interpreter, too?"

"Yes, in French. We have observers from Quebec and they prefer French. I'm here to keep them in touch with what is being discussed."

Charles made little attempt to hide his exuberance over such good fortune. "When I was assigned to this mission, I thought, oh, boy, I'm going to be spending the time with a bunch of ole' stuffed shirts. But look at me now! This is all right. But may I," holding out his hands for approval, "make a suggestion as to where we eat?"

Jeanne, glancing around, replied, "This is nice."

"You're both French, so how about some continental cuisine? Just a short walk from here is the Schneiders Hotel where I'm already on a first name basis with the owners."

Michele turned to Jeanne and quickly observed, "Charley is with Navy intelligence. This gives us an idea of the information he's trained to obtain."

"We gotta eat so let's do it right," Charles exclaimed patting his stomach, "tomorrow you'll see me shine on Navy stuff. Schneiders just a walk away. The Wienerschnitzel is superb!"

"I'm not totally opposed to the idea. What do you think, Jeanne?"

Jeanne frowned. "Sounds very German to me. We Canadians are at war with Germany."

"Hey," Charles countered, "I checked them out. It's my job. They're solid citizens. Clean as a whistle—straight as an arrow. Patriotic. There's lots of law-abiding German and Italian citizens in the U.S-and in Canada, I bet." He looked at Jeanne for agreement.

"Well that's true. For the sake of international peace, I acquiesce."

"I interpret-I can do that, too-your response as yes. Let's be on our way. Follow me," Charles impatiently coaxed, walking out the door.

"No," Michele corrected, "we walk together, we don't follow!"

"All right, all right, you know what I mean," Charles countered, shaking his head in some bewilderment. The girls smiled.

The three left and walked a few blocks to the Schneiders Hotel. As they entered, a waitress was walking toward the cash register.

"Hi, Julia. Got some new customers for you," Charles announced.

"Guten Tag, Karl. You and your friends may sit anywhere, and I'll be with you in a minute."

"See, see," Charles whispered, "first name basis. Karl. Wow. So German. She also gave me some tips on sightseeing. Brass like to tour around impressing the troops back home."

"Yes, Ensign Burns," Michele sighed, "can we please sit?"

The three selected a table near a window and ordered their dinners. For a moment, Charles sat back in his chair sporting a contented smile.

Jeanne asked of Michele, "Est-ce que Charles parle francais?" (Can Charles speak French?)

"Non!" replied Michele. (No!)

"Com'on guys, you're talking in French. I can't and I think, in the spirit of international cooperation, you shouldn't be keeping anything from me."

The girls laughed at his frustration. Michele suggested, "You should have paid more attention to your French instructor in college."

"Okay. You two know French but I'm on the inside about this conference, and I think a little discussion along these lines is in order. Not that I like to talk business during dinner, but the big meeting of your Prime Minister and our President is tomorrow. If we're going to be more than bumps on a log during this conference,

I suggest we talk a little strategy that could contribute to the outcome."

"If you were just a bump on a log during this conference, what would that mean to you?" Michele asked.

"A bump on a log? I've got a career to think of. Gotta make points. Be seen, be heard. I mean, really, what's this conference to you? You'll have a good time, talk a little French, and then head to college. I'm the one in the barrel here."

"Speaking in the broader scope of things, you don't think we have anything to lose, if this meeting were to go bad?" Jeanne inquired.

"What's to lose, you just go back."

Jeanne sat up straight in her chair, placed both hands on the table, leaned toward Charles and returned in harsh tones, "I'm proud to say, I do have something to contribute and that is the understanding between peoples of different languages. A field, in which by your own admission, you are deficient. Your concern is about advancement in your navy. To use a navy term, I harbor a concern about the life of my father who is flying with the British Royal Air Force. I don't worry about advancement, I worry about my father coming home alive."

"I, too," Michele quickly added, "have a brother who could be lost if the war in Europe boils over into the U.S. I stand a chance of losing someone precious to me and you're here- not there- worrying about advancement. So if you want cooperation, you treat us like equals and we'll see what we can do."

"Okay, okay, I get the point. Sorry if I've come across uppity. So let's talk turkey."

"Talk turkey? What does that mean," both girls chorused.

"It means let's talk business, like what's this meeting all about."

"Tell us what you know," Jeanne suggested.

"One. Hitler's Wehrmacht seems unstoppable and he's softening up England with bombs before ferrying troops across the channel. England needs men and equipment pronto. German U-boats are sinking ships right and left and the British need destroyers to protect their supply routes.

"Two. Canada is up to its eyeballs trying to meet the demands of the British government to supply those men and equipment. What if England falls? The Germans would likely cast a hungry glance at all the resources of North America and begin occupying islands of the Atlantic like Greenland, and even Newfoundland. Then it's Canada's turn in the meat grinder. The question becomes how many men and supplies should Canada send into a bad situation?"

As Charles ticked off the issues confronting the members of the conference, Michele remembered the envelope in her room outlining the U.S. position on the meetings the next day. She vowed that as soon as dinner was over, she would go back to her room and digest its contents. Obviously, Jeanne and Charles were far better informed than she.

"Three. The U.S. is in the grips of isolationism. If Roosevelt openly supplies the Brits, the national sentiment for neutrality could cost him his presidency. I know, because I'm in naval intelligence, he desperately wants to help. Like lending the British a bunch of destroyers. This agreement must appear as if the main concern of the U.S. is defense of its shores- not preparation for war. Can you add anything Jeanne?"

"Those are your major concerns. A real fear in Canada is what will happen to the British navy if, God forbid, the German manage to conquer the British Isles. The British navy is huge, and Canada doesn't have the space in its ports to anchor all of it. We would have to look to the

U.S. for the necessary dockage."

"Oh, boy, that's a sticky wicket. If the British navy berthed in U.S. ports for any length of time, it sure would look like the U.S. was taking sides. Bye-bye neutrality," Charles warned.

"Maybe the agreement has to be vague in specifics, but opening the door to secret meetings that could meet each country's needs," Michele suggested.

"Hey, we're putting the pieces together! A document loose as a goose but sets up the apparatus for cooperation and exchange all around. It's not been written as yet. I'll put a bug in the U.S. Undersecretary's ear, Preston Negley, suggesting we write a draft. Wow, that's a good idea. That's what we can do!"

"Preston Negley is the one from Washington who invited me," Michele recalled. "Maybe he'd remember my name. And Jeanne can be our Canadian counterpart."

"There! I told you if we got our heads together we'd make a mark!" Charles chortled.

The girls laughed as Jeanne added, "Don't forget your advancement was helped by two college women."

*   *   *

Back in her room, Michele sat in an easy chair facing the window. As her eyes scanned the horizon, she noticed a blinking lighthouse in the distance. It seemed to foretell, All's well! She relaxed into the chair and relished the view as if she were at a silent movie.

She gazed at a city slowly reacting to fading sunlight. Here and there house and streetlights blinked on. Automobiles, hardly visible, could be followed, once their headlights cast light on the road ahead. Vibrant colors of flowers and sky faded into increasing depths of gray.

Dawn and dusk were the two favorite passages of time for Michele. Walking to the milk barn in the morning, she could watch the day waking up. Birds singing, chirping. Cows with full bags urging the milkers to do their job. The rising sun illuminating objects as far as the eye could see. Dusk was dawn in reverse. Marvels she could enjoy daily.

After the refreshing pause, she turned on the lights and opened the envelope of documents pertaining to the conference. Reading through them, she began to see a world in greater turmoil and danger than she had ever imagined. She also noted many secret discussions had already taken place between diplomats of the U.S., Canada and England. Knowing dire consequences would descend upon anyone who revealed the contents of the documents, prompted Michele to tuck all the material under her pillow as she slipped between the sheets.

8 a.m., In The conference Room of The Hotel McConville.

Michele noted the seating arrangement as she walked into the conference room shortly before 8AM. A large, long wooden table was surrounded by two rows of chairs. On the table were two rows of cards with names indicating the seating arrangements. Small Canadian and U.S. flags indicated which side of the table the delegates would sit. Michele began looking for her name at one end of the table and as she approached the middle she spotted her name directly behind Preston Negley, the Undersecretary for Canadian Affairs! She never imagined sitting that close to the principal U. S. delegate. He was at his chair. Tall, wavy salt and pepper hair, wearing a black pin-stripped suit. Very diplomatic. He spoke.

"You must be Michele."

"Yes. You are Mr. Negley?"

"Correct. You look very patriotic in your red, white, and blue. Very attractive and very appropriate. I want you to sit behind me, because there will be French speaking participants from Quebec and I want you to keep track of their comments. It's important I know what the other side is saying to one another."

As the wall clock tolled eight, the room filled with delegates from both sides who took their places. Michele looked across the table from her chair and saw Jeanne sitting just behind the Canadian leader. Their eyes met, and Michele called across the table, "Bonjour, Jeanne!"

"Bonjour, Michele!"

A man sitting two chairs down from the Canadian leader spoke directly to Michele.

"Parlez-vous francais, Mademoiselle?" (Do you speak French, Miss?)

"Oui, monsieur, je parle francais!" (Yes, sir, I speak French!)

He continued in French. After he had spoken, Negley turned to Michele and inquired in a low voice, "What did he say?"

"He said, Not to forget France in these discussions. France must rise again because it is the beacon for Liberty, Equality and Fraternity."

"Tell him France and all the free world are upper-most in our minds."

With that assurance conveyed, Negley opened the meeting with a brief statement. "Today, we gather together to discuss mutual needs in the defense of North America in the face of Axis aggression. In this meeting we will continue discussions that have been underway for better than a year now. This afternoon will mark the culmination of our mutual cooperation when Prime Minister Mackenzie King and President Roosevelt meet in a railroad car and sign an agreement we will have negotiated. Because the political climate in the United States is strongly one of neutrality, the agreement will reflect broad, non-specific principles of defense. If it is the consensus of the delegations present here, I will ask Miss Jeanne Dupuis of Canada," pointing to her across the table, "and Miss Michele Lavern and Ensign Charles Burns of the United States to draft such a statement. When we convene at 3 p.m. after our lunch break, we can modify the document for subsequent approval and delivery to the leaders of our respective nations."

Negley's suggestion enjoyed unanimous approval. Negley continued by asking for committee reports and the morning progressed with committee secretaries reading summaries of their final reports. At times, the French speaking Quebec delegates would react to a report. Michele would lean forward as Negley leaned back in his chair to listen to her translation. Several times, Negley would whisper to Michele his reaction and then ask her to convey his reply to the Quebec delegate in French. The U.S. delegates couldn't hear Negley. They had to wait for Jeanne Dupuis to translate the French back into English for her English speaking Canadian representatives. After Negley's second such response, Michele then recognized this maneuver as a way of Negley conveying to the French delegate he held him in high regard and took his concerns seriously.

Before lunch a photographer entered the room. Negley announced a press release of the signed agreement would be accompanied by several photographs of the delegates. He organized several different arrangements of delegates. The last picture was of the various assistants and interpreters. Negley stood in the middle flanked by Jeanne Dupuis on one side and Michele and

Charles Burns on the other. When the picture was about to be snapped, Charles put his arm around Michele's waist. After the camera clicked, Michele confronted Charles, "Why did you do that?"

"Do what?"

"Put your arm around my waist. I thought it impertinent!"

"To show collegiality among the U.S. delegation. Everybody getting along, that's all."

"I hope the photo doesn't get published. It will look awkward and I'll be embarrassed."

"Don't worry. They never print pics of the peons, only the big shots."

"We've got work to do. We must get with Jeanne and draft the agreement. Should any more pictures be taken, I hope you know my attitude about collegiality!"

"Okay, okay, I get the point. Sorry, I only wanted to show friendship."

After lunch, Jeanne, Michele and Charles sat at a table on the patio. Michele raised her pencil above a blank sheet of paper and asked, "Is this a Statement, a Treaty, a Declaration? How shall we start it?"

Jeanne responded, "I like the word, declare. Like your Declaration of Independence. Shall we call it a Declaration of Mutual Defense?"

Charles confided, "Declaration is good, but Negley told me the statement should establish a Joint Board. Let's call it 'A Declaration by the U.S. and Canada to Establish a Joint Board on Defense."

"Sounds good to me," Michele said as she crossed some words out and added others, "but since we are the hosts to the Canadians, I propose that it read, 'A Declaration by Canada and the U. S'."

"Sounds like a good start to me," Charles stated waving his hand to Jeanne.

"Agreed," Jeanne replied.

Michele finished the title and suggested, "Let's write a few paragraphs about the organization of the Board and let the delegates add or change whatever."

For an hour, each wrote agreements based on decisions approved during the morning conference. After cutting and pasting the document together, a secretary typed the final version.

*   *   *

At 3PM, the conference reconvened. Michele and Jeanne handed copies of the Declaration to the members of both countries. Negley asked for comments. Minor changes were offered and incorporated. Full approval quickly followed. Jeanne smiled and nodded across the table at Michele with an expression, We did well. Michele returned the smile.

Negley then outlined the activities for the remainder of the day.   "Our Secret Service has informed me, President Roosevelt is in the area reviewing troops who are on maneuvers. At 5:45PM, he will arrive in Ogdensburg by way of Proctor Avenue. I have arranged for several automobiles to drive all of us to that point where we will join his motorcade. The parade route will be through town ending at the railroad tracks of the New York Central yards. The President will enter his private Pullman car bearing the name, Roald Amundsen, discoverer of the North Pole. There, he will await the arrival of the Prime Minister MacKenzie King. King will enter the Pullman and their conversations will be held within it. I am told the Pullman will be moved to a different location, Heuvelton, I believe, for security reasons. Once both leaders are seated in the Pullman, I will present them with our Declaration."

Northern Bend Station, A Day Later

The next afternoon Pierre and Zelia met their daughter at the Northern Bend train station. Michele was the first passenger off the coach. Spotting her parents, she waved and ran to them. She hugged each and exclaimed, "It's so good to be home. But it was exciting!"

Chatting, they began walking toward a row of parked cars. Michele scanned for the horse and buggy she expected her parents to have driven to the station. "Where's the team?" she asked.

Pierre walked ahead and patted the hood of a new Ford. "This is our new horse and buggy!" he gestured with pride.

"It's beautiful!" Michele shrieked. "Shiny black! Can I learn to drive it?"

"You drove the tractor, you can drive this. It's easy. Even Zelia drives it to the Women's Club. Tell us about your new adventure while we drive home."

As they drove back to the farm, Michele excitedly related all the events of her trip to Ogdensburg and the parade after the signing. "You can't imagine what it's like to ride in a convertible and wave to all the people standing along the curb! I felt important, grateful. To think I was granted that privilege just because I speak French. It was so easy. I only needed to refer to my dictionary twice. Words can have such different meanings. When the Quebec delegate mentioned mines, I thought he was referring to a hole in the ground. Instead, it's some kind of explosive device they drop in the water. He was kind enough to explain it to me. When I told Negley, he laughed."

Zelia touched her daughter's arm and asked, "Did you see the President?"

"Yes. Did you know that he's crippled? He can't walk and needs a man on either side to help him up stairs. I watched him walk from his car and into the Pullman. He was always smiling. We waited in our car until Prime Minister King arrived. Kinda short. He fairly ran to the Pullman. Probably anxious to see the President."

"What did you do after King's arrival," her father asked.

"We were driven back to the hotel. Walked into the dining room—we were all hungry—and you will never guess who I saw sitting at a table."

"Who?"

"Jacqueline Cochran. I couldn't believe my eyes. Just sitting there at a table. I've read much about her. She's a pilot and very rich. Owns a cosmetic firm. I admire her courage-doing things only men are supposed to do. So I walked to her table and introduced myself."

Such a bold move on his daughter's part prompted Pierre to ask, "Should you do that sort of thing? Bothering important people? What can you say to such people?"

"I introduced myself, congratulated her on winning the Bendix Trophy in 1935 and said I want to be a pilot someday!"

Pierre's concern shifted into dismay. "I had hoped that by taking navigation courses you would better realize how dangerous flying is and do something else. You *still* want to fly?"

"Yes! When I told Miss Cochran I wanted to fly, she said, when I have my license I should write to her. She wants to keep a list of women pilots. She proceeded to tell me why she was in Ogdensburg. She had learned President Roosevelt was going to review some army planes the next day and she was planning to meet with him and let him know women make good pilots, too."

"Well, you're not going to fly those army planes and get shot down. Not like my brother. And that's final," Pierre decreed.

"Daddy, that's not what Miss Cochran meant. She said if we get into a war, there will be a need for pilots to fly planes from the factories to different parts of the world, and if women did this, the men pilots would be free to do the fighting."

"This flying thing bothers me. I sure didn't raise my daughter to be way up in the sky and have something go wrong. And all over the world? It scares me just thinking about it," Pierre groaned.

"Please don't worry. Anyway, my flying lessons are on hold because the Ogdensburg trip has postponed my flying lessons until next summer. But then I want to do it."

Zelia defended her daughter's dreams. "You follow your heart, Michele. Daddy and I support whatever you want to do. We are very proud of you."

"Yes, of course, I support you. I knew the moment you sat in the co-pilot chair, when the Baron flew us to Chicago, you would be hooked," said Pierre.

Michele decided to let her father have the last word on the subject. Still, it was a dream she would work into reality. She watched a field of corn go by. "Mr. Thornburg's corn looks good."

"He spends twice as much time cultivating than I do with the tractor," Pierre observed proudly. "He's been asking me about our tractor. I bet he buys one when he cashes in his crops."

She turned to face her parents. "Have you heard anything from Wolf?"

Zelia answered from the back seat. "Yes, I saw Mercedes yesterday. Pierre," thrusting both hands forward in a hurry up motion, "can't you go faster? We aren't in the buggy."

With a good-natured glance at Michele, Pierre responded. "There's a new expression-the backseat driver. It's a person in the back seat who constantly gives the driver suggestions—sometimes orders—on how to drive. Your mother's last comment was an excellent example."

Zelia countered. "When Tim drives, we zip right along. I'm just not the pokey type." A gust of wind blew through the open back window threatening to blow Zelia's hat off. She rolled the window nearly shut.

"Yes, Mama, I'll remember that when I drive you."

Pierre admonished. "Don't you be driving fast."

"Oh, daddy, My speed will be halfway between you and Tim. Mama, you were saying about Mrs. Otto."

"Wolf and the Baron flew to California to talk to some people about building planes there. Sounds like they'll be back in a few days. When does your school start?"

"First week in September."

"By the way, Mercedes said she was impressed with the article and picture in the Daily Inquirer about your role in Ogdensburg."

Michele flushed. "Which picture? They took several."

"Oh, it showed a whole bunch of people. You were in the second row. On one side of you probably was Jeanne, and an older man on the other."

"That would be Preston Foster from the State Department. Were there any other pictures?"

"No, just the one. Your father bought ten copies of the paper that day. He's not going to let anyone forget it. He gave a copy to Father Prokas."

"He looked at the picture," Pierre added, "and said, 'Look what a fine woman she is. It seems like yesterday I baptized her. You surely can be proud of your children.'"

Michele smiled at the compliment, but her

thoughts were miles away. 'My luck, I'll be at college when he returns. I'll write him a note to call me when he gets to Trinity. Then I'll wait for his call.' The 'I'll wait' thought conjured up a second somewhat disturbing thought. 'Could waiting be my life with Wolfy?'

CHAPTER 18

CONSEQUENCES

December 7, 1941

Frederick and Annie Otto attended the 10 a.m. Mass at St. John's Mission, enjoyed refreshments in the church basement with other parishioners, then headed home.

Driving along the country road, he patted Annie's folded hands. "Gertrude's strudel was delicious. I could have eaten a second serving but it was all gone when I went back."

Annie remained quiet a few seconds. "Yes, she is a good baker. It's no wonder her husband is a bit overweight."

They laughed. Still, Frederick could detect disappointment in her voice. Ever since Emil was reported hiding in occupied France, Annie was not the same. Her cheerful demeanor had diminished despite Frederick's frequent attempts to raise her spirits. He knew his efforts were blunted since he was the main cause for Emil's absence.

In the afternoon, they attended the monthly picnic in Hangar One. A broad banner hanging from the ceiling read: Annual Sternlicht Bridge Tournament, Dec. 7, 1941. Twenty card tables were arranged in the middle of the hangar while various planes occupied the rest of the space. Teams at the tables were noisily shuffling, dealing, and playing bridge. Frederick and Annie sat across from one another.

While Frederick shuffled the deck, he remarked to an opponent, "That was a tough hand to play. I didn't think you would get back on the board but you did. Annie kicked me when I doubled. Now, we go down more than my vanity will allow me to admit."

He was dealing the cards when the loudspeaker

came to life with a trembling voice. "Ladies and Gentlemen. I must inform you that according to a radio report, the Japanese bombed Pearl Harbor this morning!"

The alarming news shattered the conviviality and the room went silent. For a moment, everyone sat frozen, horror-struck.

Annie looked quizzically at Frederick and asked, "Where is Pearl Harbor?"

Frederick gathered the cards and slid them back into their box. "Somewhere in the Hawaiian Islands. This is war. I didn't think it would start this way. We should go, Annie."

The same thought crossed the minds of others, too. The hangar emptied as families hurried home to listen to the news.

At 7PM, the telephone rang. Frederick picked it up. "Hello?"

"Baron?"

"Yes."

"This is General Wolford. You've heard the news?"

"Yes."

"Things here are happening with lightening speed. Besides development, I've been given command of procurement. General Ward has been reassigned. We need all the Airacudas you can deliver!"

"We can quickly expand to eight a day," Frederick replied in a tone steeped in confidence.

Annie knew Frederick's elated response was in answer to the request he had been longing for. A major production contract. Without similar emotion, she sat back in her chair. Frederick flinched at her detachment, yet raised his pencil to record further instructions.

"Baron, we also need a squadron of Airacudas in the Pacific—now. I can direct commission Cletus Bauerman and your grandson, Wolfgang. Bauerman,

Major, Wolfgang, Captain. Put together as many Airacudas as you can and get back to me ASAP with plans and costs. Any questions?"

"No. I'll be in touch."

Frederick replaced the phone in its cradle with an air of satisfaction. He turned to Annie elated. "We have a major Army contract to produce as many Airacudas as we turn out!"

Annie pointed a finger at Frederick. "You have a contract. You've always met Wolford's every command even if it endangers lives." She sat up in her chair, eyes narrowing. "All I've asked of you these last two years is to bring Emil home. And with your own son, the timing was never right. Always something you wanted him to get, to do—until it was too late."

"Annie, you know I'm--"

"Fred, please. Play your war games. I'm sure it will involve Cletus—your most trusted employee and Wolfgang—your own grandson of whom you are so proud." Annie raised her arms in despair. "People, even your own family, don't matter to you. Fame, contracts—at any cost. That's what is important."

Frederick knelt down on one knee and took her hands in his. "Annie, people do matter. You above all. This is what we've worked hard for. On that boat coming over here, you cooked and I stoked furnaces. Here, it's a new life, new opportunities."

She jerked her hands from his. "Don't you hear what I'm saying? I don't care about riches and contracts. I care about family. You're in your glory when you walk through the hangars and everyone hangs on your every word, or when you get those calls," she pointed to the telephone, "from some official in Washington. I'm in my glory when I have my family-including Emil."

"Annie, he's safe. British Intelligence is

working out an escape."

She stood up and clapped her hands to her ears. "Enough, enough," she groaned. "I don't want to hear anymore excuses, facts, reasons! They don't erase gnawing fear in my heart." With those last emotional words, she disappeared into the kitchen and closed the door behind her.

Frederick's first impulse was to follow and attempt reconciliation. On second thought, he knew such effort would be fruitless, or make matters worse. He would have to search for a solution to this breach in her love for him. He ached thinking the one woman whom he truly loved was deeply disappointed in him.

He stood motionless in the living room wrestling with his conscience.

"Tick-tock, tick-tock." The quiet march of the Grandfather clock entered double-time to remind him time was fleeting. Grasping at the assumption she was not beyond consolation, he turned to the other pressing matter at hand. He picked up the phone and dialed. A man's voice answered, "Otto residence."

"Henry, been listening to the radio?"

"Yes. No doubt about it, we're at war. Heard anything from Washington?"

"Got a call from Wolford. We're on top now. Got a pencil? We have to ramp up production. He commissioned Cletus and Wolfgang and they are to fly a squadron of Airacudas to the South Pacific. See you at 7 a.m

Michele Takes Wing, Too

"OK. I've seen enough. You've had enough. Solo."

The instructor climbed out of the rear cockpit and walked away from the aircraft. He slipped an evaluation sheet into his clipboard bearing the name Michele Laverne.

The lone fledgling wiped her moist palms on the seat, adjusted her goggles, took a deep breath and pushed the throttle full forward. The radial sixteen piston 350 hp Pratt-Whitney engine roared in glee spinning the three-bladed full pitched Hercules propeller into a blur.

The trainer leaped forward pressing Michele against the seat. One eye on the air speed indicator, the other on the runway, she waited until the speed passed 80 mph. With a pull back on the control stick, wheels and earth departed.

Airborne.

Airspeed 120 mph, heart rate 120 beats per minute. Alone and in full control. No more instructions. Flight now strictly an exchange between her and her bird. In view of the instructor she maneuvered the prescribed rolls, stalls, chandelles, landings and take-offs. On the first rollover, she gasped then laughed as she caught her unsecured purse that responded to gravity by falling toward earth.

Scheduled to land in thirty minutes, yet she felt like flying all afternoon, tomorrow, day and night. This is where she wanted to be. Equality with the Otto's. No longer just a farmer's daughter. The Baron would be her ticket. Pilot Wall Street execs in Sternlicht's passenger aircraft. Maybe test pilot. Sky's the limit now. She'd call the Baron for an appointment from the airport.

The instructor tired of writing out the whole word excellent. The letters ex sufficed as he described his student execute the prescribed maneuvers. A mechanic wiping his hands on a rag watched nearby. "It's a girl, ain't it?"

"Yup. That set of pig tails is as good as they come. It'll be hard to get the best of her."

CHAPTER 19

A BAD EGG AND A GOOD DANCE

Discovery in New York

The name Michele came to someone mind in New York City. The mayor of Northern Bend, the Honorable Cliff Renford, still in office until Pletz was sworn in, had stopped to eat breakfast in a restaurant prior to attending the last day of a convention attended by mayors of midsize U. S. cities. The day before, he had struck out attempting to gain a second on his motion from the floor. He was calling for a 25% rebate from the convention fee to members that attended more than 90% of the meetings. "Some token of recognition should fall to those who participate in the full length of the convention. We all know some pay their fee and then spend their time on the golf course or in bars," he argued. No sooner had the chair recognized his motion, than the President of the association took the mike and announced, "We've cut those fees to the bone. If this motion even gains a second, I can guarantee that next year, you'll be asking your City Council for an increase in convention expenses." The silence that followed was as loud as the enthusiasm to offer a second. The motion failed.

Grousing over his failure to make any impression on his fellow conventioneers, the mayor flipped through a New York paper as he munched his bacon and eggs. On the second page a photo of several people appeared under the caption: The Youth of North America Participate in Defense Declaration.

The mayor casually scanned the picture until his eyes landed on a young woman standing in the front row. "That's--that's—what's her name. Allen knows her," the mayor blurted nearly choking on a dry piece of toast. For a moment, his fingers drummed on the table as he searched his now alerted mind for her name.

Attracted by the noise coming from his table, a waitress asked, "Did you want something, sir?"

"No, no, just thinking." Then names began to surface. "Margaret? No. Mabel? Na. Michael— Michele! Michele, that's it!" the mayor shouted so loud that it startled even the New Yorkers sitting nearby.

The mayor noticed the attention directed to his outburst and apologized with, "Sorry, just thinking out loud."

Now the mayor studied the picture more closely. "Now what do we have here?" he chuckled. "Some young man has his hand around her waist. And if my memory serves me right, she goes with that Wolfgang. Where'd they get that name! She's in some little town in New York and he's -wherever. Out of sight, out of mind, they say. The ole' Baron's grandson's girl friend isn't as steady as they may think. This picture deserves to be cut out for future reference. I'll leaf through the Northern Bend papers when I get home to see if it was printed there. But not likely," the mayor said to himself, his smiling lips barely moving.

*   *   *

Months Later

Mrs. Laverne greeted the army air corps captain entering the front door. "Come in Wolfgang! So good to see you! Michele will be down in a minute. We were so pleasantly surprised to get your phone call. Please come into the living room."

Wolfgang took his hat off and slipped it under his arm. "Our unit was making a major move to a different location so our Colonel thought it would be a good time to give the pilots and air crews some furlough. Didn't take me long to find a flight back to the states. You're looking good!"

She brushed her hair back. "You always say that! But thank you."   Michele came running down the stairs. "Wolfy, it's really you!" Michele and Wolfgang rushed toward one another, but then halted in the presence of a parent.

"Oh, hug and kiss! Don't let me stop you adults. I have to check on my cake in the oven." Michele's mother exclaimed as she disappeared into the kitchen.

With such parental permission, the two did as they were told and then held their embrace. Wolfgang put his hands on her shoulders and parted them just enough to look into her eyes.   "Boy, I've waited months for just this moment. Just the thought of you gets me through each day."

Michele smiled into his eyes. "It's so much the same for me. I felt so bad I wasn't here to say goodby when you left for the Pacific. I think about you often every day. I imagine your arms around me. This moment will be another cherished memory for me. I wish this war would end."

Mr. Laverne rushed into the room drying his hands on a towel. "Just finished milking. Those milking machines are a blessing. Good to see you, Wolfgang. You look a little thin. How's the war going? Papers claim we're pushing them Japs back to where they came from!"

"Oh, daddy, he doesn't want to talk about war now!"

"It's okay," Wolfgang assured.   "You people on the home front need to hear the good news. You're right. We're pushing them back island by island. How about this? I was talking to a cook the other day and he showed me a container of dried milk that came from the Peterson Dairy Products in Northern Bend. I told the cook, 'Hey, I know a farmer who sells his cream to that creamery.' "

Mr. Laverne threw his shoulders back. "We all do what we can for the war effort. How long you got? You sure got a bunch a ribbons on your chest"

Wolfgang laughed as he brushed the brightly colored combat ribbons on his jacket. "I'll tell you about them when we have more time. I'm scheduled to fly back in three days so I have to make the most of each one. Right now I'd like to take your daughter to the dance at the Emporium. Mom tells me there is a good band there now."

Mrs. Laverne stepped up to Michele and Wolfgang and put a hand on the shoulder of each one. "You just go right now. Have a good time. Dance your feet off. Do you both good. You need the enjoyment. I'll leave the porch light on."

"Those are the kind of orders I like to hear. Miss Michele, take my arm 'cause we're a flying to the music!"

The two ran out the door, down the steps, and about half way to the car, stopped, hugged and kissed again. Laughingly, they climbed into the black Buick, and drove away.

"I couldn't believe I was hearing your voice on the phone, Wolfy!"

"Just got in this afternoon. Hope I don't look too rag-tag. The jungle steam does a number on the clothing. Didn't have time to buy a new uniform in LA. I just took every military flight I could catch."

"You look just fine. You could come in rags. Who cares!"

"When you came down the stairs-you're just beautiful-and so professional looking. In your letter you wrote about that big meeting in Ogdensburg, New York, and a trip to Washington, D.C. Are you some kind of president now or something big like that?"

Michele hugged his arm. "You're always so complementary. I just saw how the men and women dressed at the meeting and in Washington. They looked so in control-like they had goals they were reaching for. I liked that."

"Me, too, on you! Speaking of appearance," Wolfgang reflected as he rubbed his freshly shaven face, "Had a layover in Hawaii. Went straight to the BOQ (bachelor officer quarters). Check in, and stood in a shower for a half hour. Only that washed off the jungle. Ugh!"

Michele put her hands to her cheeks in mock sympathy. "Poor boy!"

Wolfgang wagged a finger at Michele. "You just never know. Now you're ferrying Airacudas. It could happen. The War Department could ask—no— order you to fly them to the Pacific. Then see what happens to your hair-do!"

Michele grimaced. "Ugh!" Silent for a moment, Michele looked out the window and then at the speedometer. "Captain Otto, how fast are you going?"

Wolfgang checked his speed and responded, "45."

Michele lightly poked his arm. "Now with the gas rationing, the speed limit is 35 miles per hour. So slow down. Don't you know there is a war on?"

Wolfgang took his foot of the gas pedal. "So that's why that guy in the plane with the big orange circle kept shooting at me!"

"Well, I'm glad he missed. Wonder who we'll see at the dance."

The Emporium

Dancing was well under way as Michele and Wolfgang entered the ballroom. The large dance floor was surrounded on three sides by two levels of tables for four. The fourth side was occupied by the band on an elevated platform playing a jitterbug. The floor was filled with dancers matching the music with a variety of enthusiastic steps.

The two paused for a moment looking for an empty table. Directly across the floor a girl, standing at a table, waved at them to come to her table. Michele exclaimed pointing at her, "Look its Cori Jameson. And she's with Carlos. He's on furlough. Let's sit with them."

They walked quickly to the table and renewed acquaintances. Wolfgang pointed to a badge on Carlos' shirt. "Purple Heart. You got in the way of some shrapnel or a bullet?"

"Everybody was green when we hit the beaches in North Africa. You know what it's like. You learn fast. It was a sniper. But I'm OK. I'm shipping back to my unit in four days. You got a tan. Is the South Pacific like the movies? "

The girls hugged the arms of their dates and listened. The band finished a piece and the players searched through their sheet music for the next arrangement.

"No, they forget to show the steamy heat and blood suckers in the movies. The hard part is when you fly out with a friend and he doesn't come back. So much for hazardous foreign travel, then pointing to the two girls, "what have you two butterflies been up to?"

Cori proudly pointed to herself. "I am the new manager of the Francis Shop! My motto is- and it will appear in our new advertisement- 'Our clothes always earn a second look!' Perfect example is the dress worn by one of our most cherished customers, Miss Michele."

The men stomped their feet for applause, and agreeably approved with "ausgezeichnet!, magnifico!"

Cori smiled at Michele. "But Michele has an exciting job. She now flies those war planes from Sternlicht to all parts of the country. You are so adventurous."

Wolfgang turned to Michele. "I had a short

conversation with the Baron when I got in. He mentioned what a good pilot you are and so dependable."

"I really enjoy it. It's like being in the middle of something so dynamic-so important. Ferrying aircraft can be grueling. You fly a plane to one place and they want you to fly their plane to some other location. I can be away for five or six days. Finding a hotel room can be a challenge in itself." Michele reached across the table and tapped Cori's hand. "But then I come home, rush to the Francis Shop and see what new outfits Cori can show me!"

Carlos, grinning, leaned over the table and whispered. "This afternoon I was in the Francis Shop like I was looking for something but I really was watching and listening to Cori work the customers. She knows how to get a sale!"

"You keep that story to yourself," Cori admonished. "I want my customers to believe I have their best interests at heart."

"And you do," Michele agreed.

Waving his hands, Carlos was about to assure his compliance, when the band stood up and began to send across the dance floor the melodious, romantic strains of Glenn Miller's 'Moonlight Serenade.'"

All four turned to their partners, and said simultaneously, "Let's dance!"

The floor was packed giving Michele and Wolfgang incentive to hold one another close as they stepped and swayed to the soft melody. Wolfgang whispered, "It's like a dream."

Michele returned, "I love you, Wolfy."

Wolfgang squeezed her hand. I love you, too, Michele."

Michele sang softly into his ear. "I sing you a song in the moonlight, a love song, my darling, a Moonlight Serenade-"

An Encounter

For two hours, the four danced, laughed, and chatted. Wolfgang and Michele stood up to enter the dance floor when a waitress ran up to Wolfgang and said, "Captain Otto, you are wanted on the telephone. It's down that hallway."

Wolfgang grimaced. "Michele, just wait at the table. I'll be right back."

"No, I'm coming with you. I want to know why someone is calling here. I pray they aren't calling you back before your leave is up."

"We'll see." The two walked down a long hallway and spotted a wall telephone at the end. Wolfgang picked up the phone, said, "Wolfgang here," and listened. His head drooped and his body rocked slowly back and forth. Wolfgang said, "Yes, sir," and hung up. He turned to a worried Michele. "Well, it's not that bad. They want me to return a day early. Something is up so my stay is one day short." Wolfgang put his arm around Michele's waist, and they turned to walk back to the dance floor.

"Hey, pal, jus' a minute!"

Startled, the two look up to see a beefy, overweight, rumpled thug standing in their way reeking of liquor.

"So I don't pass the physical and I'm stuck here while you flyboys get all the 'ttention and medals." As he took an unsteady step toward them, Wolfgang stepped in front of Michele.

"Thas right. You jus' protect the little lady. But I don' like it. I want you to know I'm as tough as you. Tougher! In fact, I'm gonna kiss her and you ain't gonna stop me!"

The brute began his advance. Michele gasped in fright. Wolfgang jerked his body upward as if to strike the villain's head. The brute raised his hands in defense, Wolfgang ducked down and drove his fist into the assailant's stomach. The brute began to cave in while exhaling a frothy wind. Wolfgang administered the *coup de grâce* with a mighty kick to the groin. Eyes popping, the brute crashed to the floor. Michele quickly stepped around the body into the open hallway. Wolfgang whispered into the brute's ear, took Michele's arm and they walked briskly back to the dance floor.

"What did you say to him?" Michele inquired.

"Now you have a good day."

"No, you didn't. What did you say."

"In words appropriate to your ears, I said he wasn't to go near you-ever!"

"Oh, Wolfy, I wish you didn't have to go back. I worry so."

"Don't. I don't want to think of you worrying. I just want to think of you pretty as a picture, happily doing whatever you are doing."

"Alright."

In Conclusion

Back at the table, Michele told the others about the encounter. "When we started back, this terrible man stopped us. He was drunk and awful. He lunged at us. Oh, it happened so fast! Wolfy hit him, oh, so hard and down he went. Wolfy whispered something in his ear. He won't tell me what he said but now I don't think we have to worry about him."

Carlos growled, "Does he need further adjustment?"

"Nah, he got the message," Wolfgang replied rubbing his knuckles in satisfaction.

"So it's Wolfy now!", Carlos chirped. "Tank would have liked to work you over with that!"

"I like the sound and if Tank—what do you mean, 'would have?'," Wolfgang asked.

Cori broke the silence. "We were not going to tell you until tomorrow. They say he was killed in action."

Carlos looked at Wolfgang. "When I heard, I called the house. His mom answered. She said all the government man would tell her was that he lost his life in a special mission serving his country. Then she started to sob, and the conversation ended. I didn't know you were in town. When Cori and I saw you coming to the table, we decided to tell you tomorrow."

"He was a good guy. Never saw him turn away from trouble. I'll bet he led the mission. God bless him," Wolfgang lamented. Then he sat up straight. "Well we can't change that and if he were here he'd be the first one on the floor, so let's get dancing!"

Later, Wolfgang and Michele drove back to the farm. The porch light dimly cast its illumination out onto the bushes and trees. The two walked up to the front door, kissed, and hugged. Michele softly touched Wolfgang's nose and expressed her wish. "Be careful and come back to me."

"I'll be back—and I'll be back to you."

Michele squeezed his hand, opened the door and disappeared within. Wolfgang, head hanging, listened to her fading footsteps. The door remained shut. He muttered, *"déjà vu,"* climbed back into the black Buick, drove into the darkness, and returned to the Pacific.

CHAPTER 20

BEDCHECK CHARLIE

Guadalcanal, October 1, 1942

The heat boiled up from the runway like squiggly vapors. This Pacific island was no paradise and sweat dripped from the foreheads of the men standing near the lone aircraft. They waited for Bedcheck Charlie, an enemy bomber that came about sunset to scatter explosives on the work area.

Today was different. Everyone looked forward to the visit by the enemy. A surprise waited at the end of the runway. A twin engine Airacuda had raced in at tree top level early afternoon, thus avoiding detection by the troops of the Japanese Empire.

Two weeks prior, the enemy shot down the last American aircraft based at the captured airstrip. Since then, Bedcheck Charlie couldn't be challenged in the air. His brazen visits were getting on everyone's nerves.

Besides taking claim to the air above, the Japanese navy's uninvited appearance prevented further supply of the landed marine and army units. Reserves of food and ammunition were running low. With it, morale was sinking. The troops felt abandoned. Something good had to happen soon.

As the sun neared the horizon, Captain Wolfgang Otto, Army Air Corps, sat in the Airacuda cockpit with a hand on the ignition switch. He waited for a radio signal from the picket ships offshore informing Sparks, a marine radioman, that the intruder had arrived. That left just enough revenge time to fire-up the twin 1200 horse-power Hercules turbo-charged engines and rise to the occasion.

Looking around, he saw anxiety, despair and grim determination on the faces of the men near his aircraft. Although astonished at the destruction he'd witnessed upon landing at the airbase earlier that morning, he tried not to show it.

Wolfgang was in the hot seat. Charlie in flames would rally the troops. If he missed, morale would ratchet downward. No way would he spend this war in a prison camp. The gunsight glistened in the fading light. He patted it and muttered, "Charlie just bought a one-way ticket."

He attempted to make light of the noisy cannon and machine gun fire, less than two miles away, by asking with mock scorn, "How do you Marines expect an Air Corps pilot to get his sleep with such disturbance in the background?" A few laughed but one red-eyed unshaven marine got right to the point. "Give us Bedcheck and we'll push that battle line out of anyone's range of hearing."

The only other sound besides gunfire was the tump-tump of a gasoline generator that served as an electrical source for the portable radio positioned a few feet from the runway. Suddenly Sparks pressed his earphones tight and listened with intense concentration. Wolfgang grabbed the ignition switch. He waited for the radioman to yell, he's on his way!

Seconds later the radioman relaxed the grip on his earphones and his body slumped in disappointment. The message must have been something else.

Wolf drummed his fingers on the fuselage. He wanted Charlie, too. Where the hell was he?

A general and his adjutant, standing in front of a tent set up for Marine Flight Operations fifty yards behind the radioman, asked the same question.

"Where's that damn bomber?" the general demanded

as he chomped on the remnants of a cigar. "I radio HQ. Desperate for fighter protection. They send me this Army kid! This fly-boy better be at the top of his game."

Wolfgang clicked on his gunsight. The crosshairs glowed green. He turned it off. As he looked down at the controls, his eyes fixed on the prominent manufacturer's label riveted to the center of the Airacuda's instrument panel. In large letters it read as follows.

The Sternlicht Aviation Corporation
Northern Bend, Indiana.
Frederick Otto, President

Sternlicht, the product of his grandfather's driving ambition. "*Baron* Frederick Otto" was what he preferred to be called. Wolfgang, in his mind's eye, could see his grandfather in his office sitting in a straight back chair answering the phone with, "Baron Otto here." Wolfgang knew why. The Baron had earned the title in Germany when be became an ace during World War One by shooting down the requisite number of enemy planes. Once in the United States he dropped the title until; his creation, the Airacuda, began to draw the interest of the U. S. Army Air Corps. Then he insisted on being so addressed as to remind all that the design of the Airacuda was the product of a veteran air ace.

The dribble of sweat running down Wolfgangs's cheek matched the feel of hot sticky controls. Air in the cockpit was close, the sinking sun's heat still relentless. He rubbed his pants. They were damp, too. If Bedcheck would show up he could get airborne and cool off.

Bedcheck always flew a Betty, code for a twin-engine bomber. Wolfgang placed a two dollar bet with the radioman that he could blow off an engine with a single salvo of 37mm shells. A gun camera would settle the wager.

Once again, Sparks pressed the earphones close to his head and listened. Then standing, he waved his hand toward Wolf as the signal that Bedcheck had been spotted!

Wolf turned on the ignition and cranked the first engine. After a sputter and cough, the engine came alive. He cranked the second engine with the same result. As the engines warmed, Sparks indicated the intruder was twenty miles offshore straight ahead.

Wolf motioned to an airman to pull the wheel chocks. He released the brakes, and pushed the throttles fully forward. The engines responded with a forward thrust pressing Wolf back into his seat. The Airacuda roared down the runway and into the air.

As dusk had already cast a gray blanket close to the earth, Wolf flew low within its cover enabling him to engage the bomber head-on from a sharp climb. Approaching undetected out of the dusk, Wolf could fire into the cockpit. He would rather blow a wing or motor off letting the pilot fend for himself. Wolf abhorred seeing a mangled body. But base morale demanded a decisive, spectacular kill.

Wolf headed out over the ocean. The Airacuda was primed for a fight. The engines hummed and the eager gun lights glowed green. Now to find Bedcheck.

He scanned the horizon to find a single plane in expanding dusk over an endless ocean. Wolf saw the beach recede behind him. Still no sign of Bedcheck. Had he changed course?

Probing the union of illuminated sky and the vast expanse of darkness, bingo-go, Wolf caught sight of a twin-engine bomber headed inland. Wolf remained within the cloak of dusk until the two aircraft were less than a mile apart. Then he pulled the Airacuda into a steep climb. At a distance of a thousand yards with the bomber dead center in his gun sight, he released a three-second salvo from his armada of four 50-caliber machine guns and two 37-mm cannon. Their simultaneous discharge sent a shudder through the Airacuda. Judging from the trajectory of the tracers, Wolf gauged the first few bullets would spray in front of the unsuspecting pilot but the rest should rake the fuselage. To make certain, he fired a second salvo.

As quick as his mind formulated the sequence, his hail of steel hosed the fuselage from forward cockpit to tail assembly. Wolf banked sharply to escape the impending explosion of the bomber's cargo. In an instant, Wolf watched bits and pieces of the bomber spit into the air as his calling cards made deadly contact. A fraction of a second later, the contents of the bomber detonated in a spectacular ball of fire. Wolf watched remnants of the twin-engine trespasser spiral in wide circles downward. Some parts splashed into the ocean close to a picket ship. Wolf could imagine the message Sparks was hearing now.

Mission accomplished, Wolf returned to base. As his motors died down, Sparks ran to the Airacuda shouting, "You got him good, but you owe me two bucks!"

* * *

While lying in his bunk, Wolfgang ruminated over the day's victory. Flaming the bomber was another time he had carried out 'ole Baron's wish. He could hear his grandfather's voice repeating the wish.

"The Airacuda is the best," he said as Wolf left for the Pacific. "You'll have the honor of proving it again. Oh, how I wish I were in your shoes! The Washington brass claim I'm too old, bad heart, and more valuable here, designing the next generation of aircraft."

Wolf remembered how the Baron stepped back a few feet, pointed to him, and set his jaw. "But you're an Otto following in the footsteps of the Baron!" Whenever he uttered the name Otto in the context of a lineage, Frederick's body seemed to expand with a confidence inherited from generations past.

"I'm World War One with a dream and you're World War Two making it come true. There are people, and then, there are people with fire in their bellies. You've got fire in your belly and that fire will bring you home to take over the reins of Sternlicht. Remember that fire will make you, no matter what the odds, the hunter. The hunted perish, the hunter survives."

Wolfgang stared up at a bug walking across the top of his canvas tent. Canvas. The idea of canvas brought forth the image of a canvas upon which his grandfather had painted his goals and the images of those persons who would help him—come hell or high water—bring them to fruition. Wolfgang could see himself, Cletus and other test pilots, in the center, with the Baron in the background. Above was the outline of an Airacuda. No where in the scene could he find Michele. He tried to paint her in. A fuzzy portrait was the best his mind could accomplish. Her absence would not allow a clear image. The emerging reality of his existence on the island was wrenching as he gripped tight the edge of his cot. He clenched his eyes shut in an effort to dream of other things.

*   *   *

The next day, Wolf watched as Major Bauerman

flew in with three other Airacudas. "We spent a couple of days chewing up some Jap positions on the northern end of the island where they're adding reinforcements. When we got there, they were bringing in troops during the day. It was a turkey shoot. They started coming at night and we couldn't see them. To counter their tactic, the Navy brought in PT boats and we left. How you doing?"

"I got Bedcheck Charlie. He was the nuisance night raider in these parts. Came in at dusk, slow, like he was sightseeing. He never knew what hit him."

They chatted in the mess hall while eating a lunch of egg from a dried concentrate and Spam. Wolf grimaced at the pale green preparation on his fork. "When I get back to civilization I'm gonna put the fresh egg on a pedestal. This stuff is awful!"

"Bet even the cooks can't eat it." Cletus held a portion up on his fork. "This is so bad it'd gag a maggot!" They laughed.

Spreading the remnants on his plate between two slices of bread, Wolf finished the meal as a sandwich.

"An AP photographer took some shots of me in front of the Airacuda when I got back." Cletus related smiling. "They'll be front page in the States in a few days. Should make the Baron happy."

Wolf noted Cletus was using the title Baron. In the past when speaking to Wolf, Cletus would refer to your Grandfather or Grossvater. Now Frederick Otto, champion of the Airacuda, was the Baron and Cletus, Wolfgang, and other selected pilots were to prove him right in the field of battle. Wolf sensed that Cletus's ambition was more about proving the superiority of the Airacuda than destroying the enemy. If that were the case, Cletus would select missions based on the potential for a spectacular kill guaranteeing front page news.

Wolf was not opposed to danger, but unnecessary risks for the sake of bigger contracts would cross the line. There was someone back home to whom Wolf wanted to return to, to be near, to hold. But,to decline accompanying Cletus anywhere would reflex on his own image. And that wasn't going to happen.

Wolf wrote to his parents whenever time permitted.

October 12, 1942

Dear Mom and Dad,

Arrived safely on the island of ---censored---. Went first by troopship to Australia and then flew here.

Bagged Bedcheck Charlie, a lone bomber that flew nuisance raids here each night.

Cletus is now a Lieutenant Colonel and commands my squadron. He is fearless.

Fly daily, some short, some long missions.

Miss you all. Enjoy your letters.

Michele wrote from San Diego. Had flown an Airacuda there. She is something special. She must get calls from guys all the time. I miss her—miss home.

Love, Wolf

*   *   *

Jan. 30, 1943

Dear Mom and Dad,

Got your letter about the Victory Bond Rally at Sternlicht. Bet every doorstep was scrubbed-snow or no snow!

Had to be exciting when Kathleen brought the Rockettes there to perform. And Mom, you with the high kickers, bet you were the prettiest one in the line!

Michele wrote that you introduced her to Kathleen. Thanks for taking her to the rally.

Played touch football with guys I played against in college. Popcorn Grant from Michigan, and Freddie Mr. Outside Watson from Purdue. Had a great time with Popcorn when I sailed to France. A character. The next day, they flew a mission to ---censored---and never returned. Crews missing every day. It's a meat grinder. I don't like getting to know pilots too well because it's tough if they don't come back. I hope the New Year ---censored---

Love, Wolf

*   *   *

The former mayor of Northern Bend sat alone at supper. His wife and son had left for work. Proper employment eluded him. Factory work was beneath him and none of the office positions appeared suitable to his imagined managerial prowess.

Hearing a thump on the front door, he got up and fetched the evening Northern Inquirer. He scanned the front page as he walked back to the dining room. The headline brought him to an abrupt stop when he read

Local Pilot Shoots Down Marauding Bomber.

In the center of the page was a picture of Wolfgang standing in front of an Airacuda.

Dejected, Clifford slumped into a dining room chair. His mind raced. Talk about breaks! Flies around, pulls a trigger and gets his picture on the front page. I faithfully served a community, shot down rotten development scams and get dumped at election.

He drummed his fingers on the table as he read the accompanying article. To him it was blah-

blah until he reached an inspiring paragraph.

If you would like to congratulate Capt. Otto his address is as follows:

Capt. Wolfgang Otto, AO3043555
Division 40, Unit 369
Pacific Theater 4
APO San Francisco, Cal.

Smiling, he added and stirred another teaspoon of sugar to his coffee. The fixings for a timely celebration. "His address, how fortuitous. I'll send him a picture that'll wipe that smirk off his face." Then he raised the cup to his lips and savored each sip of the sugary beverage.

*   *   *

Wolfgang sat on a cot cleaning a Colt 45. His hair was matted, his flying suit soiled, and his shoes rested on some small branches to keep his feet out of the mud. Hearing footsteps, he turned his head toward the open end of his tent.

Colonel Bauerman lifted the tent flap and stuck his head in. "Got a minute?" Cletus asked.

"Sure, come on in. Have a seat—such as it is," Wolf returned waving his hand at an empty cot.

Cletus, looking no less grimy, sat down on the cot and put his feet on the branch mat. "Like your flooring. Gives your apartment an earthy look."

Wolfgang smiled weakly.

Cletus clasped his hands and rested his forearms on his knees. "Just returned from Operations. Headquarters handed Ops a mission. I'm calling the squadron together and asking for volunteers. I don't want you to do it. It's chancy and the odds aren't good for returning."

Inside his heart, Wolf just wanted to go home but pride and honor ruled. "Colonel, where you go, I go. Don't favor me, it's not fair to the rest."

Cletus edged closer to Wolf. "When we're alone, call me Cletus. We've been through too much together for such formality. I don't want us both gone. It would devastate the Baron and your family."

"Frankly, Col-Cletus, between you and me and the lamppost, I think the Baron would survive such news a lot better than our families. His life is the Airacuda and if we aren't around to fly them, he'll make sure his flying schools turn out plenty that can."

Wolf paused but Cletus didn't respond. To avoid the appearance of pushing Cletus into reaction, Wolf asked, "What's the mission?"

Cletus sat back on the cot and brushed a mosquito from his sweaty forehead. "Code intercepts indicate the Jap battleship, Nakota, is being serviced to steam into our region and block our reinforcements. A real snake in the grass. If we can stall its departure, Ops will have time to fly in some B-17's to send it to the bottom where it belongs. It's armed to the teeth against air attack. The mission will be hairy."

Wolf stood up and gestured for Cletus to lead the way. " Let's go to your meeting and plan the surprise."

In Operations, Cletus explained the mission to an audience of three Army pilots and Wolf. "Our mission is to skip bomb ordinance into the battleship Nakota's steering mechanism to keep it in port until B-17s can sink it. It bristles with antiaircraft guns. I expect 50% loss of our force. My plan is to attack with four Airacudas. One of you can't go. Which one will that be?"

An Army pilot turned to one of his companions. "You've got a wife and kids. You stay."

The pilot, with a family, sat for a moment

looking at the other pilots. He rose, said, "Good luck, guys," and left.

Cletus began outlining the attack to the remaining two Army pilots and Wolf. "We'll approach low at sunrise so their picket ships might miss us. Above all, maintain radio silence. If you get separated, navigate yourself back to base."

He gave each a map with a picture of the harbor where the Nakota lay at anchor. "Captain Otto and I will enter the harbor from the east on the deck. You two," pointing to the army pilots, "from the north diving from an altitude of 10,000 feet. We'll all aim for the stern of the ship. By approaching from two directions, they should get confused about their targets and some of us'll get through."

His audience of three sat in silence examining the steel giant and its lethal umbrella. Cletus could only sympathize with their thoughts. To introduce some sense of hope he offered, "The moment you're in range, fire every gun and drop all your bombs. Don't even think of coming back for a second run. It'll be over in seconds and we'll all be back in time to enjoy Cookie's splendid lunch cuisine. We'll nail that sucker and raise the morale here and at home. See you at 0300."

That night, Wolf lay on his cot staring at the tent top. A light rain commenced and soon beads of water formed on the inside of the canvas. As the spheres of water grew too heavy, they plopped onto the two pilots below.

The lieutenant in the other cot complained, "What a hell of a way to get some sleep before three o'clock in the morning! It's hot enough in here and then to be wet and hot?"

"As they say," Wolf lamented in muffled tones, pulling a blanket over his head, "Into each life some rain shall fall!"

"Thanks for the comforting thought."

"Hey, you can always write home about our indoor plumbing!"

"Damn! And I passed over the chance of being an instructor at Randolph Field in San Anton."

Lying under a damp blanket in the hot, humid tent, Wolf listened to several voices speaking to one another in that little room in his cerebrum. Each claimed the truth.

"Raise the morale back home? To 'Ole Cletus back home means the Baron. The Baron will pop a button when he reads of the Airacuda's daring exploits."

"Cletus wants to run Sternlicht when the Baron retires."

"Cletus has never shaken the mayor's charge of criminal behavior. It's a blot only daring exploits can erase!"

"Daring exploits—but at what price?"

Wolf didn't like where the conversations were going and angrily intervened. "Not me, I'm getting back. Got other plans for my life." He angrily pulled the blanket down from his eyes. Rolling to his side, he looked at Michele's picture sitting on an empty ammunition box next to his cot. Even by squinting, the darkness in the tent prevented him from seeing her face. Only the frame was discernable. The inability to catch a reassuring glimpse of the woman, whom he longed for, was troubling.

A voice in the little room in his head popped up, "Out of sight, out of mind. She's no longer there for you!"

This thought could be real! His heart began to race. He grabbed his flashlight and aimed it on the frame. Her radiant smile erased all negative thoughts from the little room. Silent comfort prevailed and Wolf fell back onto his cot sound asleep.

*   *   *

At 0245, a sentry roughly wiggled the rain-laden flaps of Wolf's tent and shouted, "You guys awake?"

The action sprayed drops onto the sleeping occupants. The sentry ignored their disgusted reaction. "Up! up now! Cookie's got breakfast on the table." The two tent mates grunted and swung their feet onto the dirt floor.

An hour later, four Airacudas lifted off the coral runway. They rose to 100 feet over the calm sea and set course toward the venomous adversary, the Nakota.

CHAPTER 21

IT DOESN'T MATTER ANY MORE

"Don't worry so, Henry, he'll come back. He's flying an Airacuda." The Baron searched through the contents of a desk drawer and drew out a picture of Wolfgang in a football uniform. He handed the picture to Henry. "There he is in the armor of a gladiator. A picture of confidence." Then pointing to a picture on a shelf behind him, "Today he wears the uniform of the Army Air Corps. Same air of confidence. He's an Otto."

"That Army picture was taken before his friend, Popcorn was killed." Henry's voice faltered. "I still fret over the hurried commission and sending him to the Pacific before he had a chance to get some advanced training. Get eased into it rather than rushed."

"He'll cut his teeth in the Pacific," the Baron countered. "Like a trooper. He'll show what the Airacuda can do. I hate war but December 7th got us one big contract, Henry. Don't forget we're in a competitive business. It's dog eat dog. Furthermore, lot's of employees depend upon us."

To accentuate a principle underlying the decisions made in his office, he broadened their responsibility. "Not only employees but their families and all our subcontractors and their families. We stumble and a lot fall. Our business shoulders greater risk than most but that adds an element of excitement to the challenge." The Baron stood up, placed both fists knuckles down on his desk and leaned toward Henry. "I can't fly anymore but I still relish the power of this office. Believe me, Wolfgang Otto is a survivor. Now let's hammer out the details in this renewal proposal. I want to hand it to General Wolford in person."

Later in his own office, Henry gazed out the large window overlooking the Sternlicht complex. The scene took him back to a Saturday afternoon when he was listening to a radio broadcast of a football game between Michigan State and Trinity University four years ago. Wolfgang was a freshman at Trinity, a member of the football team but had yet to play. Henry didn't expect to hear his son's name until his sophomore or junior year but tuned into the games anyway.

"Beautiful day for a football game, folks," the announcer proclaimed. "The sun is shining and the temperature is 50 degrees. Whale of a game but Trinity is taking it on the chin. They're down twenty to zip. The way State's Popcorn Grant is charging through the Trinity line, I think the point spread is gonna get larger as the day gets longer."

"It's Michigan's ball on Trinity's 20. First down. Michigan's out of the huddle. Now in a tight T formation. Their center has his hands on the ball. Wait, there's commotion on the Trinity side line. One of their players just ran out on the field—no, he ran back. Trinity calls a time out. Some confusion down there."

Henry pushed some papers aside and drew his desk radio close and turned up the volume. His ears perked up when he heard the announcer ask in a low voice, "Who's the kid in the number 38 jersey? The one that ran out on the field?" A pause as Henry could hear papers shuffle. Then he heard the announcer whisper disbelief. "Otto Wolfgang? What kind of a name is that?" In a louder voice, "Number 38 Otto Wolfgang--" A frantic voice in the background corrected him, "Wolfgang Otto, Wolfgang Otto!"

Henry grabbed the plant microphone and placed it in front of the radio. The announcer's voice boomed out over the factory's loudspeakers. Work

stopped as everyone was eager to hear what Wolf
might do.

"I mean Wolfgang Otto is in for number 15, Ed
O'Hara at defensive back. There is still some
turmoil on the Trinity side. Guess arguments are
inevitable when you're down 20."

"Back to the game. State out of the huddle,
again a tight T formation." The announcer's voice
rose with excitement. "The quarterback has the
ball, it's a handoff to Popcorn who is charging
through a hole in the Trinity—WOOOA—Popcorn was
stopped--WOW—dead in his tracks at the line of
scrimmage. What a jarring tackle!"

Again in a low voice, "Name of tackler?" Now
the announcer's voice expressed surprise. "Number
38, the new sub for Trinity. What a lucky tackle
by Otto Wolf-sorry-Wolf Tack-Wolfgang Otto. I'll
get it right yet, folks.

"Michigan back in the huddle. They look
determined. Trinity lines up once more. Michigan
up to the line of scrimmage. Single wing to the
right. Numbers 38 and 16 defensive backs keep
moving from side to side. Must be confusing to
the offense." In a low voice, "Are they allowed
to do that?"

Back to the microphone. "It's a long count.
Michigan quarterback maybe changing signals. The
ball is snapped. There's a mixup! The ball is
loose. Trinity recovered!" the announcer shouted.
"Number 16, Jack Harrison's tackle caused the
fumble and number 38 Otto fell on the ball. It's
Trinity on their own 25. Trinity's sideline is
going wild. Those last two plays have fired up new
life into the Trinity team."

Such was Wolfgang's first venture into
collegiate football and Henry could still repeat
the announcer's descriptions word for word.

The picture of his son that the Baron had
fished out of his desk was well known to Henry. He

wished that Wolfgang were still in the football
uniform rather than the one he currently wore.

*   *   *

Wolf glanced at the map and reconnaissance
photos he had received at Cletus' briefing. He
traced the U shape of the island with his finger.
The two sides of the U appeared thin with the
harbor lying between them. Cletus had plotted the
attack to approach low over one arm of the U so a
quick location of the ship was essential. He had
drawn a line between a tower on the approach side
of the U to a large hangar on the exit side. The
ship lay on a point in the middle of the line.

Although the sun had yet to peek up from behind
the horizon, enough day had dawned that Wolf
could make out the island just ahead. At 410 mph,
they were closing fast.

Four miles from shore, Cletus wiggled his wings
and the two lieutenants pulled their Airacudas
into a steep climb and banked north. Both Cletus
and Wolf reduced speed allowing the two to gain
altitude and position. Wolf then dropped behind
Cletus to avoid any collision as they maneuvered
in their attack.

The island rushed up to meet them. Wolf spotted
the tower directly in front. He could see men
tending some boats near the shore. He grimaced
at the smell of dead fish.

Thatched roofs, tents and a tower zipped
by. An alarmed face of a man climbing a ladder on
its side. Tracers spewing from a machine gun nest
atop the tower stripped paneling from Cletus'
Airacuda who then banked to the right to line up
with the lone hangar across the harbor.

Wolf followed and spotted the battleship lying
at anchor. Doubt rushed through his veins. It was
a mountain of steel.

A destroyer lay near its bow. Bright lights flickered on both ships as their antiaircraft batteries zeroed in on the intruders. The air quickly filled with smoky flak and tracers. Wolf tensed in anticipation of hits.

The sound of razor-sharp metal from exploding shells striking his aircraft reminded him of hail clanging on the tin garage roof at home. Only this hail of gunfire was tearing holes in the vital organs of his Airacuda.

Jesus, Mary, and Joseph, just let me get through this!

A deadly contest now between a rising wall of fire and four resolute bombers. Some enemy fire concentrated on the low flying lead bomber. Other fire appeared directed upward. Back twenty yards, Wolf watched in alarm while bright puffs of exploding and penetrating shells peeled away wing and motor parts from Cletus' Airacuda. Close enough, Wolf began firing his 50's and 37-mm at the gun emplacements. He could see tracers from other Airacudas striking the battleship as well. An explosion in a gun emplacement blew a four-barrel battery into the air.

Cletus' Airacuda was being peeled like an orange. Wolf could only watch. "Drop your bombs and get out!" Wolf shouted into his mike.

An Airacuda diving from above trailing black smoke crashed into the battleship. A sheet of fire and shredded wreckage engulfed the ship's stern. One lost.

Wolf expected Cletus to release his bombs and pull away. Too late. One engine blown away, Cletus, Major Cletus Bauerman, the Baron's most trusted confidant, Wolf's hero, drove his bomber straight into the steering mechanism of the flaming battleship. In anguish, Wolf could only cry, "No, no, Cletus."

Now it was Wolf's turn. His Airacuda damaged

but still flying, he released his two bombs and banked away though a dense cloud of flame, smoke and debris. Tears ran down Wolf's cheeks as he glimpsed through a rear view mirror the carnage behind him. A man he much admired gone. Forever.

'Must stay alert,' Wolf rallied.

Over the hangar now.

Men running to aircraft.

A plane taking off just ahead.

Wolf dropped down to a few feet off the runway.

A short burst from the Airacuda and the plane careened uncontrolled.

Its wing tanks aflame.

Wolf continued low and straight beyond the island.

Looking to the right he saw a second Airacuda close by.

Four in, two out.

War, personal ambition, and misfortune took its toll with no apologies.

That evening Wolf penned a letter home.

Feb. 1, 1943

Dear Mom and Dad,

Tonight I can hardly write but must. Cletus was killed in heroic action -censored--. We attacked -censored—and he crashed -censored--. Our CO wrote to his wife so you may know before this letter. A Major -censored--has taken his place. He's new, fresh from the States, green. Talks about promotion. Anxious to get into battle. I don't want to get to know him.

Have a new tentmate who isn't a pilot. A Navajo, 2nd Lt.--censored—from New Mexico. His role is to -censored--. Great guy. Carries an eight inch hunting knife. Any Jap that sneaks into this tent won't come out alive!

Haven't heard from Michele. Mail gets lost when -censored--. Moving to a new base on--censored--.

Love you, Wolf

A Month Passes

One evening, Wolf returned to his tent sweaty, grimy and exhausted from two strafing missions.

A strong acrid smell of mildew greeted him as he raised the tent flap to enter. In the dim light, he saw two letters on his cot. He sat down and picked them up. One was in a plain white stamped envelope with a typed address. The other a V-mail from his mother whose European penmanship he could always recognize.

The plain envelope puzzled him. No return address and typed. Which to read first? He started to open his mother's letter but the typed address was so unusual that he laid down his mother's letter and opened the plain envelope. He withdrew and unfolded a newspaper clipping.

What he saw stunned him. He blinked hard hoping each momentary darkness would alter the image before him. But each time he looked, the picture remained the same. It was a newspaper photo cut from a larger picture. Obviously, the intent was to focus Wolf's attention on two people in a group of many. Right in front was Michele standing next to a naval officer. The crushing content of the photo was that the naval officer's arm was around her waist and she was smiling!

Wolf looked at the smile in the picture on the ammunition box and then back to the smile in the clipping. Exactly the same. A smile for all, not him alone!

Holding the picture, he stood up but his legs wobbled and he sat down again. In disbelief, he searched about for something that would dispel the burden of disappointments that were scarring his life. Mumbling, he pulled a duffel bag from beneath his cot and opened it. Rummaging through the musty contents revealed no answers.

Even a review of Michele's letters held no clue. They expressed only the excitement of new adventures. After looking at the clipping once again, her 'Always, Michele', seemed no more personal or exclusive than her smile. He sensed the relationship severed. He folded the picture and placed it back in the plain white envelope. Now she was truly gone. He removed her picture from the ammunition box, placed it between clothing in the duffel bag and shoved his lost treasure beneath the cot.

Staring at the dirt floor, he reflected on the events that led to his present situation. Maybe it was for the best. The chance of getting out alive here wasn't that good, anyway. He couldn't confront Michele about this. Her confirmation of his assumption would be too much. He could mention it in a letter home and maybe Mom would talk to her.

He knew of men in his unit who had received the Dear John letter stating that their girl friend or wife had fallen in love with someone else. Most letters would end with, "I hope you'll understand." Understanding how a person safe back home could discard someone they once loved who was risking danger every day was beyond Wolf's comprehension. So the newspaper clipping hit doubly hard.

Should he read his mom's letter? It could bear more bad news and he'd had enough of that. A big band arrangement rose from a Victrola a few tents away. "Turn it up!" Wolf heard someone shout. Some shuffling and the music rose clear and melodious. Wolf drank in the soothing, mellow strains of a slow dance.

Wolf laid back on his cot and called out, "Star Dust by Hoagy Carmichael!"

"Yah," a voice from another tent agreed. "Always saved that one for my girlfriend on my dance card."

Wolf knew the music well and quietly sang the lyrics along with the melody.

"*Sometimes I wonder why I spend the lonely night dreaming of a song?*

The melody haunts my reverie,

And I am once again with you-"

Wolf stopped. The words with you just didn't ring true anymore.

The tent was hot and stuffy. He stepped out and was greeted by an ocean breeze that brushed across his face. Even though warm and humid, it beckoned him to the water's edge. After a short walk to the beach, he removed his shoes and socks and stood ankle deep in the cool Pacific water.

The sea was calm. Small waves slapped quietly upon the sand. The breeze led him to the beach and the dark blue expanse before him offered eternal peace and escape from the wrenching loss of friends and the carnage of battle. But most of all the loss of the love of his life.

A solution lay before him. It would be over in a few minutes. The option grew more appealing with each passing second.

As he lifted a foot, a voice barked from the beach, "Halt! Don't move. What's the password? Identify yourself!"

Startled, Wolf was momentarily speechless. Shaking himself back to reality, he replied, "Red Socks, Captain Wolfgang Otto, 37th Special Wing Unit!" He turned to look into the barrel of a Thompson submachine gun.

The sentry relaxed and returned the gun to his shoulder. "Thanks, Captain. Corporal Parks here. Some Japs been sneaking ashore at night and knifing men in their tents so I get nervous when I see a lone person on the beach."

"I'm glad you're diligent in your duty, Corporal. My tent is close to the beach. I just came down to cool off. Feels good to stand in the water."

"You have a good night, Sir, I gotta go. Got more beach to cover."

　　　　The Corporal impressed Wolf. Who knows, he could have major troubles in his life but he keeps plodding along. Step by step until things hopefully improve. Maybe the more sensible course of action. Michele couldn't be the only person he could love. If he got back.

Later Wolf penned another letter home.

July 1, 1943
Dear Mom and Dad,
　　This war just grinds along. Miss you so. We're finally pushing the Japs back. Carried out missions over ---censored--- Major ---censored---lost at sea. New replacement. Can't think of his name.
　　Got a letter without a return address that had a newspaper clipping of　　　　　Michele standing next to a naval officer who had his arm around her waist. I don't know who sent it but I understand. I never asked Michele to go steady or be engaged. She is free and I wish her the best. But I ache with her loss. I love you, Mom and Dad, but now my life seems empty. We're on the move again. It doesn't matter. I don't - censored--.
　　Love, Wolf

Chapter 22

A FIERY ENDING

"Henry, please come home. I'm frightened. We just received a letter from Wolfy. He sounds very despondent."

"Be there in a couple hours. Don't worry so. Sometimes you read into his letter more than he means."

"I don't think so." Mercedes began to sob.

"I'll be right there."

After reading the letter, Henry had to agree that the tone of the letter was one of depression. Rubbing his face in disappointment, he asked, "I wonder how Michele would respond to a question about the picture. Who'd it come from? Can't remember it ever appearing in the Daily Inquirer."

Anxious, Mercedes sat on the edge of the sofa. "I can only suppose it was taken when she was in Ogdensburg or Washington. She must never have said anything to Wolfy. Not like her. I thought she loved him."

"Well, we can't sit here guessing. Let's call Michele and simply ask. Then we'll know one way or the other."

"You'll have to talk with her. I couldn't bear to hear her say she loved someone else."

"Okay, I'll call." Henry thumbed to the L's in the phone book. As his index finger traced down a column of names, he noticed his hands tremble. "The worst crises are family," he mumbled.

"What did you say, dear?" Mercedes asked.

"Just reading their name and number to myself."

Henry lifted the phone and dialed. He heard clicking, a pause, then ringing. He leaned against a wall for support and glanced at the grand piano while waiting for a response. The piano looked forlorn.

A woman's voice answered. "Lavern residence."

With the truth now eminent, Henry tensed, stood straight and gripped tight the phone.

"Zelia, is that you?"

"Yes."

"Zelia, this is Henry Otto."

"Henry, it's a pleasure."

"Zelia, I need to talk to Michele about Wolf."

Henry heard a horrified gasp on the other end and then a muffled, anxious voice. "Oh, God, I hope he hasn't been killed. Michele would be heartbroken!"

"No, thank the Lord, but he wrote a letter in which he now believes Michele only thinks of him as a friend—nothing serious. He just sounds so negative, so down."

"No, no, that's not true. Here, here is Michele. Speak to her!"

A pause, then a voice that Henry and Mercedes always looked forward to hearing, a person to be near. Youthful, with that hint of Parisian accent. Usually spirited, this time concerned.

"Mr. Otto, this is Michele. What's wrong?"

"Michele, it's a delicate matter and I-we just need the truth. Whatever it may be," Henry now steadied the phone with both hands, "so we can respond to a letter from Wolf we just received."

"What did he say?"

"He wrote that he received a white envelope with no return address that contained a newspaper photo." The last word brought a disheartened gasp from the other end.

"Of you with a Naval officer's arm around your waist. Wolf now thinks that you don't care for— or more to the point—love him anymore. Thinking of him more as just a friend. I hate to be so intrusive into your-"

Henry could hear soft, pleading, "No, no," as he spoke.

"-private life but it involves our son."

"Mr. Otto, I do love him." Henry hurriedly mouthed the words, "She loves him," to Mercedes who smiled and sat back in her chair relieved.

"He is the light of my life. That can only be from a picture taken of all the participants in the Ogdensburg Conference."

Her voice rose in anger. "Just as the photographer shot the picture, that naval officer put his arm around me. I told him I didn't appreciate that. I was so upset! He thought it funny, I didn't. The officer assured me that the photo would never be printed. But it must have been in some paper."

"Must have and some anonymous person sent it to Wolf. He wrote there was no message in the envelope, just the picture. I guess someone who wanted to put a wedge between you and Wolf. Hurt you both."

"Oh, I didn't send the picture. In fact, I never received a copy of any that were taken. Mr. Otto, what did he write? Please read his letter."

Henry read the letter. Michele repeatedly whispered, "No, no."

"I love only him. Please tell that to Mrs. Otto, too. I can see how he could form a different impression after receiving the photo."

Speaking with such emotion, Michele was forced to pause and take a deep breath. Then she continued. "That picture has haunted me. I wanted to take that plate from the photographer but once the pictures were taken, he just disappeared. Then everyone was in such a rush to get home. I must do something but I'm not sure a letter will suffice. If only I could see him, hold him and tell him how much I love him."

Henry related their experience with letters. "They move the base so often that some of our mail doesn't catch up with him for weeks." Then

Henry offered a suggestion. "Maybe the Baron could get word to him through his contacts in the War Department."

"No, Mr. Otto, I must do this myself. It has to come from me. I need to see him. He's never mentioned a furlough?"

"Small chance of that. Things are still pretty desperate out there now." "Mr. Otto, I just had a thought. It may or may not work but at least I'd be trying."

"What's that?"

"At the Christmas Bond Rally, Mrs. Otto introduced me to Kathleen Temple. While talking with her, she mentioned that a dance group in New York was putting together a musical review to entertain troops in the Pacific." Her voice began to exuded confidence. "I can sing and dance while twirling a baton. If I could speak to her she might think that novel enough to suggest I travel with the troupe."

Her idea seemed farfetched to Henry. "There are hundreds of bases out there. Slim chance."

Michele persisted. "I could be lucky. At least I'd be doing something positive."

"The routine sounds novel enough. Just a moment, I'll have Mercedes give you her telephone number." Warming up to Michele's inspiration, Henry hit on an approach. "Better yet, let Mercedes talk with her first. Give you an A+ report card. That should peak her interest. Then you can come on with charm and enthusiasm."

"I just know it'll work. I'll be home all evening, Mr. Otto."

"Good, we'll be in touch one way or another."

                        *   *   *

Michele was appalled at the miserable conditions in which the troops lived, fought and died in the

Pacific. She wrote home about her experiences.

Dear Mom and Dad,
July 10, 1943   -
Somewhere in the S. Pacific
You can't….censored … drenching rain will
transform one base into a sea of ankle-deep mud.
Only cots in the tents kept the occupants from
sleeping in a bed of water. The next base can
be hot, sticky, and damp. Wolf was right. This
jungle's steam, heat, and bugs are not Hollywood.

> *Looking fresh and attractive is only*
accomplished by carrying my uniform and boots in
a waterproof bag. Just before show time, I change
in some makeshift dressing room. If the stage
lacks a roof and it rains there is no choice. I
go out casting water from the twirling baton and
sloshing across the stage best I can! We pray the
next day is sunny so clothing dries out.

Shows are never cancelled because of weather.
If the GI's know a troupe has arrived, anyone off
duty hurries to the stage and waits boisterously
for the show to begin.

No two shows are the same. At one base that had
a large hospital, only wounded were allowed in
the front rows. There I performed to an audience
wrapped in bandages who had arrived by crutch,
wheelchair and gurney. They had risked their
lives for me and now were applauding as I did
something so insignificant in comparison as to
catch the baton after a high toss. I struggled
to hold back tears.

Another time, a Japanese soldier dazed from
fierce combat no more than two miles away, wandered
into the base and sat down to watch the performers.
Engrossed in the show, no one took notice of his
oriental features and tattered uniform. But when
he began to laugh and shout encouragement in
Japanese, those sitting next to him recognized

the presence of an enemy in their midst. A brief commotion ensued. The show stopped momentarily while the disappointed prisoner was hustled off. Then the clapping renewed and the show resumed.

At every base I ask about Wolf. I think his unit was moved from a base just a week before I got there. So disappointed. They won't tell me.

Love you and miss you.

Love, Michele

This evening Michele planned her act for a stage that had been assembled from six trailer flat beds placed side by side. The runway was only a quarter of a mile away, and planes came and went during the performance. Michele could only laugh at the difficulties the performers had to overcome in the makeshift, primitive conditions. During occasional noisy take-offs and landings, the band just played louder and the singers shouted the lyrics. The crowd loved the show and for an hour or so the war became very distant.

A young corporal was stationed at the bottom of the steps leading to the stage to help performers up and down the rather treacherous stairs. Michele was the next act and once again attempted to gain some information regarding the major reason why she joined the troupe.

Glancing at a bomber landing, she asked, "Does this go on all day?"

"Day and night. I'm an engine mechanic. Just got off duty. Our plane was pretty shot up but I finished my work early and got to come here. "Just a minute." He ran up to the stage to help a dancer come down. He insisted on holding her hand as she descended. Again at the bottom, he stepped close to Michele. She heard him take a deep breath. "Lucky me," he grinned, "Sargent Johnson ordered me to help you all up and down the steps. Always wanted to be backstage to see what happens. Had to come to this heap, ah, coral to get the chance. Where you from?"

"Northern Bend, Indiana."

He looked at her hair, her uniform. "You got a steady?"

Michele smiled. "Yes, he's a pilot in the Air Corps."

He turned to look at two burned out skeletons of planes lying nearby. "Glad I stay on the ground," he murmured. Looking back at Michele, he sought to continue his exclusive interview. "Ah'm from the great state of Texas, Austin, Texas, to be exact. You'd like it."

Michele wanted to get back to her line of questions. "Just bombers at this base?"

"Nope, there's a special fighter-bomber unit at the far end of the runway." He pointed to a group of tents and aircraft in the distant. In the dusk, she couldn't make out the shape of the aircraft. "Ah hear they take on special missions. Six or eight go out and half get back. Those that do, get tore up pretty bad. Group went out about 1500 today. Should be comin' back soon."

A four-engine bomber landed in a frothy swirl of coral dust. The corporal raised his voice to continue his conversation. "Lots of pilots paint names on their planes but this group had a wolf's head on theirs. Call themselves the Wolfpack."

"Wolfpack?" Michele shouted as her eyes darted between the corporal and the stage. The present act was nearing the end of its routine, and she was getting close to answers she had come so far to hear.

"Yup. Special group. Keep loosing planes but they just fly new ones in."

"Do you know the names of any of the pilots?"

"Well, there's a Captain-"

The loudspeaker drowned out the corporal with the announcement, "The next act is the gorgeous and talented cheerleader from Indiana to lead you guys in the fight songs from Southern Cal, Minnesota, and Trinity U!"

The crowd went wild in anticipation.

Heart racing, Michele put her face close to the corporal's. "Captain who?"

The corporal opened his mouth to answer when a surly voice from the top of the stairs bellowed, "Corporal, let her come up!"

Michele looked up into the face of a beefy red, thick chested marine pointing to the dance group exiting across the last flatbed.

"O.K., Sarg, she just-"

The band began her number.

"Don't give me lip. Get her up here!"

Michele ran up the stairs and was met with an earth-shaking din of cheers. She spun her body around twice and stopped. Swaying to the music, her long fingers pointing to the crowd, she twirled the baton with the other. Then she flung the silver rod flashing high into the air, spun around twice again and caught the baton behind her back.

Her spectacular entrance brought the camp to its feet, swaying and singing along with Michele as she waved encouragement to the band and crowd.

"tang..tung...tung...rrrrrRRROOORRRrrroooo" An engine laboring to start, run and then die was a sound Michele immediately recognized from that day on the bank of the Northern Bend River.

She froze and turned to the sound of aircraft struggling to reach the runway.

The crowd, too, fell silent and turned to look.

Just offshore, two aircraft could be seen emerging through the dusk approaching the runway. Both trailed thick, black smoke. Fire flickered from both engines of the lead plane and the tail of the other.

Michele, center stage, baton in one hand, the other on her lips, stood horrified. Both aircraft had propellers on the rear of their motors. They were Airacudas.

"It's the Wolfpack," the corporal yelled, "they'll never make it!"

Michele was stunned at his prediction. Tears flowed from her eyes.

The first aircraft, black smoke billowing from flames engulfing its engines, failed to reach the runway and slammed into a sand bank on the beach. BLAAMM. The plane exploded in a belching burst of thunder flinging parts within yards of the crowd. The cockpit disintegrated in a blinding flash.

All could only watch as the second Airacuda clawed its way through the air to reach the white coral runway. A three-second final surge of the failing motor enabled the crippled bird to crumble onto the hardened surface. Screeching forward, the flaming section of the tail broke away from the fuselage.

For a moment, Michele sensed relief that the cockpit was free of flame as it slid down the runway skidding from side to side.

A second later, she dropped the baton in despair as she watched a collision as the fuselage swayed into the path of the trailing, blazing tail. Once again united but now in a deadly clutch, the wreckage ground to a searing halt.

A fire truck raced to a point just short of the flaming hulk. One man pulled a hose from its water tank and began spraying the inferno. Two other men in asbestos suits jumped onto a wing, ran to the cockpit and slide back the canopy.

As they reached in to pull the pilot free, Michele raised her arms to help them in their task. After a brief struggle, they hauled a body out and lowered it down to two medics who placed it onto a stretcher. Anxious to escape the scorching heat, the stretcher was put into the ambulance, and it sped away, its lights flashing a clear path to the base hospital.

The men on the wing jumped down and ran. None too soon. The gasoline tanks heated to boiling, burst into flame and flung blazing fuel across the wreckage

Pilot saved, the firemen retreated. "Let'er burn. Save the water," the fire chief commanded.

Michele ran to the edge of the stage to repeat the question to the corporal. He was nowhere to be seen. She stood alone on the stage. Everything seemed distant. Sounds were dim. She struggled with the possible consequences of what she had witnessed. Was Wolfgang in one of those planes? If he was in the first one she had lost the chance to mend his broken heart, to enjoy forgiveness in his eyes. But what if he were in the second plane and still alive? Or maybe neither.

A familiar voice barked an order. "When those hulks burn out, bulldoze'em out of the way."

She turned to see the beefy, red-faced sergeant yelling orders to a group of men. She ran to him. "Sergeant, I think I know that pilot. Where'd they take him in that ambulance?"

"To the hospital."

"Where's that?"

"Look, lady, I've got to get that runway cleared. Get back with your troupe."

"No, I've got to go to that hospital. You must take me!"

"You must take me? I give the orders!"

Michele began to sob frantically. "Yes, please!"

The sergeant, embarrassed that he had made one of the performers cry, shouted to a man standing nearby. "Jackson, take over. I'll be right back."

Without looking at Michele, he waved his hand at a vehicle. "Climb in the jeep."

As they left, she saw the stage pulled apart and the flat beds being hauled away. The show was over. Several four-engine bombers circled overhead waiting for the runway to be cleared for landing. The crowd was gone. It was back to making war for them. But Michele was on a mission, too. She had to see the second pilot.

The sergeant pulled up in front of a large tent. A corporal stood guard. As Michele and the sergeant approached, the guard blocked the entrance.

"You can go in Sarg, but you know the orders, civilians without a pass stay out."

"I gotta take her in. She knows the pilot."

"Sarg, if I let her in, the Colonel will have me diggin' a six by six!"

"Who's the rear guard?"

"Private Bixby."

"Get back in the jeep."

As they drove around the circle of tents, the sergeant spoke in a growl. "Privates are too new to say no to a hot tempered 3 striper. They know that'll get 'em a week scrubbin' latrines with a toothbrush."

The sergeant deliberately increased speed as they rounded the back corner of tents. "Jump out and follow me as soon as I stop."

Slamming on the brakes raised a cloud of dust near the back door. They ran up to the guard who had lowered his gun across the entrance.

"Private Bixby?"

"Yes, sir."

"Stand back!"

"Ah, yes, but Sir!"

"Comin' through. I'm in charge!"

The guard had heard of the horrors of special latrine duty so three stripes was sufficient cause to raise his rifle. The two disappeared into the tent.

They hurried between two rows of cots filled with injured and sick GI's. At one cot, several medics in sweat-soaked T-shirts were attempting to create an airway in a patient struggling to breathe.

Someone demanded, "Lungs full of blood. Gotta get him to surgery."

Michele could see his mouth was full of bloody froth. That was the red she had seen on Bauerman's face as he fought to keep his smoldering Airacuda airborne. She had seen cows struggle to stay alive but this was a first with humans. She paused as the struggle, the shouts, the urgency gripped her.

She felt herself jerked forward by a callused hand. "We gotta get out of the way. Keep goin', this ain't our problem."

They exited into a small open area surrounded by tents. The sergeant whirled around looking for the right one.

"That's ours," as he jerked Michele toward a sign that read Emergency. This tent was brightly lit and shadows darted back and forth about a seated shadow that didn't move.

What she might see. Horrible burns? Terrible, bloody wounds? Disfigurement? She hesitated. Maybe she'd rather not know.

Too late. The sergeant pushed the flap aside and pulled her in.

There were two patients. One on a gurney with a sheet pulled over its head. It was unattended. With boots sticking out from under the sheet, Michele could only imagine the patient beneath was dead. Dear God, let it not be Wolf.

Burnt flesh stung Michele's nostrils.

The other patient sat on a chair, head bowed with his back to Michele. His clothing still smoldered, his head black with soot. As yet no distinguishing characteristics. To Michele, it could be anyone.

"Captain, could you turn your head so I can cut away your jacket and shirt," a corpsman asked. The person's head slowly turned. Still no recognition until Michele saw a scar that ran from his mouth to his ear!

Michele muffled a scream, then called out, "Wolfgang!"

The unexpected outburst startled the tent occupants. As Michele came closer, the treatment team stepped aside opening a path to the seated pilot. Wolf looked up to the source of that voice, that fragrance and saw Michele in a cheerleader uniform.

For a moment, they were back together again on the football field.

"Wolf, are you Okay?"

As if in a dream he asked, "Did you bring a pail of water?"

Profoundly relieved to have found him, she dropped to her knees. "Wolfy, I've been searching for you to tell you something. I've never-"

"Michele," Wolf interrupted as he took her hand, "if there is someone else in your life, I understand. I received a picture of you with a naval officer. You looked so beautiful, so full of life and he so sharp in that uniform. I just felt unequal, undeserving of you."

She placed her hands on his blackened cheeks. "Wolfgang, look at me!" Their eyes met. "His arm around me in that picture was done without my permission or encouragement. Not for a moment was he anything in my life. From the day you looked up at me on that football field, you became the sole love in my life." She brushed hair back from his eyes and kissed him on the forehead.

"Michele, Michele," he whispered. Now the words Wolfgang had longed to hear floated melodiously about in his brain.

As he sat there covered with the debris of a fiery crash, he felt his life began anew. Once again, adrenaline reserved only for moments like this, flowed from that same deep recess in his body restoring his energy, his hopes, his confidence.

Wincing, he rose, took Michele into his arms. He in hers. Looking into her tearful eyes, he spoke passionately. "I love you, too, Michele and nothing—but nothing—shall ever come between us."

With a radiant smile, she laid her head on his shoulder.

In one another's arms, they began to sway from side to side singing, "I sing you a song in the moonlight, a love song, my darling,-!"

www.ingramcontent.com/pod-product-compliance
Lightning Source LLC
Chambersburg PA
CBHW021515240626
47154CB00002B/634